In the Shadow of Kirinyaga

novel

Sophia Mustafa

© 2002 Sophia Mustafa

Except for purposes of review, no part of this book may be reproduced in any form without prior permission of the publisher.

We acknowledge the support of the Canada Council for the Arts for our publishing program. We also acknowledge support from the Ontario Arts Council.

Cover photo: "Woman on the Isle-de-Gorée near Dakar, Senegal" by Paul Nieuwenhuysen

National Library of Canada Cataloguing in Publication

Mustafa, Sophia
    In the shadow of Kirinyaga / Sophia Mustafa.

ISBN 1-894770-03-X

    1. Muslims—Kenya—Fiction. 2. East Indians—Kenya—Fiction. I. Title.

| PS8576.U77I5 2002 | C813'.6 | C2002-905154-1 |
| PR9199.4.M88I5 2002 | | |

Printed in Canada by Coach House Printing

TSAR Publications
P. O. Box 6996, Station A
Toronto, Ontario M5W 1X7
Canada

www.tsarbooks.com

To my deceased parents

Mohamad Hussein Butt who instilled into me

a spirit of religious and racial tolerance

and

Sardar Begum Butt who taught me perseverence

CONTENTS

Introduction	*vii*
1 Mussavir	*1*
2 Shaira	*10*
3 The Township	*17*
4 The Journey	*30*
5 The Meeting	*38*
6 Morning with the Guests	*48*
7 The Geet Ceremony and the Snake Drama	*57*
8 The Ghai Girl's Wedding	*69*
9 The Proposal	*77*
10 Latif Warns Mussavir	*83*
11 The Telegram	*98*
12 The Walk	*104*
13 Shaira in a Dilemma	*116*
14 In Nairobi	*123*
15 Catching the Thief	*131*
16 Latif's Mehndi and Rukhstana	*139*
17 The Auspicious Day	*148*
18 The Announcements	*157*
19 The Dream	*163*

20 Mombasa Island *168*
21 Mussavir Writes *177*
22 New Home and Neighbourhood *185*
23 Letter from Addis Ababa *192*
24 Muharram *196*
25 Casualty *205*
26 Hibba's Misfortune and Zaffer's Visit to Mussavir *215*
27 The Letters *226*

Acknowledgments *236*

Introduction

EAST AFRICA COMPRISES three separate countries: Kenya, which used to be a British crown colony; Uganda, once a British protectorate; and Tanzania, itself consisting of Tanganyika, formerly German East Africa and later a British trust territory, and Zanzibar. This geopolitical area is mainly populated by African peoples hailing from many different ethnic and language groups though sharing something of a lingua franca in Kiswahili—a consequence of Arab melding with and subsequent domination of the East African coast prior to and during the period of European colonization.

Since the late nineteenth century, however, this area has also been populated by small European and Asian communities, the latter of which are divided into many language, religious, and caste groups. In the East African context, *Asian* refers exclusively to peoples ancestrally from the Indian subcontinent.

Of the several books about East Africa that I have read, those by Europeans have tended to focus on topics such as the colonial administration, histories of the colonial era, world politics, and increasingly, game, wildlife, and safaris. While some of these stories have also tried to address the Mau Mau rebellion and period of the Emergency in Kenya, they have almost always been from the perspective of the white settlers. In such works East African Asians have always been a peripheral people working for the railways and at petty trading and business.

African writers have written about colonialism and its evils, of their sufferings and hardships, and of their exploitation by both the land-grabbing Europeans and Asian racketeers. There have, however, been some African writers who have paid tribute to the few Asians who supported them in their struggles for independence, but, by and large, Asians have appeared as stereotyped and marginal characters in African-authored writings.

Of the East African Asians who have written about East Africa, with the notable exception of the comparatively recent and excellent books by MG Vassanji, very few have really ventured into fiction. Most of their writings have been academic, covering politics, history, and culture. Theirs has been a primarily scholarly interest in Asian contributions to the economic development of the area, with a sociological focus on the extraordinary insulation of the various subgroups that make up the larger Asian community.

In my work, I attempt to write about East African Asians as a people who migrated to East Africa for a variety of historical reasons, transplanted themselves, and adopted the new countries as their homes. I try to explore how and why they lived in watertight cultural compartments which often left them ignorant of or indifferent towards what was going on around them. Hence I am interested in the efficacy and constraints of arranged marriages, and parental attitudes towards sons versus daughters and daughters-in-law, and the pitiless social insularity that results. In this novel I deal with the consequences of one family choosing to stay in a rural area while another opts to move to an urban setting during the period from 1935 to 1937, when the Italian-Abyssinian war took place. This war was waged many miles away, and lasted only seven months, but its repercussions are illustrative of the vulnerabilities of colonialism's new worlds: mine and my people's.

Sophia Mustafa

Circumstances drive us on
In narrow paths by kismet hewn

For Fate has ways we cannot change,
While weakness preys upon our will;
We bolster with excuse the self,
And help that fate our selves to kill.

                                              KHALIL GIBRAN
                                              The Procession

1

Mussavir

"THIRTEEN! SHE'S THIRTEEN and you want me to marry her?" Mussavir wondered if he'd heard his mother correctly. "I'm already twenty-two, Mama!"

"So what? You're only nine years older than she," Ayesha said, shrugging her shoulders. "Your father is twelve years my senior. A full twelve years. I was five, your father seventeen, when our parents announced our engagement."

"For heaven's sake, Mama! You were at least sixteen when Abu married you. And lest you forget, those were Victorian days! You can't be serious, Mama." Mussavir scowled, showing furrows on his broad forehead. Tall and well built in his grey flannel pants and blue polo shirt, he had inherited his mother's dark intelligent eyes, deep set in his handsome young face.

A naughty smile played in the corners of Ayesha's fine lips. She seemed to enjoy seeing her first-born so excited. It reminded her of his childhood. He would get worked up and object to all her demands, then turn around and do exactly what she wanted. Ayesha had sharp features and a pleasant smile. She was of medium height, with a slender figure. Not yet forty, she was the mother of three grown-up sons and two teenage daughters.

"Traditions and customs have not changed, my son," she said as she hurled her blue dupatta over her shoulder. She was wearing a blue printed shalwar kamiz.

"Mama, this is the twentieth century. It's 1935! Times are changing. Young men are beginning to marry girls of their *own* choice even in India! Muslim boys name and choose the cousin they want to marry."

"Have you any cousin in mind then?"

"Cousin in mind?" Mussavir glowered. "Certainly not. I told you long ago. I *don't* want to marry a cousin." Turning his head, he looked out the window towards Mount Kenya, as if hoping to find a witness in the great mountain. Though wisps of cloud shrouded its lower slopes, the mountain's twin snowy peaks were clearly visible that morning from the house in Nyeri, where Mussavir's parents and two sisters lived.

"Then why do you feel so strongly about our choice?"

Ayesha's question made him turn and look at her again.

"Mama, I never said I'm against you choosing a girl for me," Mussavir said, now in a calmer tone. "It's a privilege I've no intention of denying you. But I do have a right to refuse if there's something I'm not happy about, haven't I?"

"True. But what are you unhappy about, son, when you've not even heard all about her or set eyes on her?"

"She's far too young, Mama," Mussavir said with irritation.

Ayesha was sitting opposite him at the long breakfast table. The poky room had pale green walls, with a four-inch black skirting from the cement floor.

"We're not asking you to marry her tomorrow. We only want you to be engaged to her." Ayesha picked the brown enamel teapot with the padded red tea cosy and poured tea for him, then filled her own cup. They had finished eating the parathas with fresh local honey that Ayesha had served for breakfast that morning.

"I couldn't marry her tomorrow even if I wanted to, Mama. I am off to a war front, as you jolly well know."

"That's not the only reason, son. Her mother won't give her in marriage yet. She's appearing for a Cambridge examination next year."

"Appearing for a Cambridge examination?" Mussavir raised his eyebrows. "What Cambridge examination can she appear for at thirteen? Unless she's a churail."

"She's not a she-devil. She's absolutely normal," Ayesha added seriously.

"But Mama, why do you want to tie me to such a young girl? Don't tell me older girls are in short supply here! I'm sure this one still plays with dolls."

"Not this thirteen-year-old. She's grown-up. Mature. Wholesome and good. A girl who has had some schooling. She's clever, smart, well-mannered, and fully able to shoulder responsibility."

"That still does not alter the fact she's only thirteen years old. Look at our Hibba, Mama, she's nearly fifteen. Is she ready for marriage?" Hibba was the elder of Mussavir's two sisters. "Why do her parents want to marry her off so young? Why are they so fed up with her?"

"Fed up with her? Far from it. She has no father. He died when she was seven. He was a good friend of your father. We both like her very much; in fact, we should be lucky if we can persuade her mother to agree to the rishta."

"Why don't you reserve her for either Zahir or Ta'Ha?" Mussavir said, goading his mother. Zahir and Ta'Ha were his two younger brothers, both studying in India.

"Zahir is already fixed. Inshallah, he'll marry my brother's daughter after his studies." Ayesha paused. "Ta'Ha, alas, does not show promise. He may not even complete his studies," she said, smoothing the white tablecloth. "To get her we'll have to offer our best and ablest son." She smiled as she looked at him. Her face warmed up with motherly pride.

"So I'll have to be the sacrificial lamb?" he asked, pointing a finger at himself.

"Perhaps," his mother said, tilting her head and smiling again, showing her gleaming white teeth, "you'll make . . ." She left the thought unsaid. She realized she must not banter with him as she often did. Of all her children he was the only one she could persuade to do what she liked. He was the most considerate and affectionate of her five offspring.

"Yes Mama, go on. What will I make? A good martyr!"

"A good husband, Beta. I am absolutely sure of that."

Mussavir looked up towards the white ceiling. There were black marks on it from the leaking roof, caused during the long rains. "Ya Allah, help me! What did I do to deserve this?"

"Destinies are made in heaven, my son. We think she's the right girl for you," his mother said slowly.

"I thought one makes one's own destiny," Mussavir murmured, then paused. "What's she called, this wonderful creation of God?"

"Shaira."

"Shaira? Is that her real name?"

"Yes."

"Shaira?" he asked again. "Meaning a poetess!"

"Yes, what's so unusual about it?"

"I'm called Mussavir. What a pair we'd make: painter and poetess."

"A good combination, son. Artist and poetess. 'Mussavir' doesn't exactly mean a painter. It refers to anyone who draws or fashions pictures, landscapes, and portraits from memory and sight." Putting out her hands she grasped her loose long hair, shampooed that morning, and braided it into a single plait. Streaks of grey shone like fine silk thread against the massed blackness.

Mussavir laughed. "Parents when naming their offspring never give a thought to what the children will think of their names in later life, do they? Alas, if only they stopped at that. No, they have to push further and even decide who their children should marry."

"I'm beginning to suspect you have some girl in mind, other than a cousin," said Ayesha.

"No Mama, I've told you I haven't. Allah kassam!" He raised his hand as if to affirm. "Listen Mama, I've told you I'm only twenty-two and have been busy studying. I really had to slog and sweat to get through. I had no time to think of marriage. I haven't even had time to breathe, and Abu wants me to go to this war in Abyssinia. I am not cut out for the army, let alone being excited about going to a war between the Italians and Ethiopians, who are not even my distant cousins! You know I've agreed because Abu committed me to it. Now, on top of all that, you both want me to tie myself to a thirteen-year-old girl you are so enamoured of. You want me to be engaged before I go. Suppose I get killed or maimed? Have you thought of that? I don't think it's right to involve such a young girl in all that."

"Mussavir, shut up. Don't talk like that, son," Ayesha reprimanded and her mood changed. "It can bring bad luck. God forbid. Life and death are all in Allah's hands. One can die before going to a war too. Inshallah, you'll come back in one piece, my son." She added gently, "You'll not be fighting. Only looking after the sick and wounded. In a hospital."

"But bombs can fall on hospitals, even on field hospitals and tents. Do you realize there will be bombs, Mama, not only guns and swords? And it's going to be a dirty war, I tell you. The Italian armies with tanks and guns, lorries and airplanes are travelling through the Suez Canal as we speak. They are not carrying arms for an exhibition, Mama. They are going to use them."

"Let's not talk about war. Please. There are other pleasant things to talk about," Ayesha said, suddenly paling with the realization that there was truth in what Mussavir had said.

"I suppose by pleasant you mean my marrying this thirteen-year-old Shaira?" Mussavir said. He knew his mother was not happy about his going to war. She looked pained when he talked about it.

"Right. We feel the nikah should be performed. You can then go to Abyssinia, she to her studies. The rukhstana can take place when you return." Ayesha quickly added, "She's very attractive. Don't reject her before you've even seen her, son."

Mussavir was thoughtful for a moment or two. Then he asked, "Will they allow me to see her? And talk to her? Being only thirteen, she can't be wearing the veil."

"She wears a burqa and is in purdah."

"In purdah? Already, at thirteen?"

"She wore the veil at eleven."

"Mama! That's cruel, really cruel. Wearing a veil and observing purdah at eleven. Talk of marriage at thirteen. Poor girl. I am beginning to have sympathy for her."

"A good sign, son!" Ayesha smiled, a twinkle in her eyes.

"Really, Mama. How I wish you'd stop joking and teasing me."

Sophia Mustafa

"I'm not joking or even teasing you, Beta, I'm serious. Think it over. Give me your reply when you've seen her."

"And how, if I may ask, will I see her?"

"She's coming with her mother and sister for the holidays next week."

"Here?"

"Yes. We've invited them all."

"From Nairobi?

Ayesha nodded.

"You really are serious, Mama."

"I told you so," she said as she got up and collected the honey pot and the remaining parathas to put them away in the kitchen.

"Mugro," called Ayesha, "ondoa viombo," and Mugro the houseman came in with an empty tray and started to clear the table. A native of Kiambu, Mugro had worked with the family for many years. Short and plump, with distended earlobes reaching almost to his shoulders, he wore a pair of Mussavir's father's old khaki trousers and a cast-off green army sweater. Nyeri, almost in the shadow of Mount Kenya, could be cold.

Mussavir's father, Dr Mohammed Bashir, one of two surgeons at the Nyeri District Hospital, was recruited by the colonial government from India before the First World War and had come out with Ayesha to Kenya when it was still called British East Africa, before it became a crown colony in 1920. Mussavir was born in Nairobi. Later Dr Bashir, like other doctors from India, lived in many small rural places. Their sons and daughters were all born within the first ten years, in different towns in Kenya. The small townships had no schools. There were day schools in Nairobi, as well as in the bigger towns, for Asian boys, but no boarding facilities. All schools ran separately on a racial basis, according to government policy, with different education systems for each of the three main races: European, Asian, and African.

Dr Bashir taught his sons at home and later sent them to India at an early age to study there. Mussavir qualified as a medical doctor in Delhi at just about the time that Mussolini's armies invaded Abyssinia. He returned to Kenya to join the medical department like his father. The Red Cross Society was recruiting volunteer doctors to help in Abyssinia and Dr

6

In the Shadow of Kirinyaga

Bashir had put his son's name down without consulting him. He persuaded Mussavir to go, arguing that his son's contributions would only enhance his prospects for a good job. Mussavir had no alternative but to honour his father's commitment. Waiting to hear from the authorities about his journey to Abyssinia, he was staying in Nyeri with his parents and young sisters and studying the English papers and books on Abyssinia which his father had collected from his European colleagues.

The house, a stone bungalow, stood in the complex of the Government District Hospital, on top of a hill overlooking the valley and river. The house had a breathtaking view of Mount Kenya, which the Kikuyu, living in its foothills, knew as Kirinyaga.

As Dr Bashir started work early, Mussavir never saw him for breakfast except on Sundays. Sometimes he visited the hospital and watched his father operating on patients, but he normally had his breakfast alone or with his mother. Once the matter of his work was finalized, Mussavir knew the next item on his parents' agenda for him was his marriage. He was glad it was his mother and not his father who had broached the subject. He could communicate better with Ayesha. He was not that free with his father, except when talking about medical matters or current events in East Africa, India, and the world.

After sampling the paper, Mussavir rose from the breakfast table to fetch his cigarettes from his room. He had to pass through the small living room, where his two sisters were busy at a side table, doing homework assignments given by their father. An early riser, Dr Bashir spent an hour with his daughters giving them instructions for the day. Hibba was fourteen, Farida twelve. There were no schools for Asian girls in Nyeri. Dr Bashir coached them in English, arithmetic, elementary history, and geography in the evenings after supper, according to a set timetable. Ayesha instructed them in Quran reading, Urdu, sewing, knitting, and household chores.

Farida, who looked very much like Mussavir, with her fair skin, thin nose, and sharp sparkling liquid eyes, was yawning and looking bored. Hibba was absorbed in her work. She was tall for her age and darker than Farida. She had a longer nose like her mother's.

7

Mussavir smiled. He understood his younger sister's difficulty well, and he felt sorry for both his sisters. They would not have long to study if their parents were thinking of marrying them off before they were even fifteen. The poor girls would not have much of a childhood.

He walked slowly through the living room, which was not only small and inadequate but also totally unimaginative like all government quarters—a cream-walled rectangular box with heavy wooden furniture, easy chairs, and a long piece of brown and yellow linoleum spread from wall to wall, with a red Indian darri thrown over it. His mother's handiwork—embroidered cushions and white crocheted chairbacks plus numerous family photos on the walls—made it look homely, even cosy, as far as the family was concerned.

Mussavir moved to the front veranda, the nicest place, with a view of the valley dotted with green juniper bushes and pepper trees. The Nyeri River, flowing from Mount Kenya, was moving slowly to the plains below. At that time of the year the water was sparkling and limpid, not muddy as in the rainy season.

The garden was bordered with a plum togo hedge with dark green leaves and blue flowers. Mussavir lit a cigarette and threw the extinguished matchstick into the garden. He looked up at the mountain, then down on the river. Then he skipped down the steps and walked across the lawn to the flowerbeds.

Pink balsams and deep red and yellow dahlias were all in full bloom. Mussavir's eyes focussed on the red and yellow snapdragons in the other flowerbed. A huge jacaranda tree stood in all its glory showering the lawn and paths with purple blue petals. Nandi flame trees dotted the drive to the hospital, a big white building with a green galvanized roof. A few prisoners in white khadi shorts and smock, guarded by a police constable-in-arms, were sweeping the leaves on the driveway as well as mowing the lawn by swinging the long and sharp iron fiakas over the grass. Other prisoners swept the cut grass with hand brooms made of long bristles. They also helped tend the gardens of the administrative officers and the doctors.

Out of all the places they had lived, Nyeri was the most picturesque and cool. Kirinyaga with its two silvery snow-capped peaks gave it added glamour.

In the Shadow of Kirinyaga

Mussavir thought about what his mother had told him and tried to picture the thirteen-year-old Shaira. He found it hard to envisage a girl that young being mature, attractive, smart, and about to sit for an overseas examination equivalent to matriculation. He had known all through his college days that eventually he'd marry a girl chosen by his parents, according to custom and tradition, and he had no objection to that, knowing that his parents would consult him. He was not a rebel but felt there was no hurry. The age of the girl bothered him. Early child-bearing could ruin a woman; it was a pity how few of his people realized that. However, there was one saving grace. He was going away for two years. If he came back alive, he could get the time extended by another year or so. In that event he would marry her when she would be at least sixteen. But then, he thought, he had not even met her yet. He might not like her at all, would perhaps have to reject her outright.

He walked to the edge of the garden, halfway down the slope, which led to the riverbank. A cluster of Kikuyu women from the parish across the ridge were standing knee deep in the water and bashing their soaped clothes using the round stones as slabs. Others were scrubbing their own muddy feet as well as their children's. Mussavir was reminded of women and young girls in India who, in colourful saris, washed clothes in the village ponds, then drew water from the well and carried the earthen pitchers up the ridges to their homes. But the Kikuyu women's dresses, though colourful, were shapeless and made from coarse material. Their multi-coloured scarves stood out. The young girls were plump, some even fat, not graceful like their rural Indian sisters.

Across the river and the ridge, a scattering of goats grazed with flowering shrubs in the background. The bells tied around their necks jingled as they chewed. Totos in brown shukas, knotted on one shoulder, looked after the goats. When the wind blew, their naked ebony bodies were revealed.

Mussavir turned back and walked up to the house on his way to town and the stores. Getting his jacket and calling to his mother that he was going out, Mussavir left by the back door. He loved going to the small Nyeri township. He made his way down the slope and, crossing the main highway, stepped onto the red road leading to the town.

2

Shaira

SABRA TIPTOED INTO the bedroom she shared with her daughters, Shaira and Huma. A tall woman with a good figure, she looked much older than her thirty-five years—somewhat haggard and her hair practically grey. She picked up the small alarm clock from the bedside table and set it for predawn. She always got up before the clock chimed but felt safer setting the alarm too. Pulling her grey shalwar kamiz from the peg behind the door, she changed and got into bed with eight-year-old Huma. As she pulled the white quilt up to her shoulders, she gently called, "Shaira, are you awake, Beti?" and lay back on her pillow.

"Yes, Ami," replied Shaira from the other bed as she turned to face her mother.

Sabra had rearranged the bedroom since her husband's death five years ago. The triple-mirrored dressing table was placed between the twin beds in the main bedroom.

"I suppose the boys are all asleep now."

"Yes, Ami. I can hear Majid snoring already." She chuckled lightly. Majid was the elder of her two cousins, on holiday from Mombasa.

"Good. I want to tell you a few things I might not have a chance to tell you later."

"Yes, Ami." Shaira raised herself and pushed back her long black glossy hair. She had brushed it before going to bed.

"In Nyeri, apart from Dr Bashir, his wife Ayesha, and the girls, there'll be their son too."

"Ta'Ha? When did he come?"

"No, not Ta'Ha, but his eldest brother, Mussavir." Sabra paused, then added, "You haven't met him. He was studying to be a doctor in India."

"Ah yes, Hibba showed me his photo once. But how do you know that, Ami? In her letter Hibba only asked that I take back a few silk skeins for her. She didn't say her brother was home."

"His cousin Latif told me Mussavir came home about a month ago." Then, before Shaira could respond, Sabra said, "Hibba has asked you to get some thread, did you say?"

"Yes, Ami."

"She has left it to the last minute, I must say."

"Yes, but I can get it tomorrow."

"Would Labbo's mother have some?"

"No, Ami. Labbo's mother only stocks DMC cotton. I'll have to go further to the city as Hibba wants silk skeins. I'll try and get them from Naqi Brothers on Government Road."

Labbo was an old student of Sabra whose mother ran a small haberdashery store in one of her bedrooms where she sold cotton and other fabrics to women who did not like going to the shops in the city.

"You'll need some money, won't you?"

"I suppose so, Ami. It won't be much though. About fifteen cents a skein and she wants ten skeins."

"Well, take two shillings from my purse and get twelve skeins to be on the safe side," Sabra said, as if relieved the matter of the thread was finally decided.

"Thanks, Ami." Shaira was about to bid her mother good night when she spoke again.

"About Nyeri, what I wanted to say was that it might be difficult for you to observe purdah from Mussavir in the Bashir household. The house is small and will be quite crowded with so many of us. Nevertheless, I want you to keep away from Mussavir as much as possible. Don't talk freely with him. Cover your head with your dupatta all the time. And wear your blue chador on your shoulders."

"Why, Ami?" Shaira asked, surprised at her mother's peculiar demand. "I mean . . . is he . . . is he a makora? Is there something wrong with him?"

"No, for heaven's sake. Nothing's wrong with him, and he is not a bad-charactered boy, but he *is* a grown-up man now, and you are supposed to observe purdah from him."

"Oh, I see . . . but it's hardly polite to be guests and want things our own way. Do you want me to remain indoors and eat in the kitchen too?"

"No, for goodness sake, that won't look right. I don't want you to remain indoors or eat in the kitchen or sit by yourself. Move about. Only try and have your back towards Mussavir if he's there. Talk to him only when he addresses you. Be reserved. And careful. Surely you know what I mean."

"I am sorry, Ami, but I don't know what you mean. Wouldn't it be better for me to not to appear in front of him at all? After all, I am in purdah. They'll understand. To turn my back, to play hide and seek, to wear a shawl all the time sounds funny."

Sabra stared hard at her daughter. "The real problem is that you look much older than your thirteen years. I wish to God you'd not grown up so quickly." Sabra sighed, as she always did when she commented on Shaira's growing up, as if it were the world's worst crime, and only Shaira had ever committed it.

Shaira was tall and slim with a rosy complexion and liquid eyes, a fully developed bust, and a good figure. She could easily pass for sixteen or even more.

"Then leave me behind, Ami," she stated in a voice that was louder than usual. "You'll have no worries. I can't embarrass you if I'm not there."

"I can't do that. Both Bashir and Ayesha will be disappointed. They are expecting you, and I can't manage the children on my own." Sabra paused, collecting herself. "Sometimes you amaze me, Shaira. You are a good and obedient girl. I've brought you up well with due regard to religion and culture. You have a good brain or you wouldn't be two grades above your age group, but it's a pity you fail to understand or think out the simple things of life and growing up. I can't spell out everything." She grimaced. "Oh how I wish . . . anyway, we shall see how it goes. Just be a bit careful." Before Shaira had even caught on to what her mother was aiming at, Sabra changed the subject, asking, "What else did Hibba say in her letter?"

"Hibba? . . . Yes, she said there's going to be a marriage in Nyeri during our stay there. She suggested we take suitable clothes for that too." Shaira wondered if her mother also had other ideas about her wardrobe.

"What have you packed then?" asked Sabra.

"My pink suit," Shaira said hesitatingly, "and Huma's tariwalla orange."

"That's fine. Why didn't you tell me earlier? I'd have got some jewellery out for both of you. Remind me when we get up. What about the boys' packing?"

"I got them to pack their clothes in the small tin suitcase. And Mwangi is going to lay out the vegetables and fruit we are taking for our hosts in a wicker kikapu. He said we'll have to keep it at our feet, the sun will spoil it if we place it on the roof of the bus."

"He's right. I told him to pack our food for the journey in the picnic basket. Make sure he does not forget drinking water," Sabra said in a sleepy voice and yawned.

"Very well, Ami."

Shaira was about to bid her mother good night when Sabra put out her arm and turned off the bedside lamp. A fisi howled just then. It was a moonlit night and hyenas came out early on such nights. Because Sabra's house was the last in the row they often ended up there and stood howling at the moon. Sabra covered her head with the quilt and pressed her ear against the pillow.

Shaira was aware of her mother's disappointment at her growing up fast; she was also used to her outbursts. Shaira tried not to annoy her. An intuitive sense made her realize that being a widow and having had to work hard as a teacher and rear her brood of children, Sabra was prone to irritation and abrupt demands. But at times Shaira felt her mother asked too much. She could not defy her outright—that was not acceptable from respectable and well-brought-up girls—but she couldn't help feeling annoyed. She was looking forward to this holiday in the beautiful countryside. Her mother was now going to make it difficult for her. Shaira brooded and wondered why her mother was so particular about purdah in Nyeri from the son of such good family friends when she never bothered about her observing purdah from Latif, Dr Bashir's nephew, and other neighbours' sons, all grown-up men too, when they visited her brothers. She was only thirteen and already shouldering more responsibilities than other girls and doing things that even older girls in the community did not do. She was made to wear the veil much earlier than the others. She felt a pang of self-pity, but then tried to shake it off. If her mother had it in her head that she must observe purdah or semi-purdah in Nyeri, from this Mussavir, then she'd have to obey. That was the custom, however much she disliked it. But there was one respite. Her mother's moods changed often. It was possible once she was in Nyeri she would forget all about it. Shaira pulled up her quilt when the hyena howled again. She could hear dogs barking and in the distance the singing of the Africans who usually sat outside their huts roasting and eating sweet potatoes and corn on the cob well into the night. Turning to her side she tried to sleep.

The next day they made all the purchases. By evening the packing was done too. They pulled the big trunk out from under the bed—the family had brought it from India almost two decades ago and it was now used as a bottom drawer for the girls. Sabra opened the huge padlock with an iron key and handed over gold bangles, earrings, and necklaces to Shaira to pack along with the clothes. Sabra had stopped wearing ornaments after her husband's death. The girls used the smaller pieces for festive occasions; Sabra had deposited the heavier family jewellery in the bank for the marriages of her offspring.

In the evening there was an air of excitement in Sabra's household. Huma, Honey, and their two young cousins, bathed and in their nightclothes, were ready for bed. Zaffer, Sabra's eldest son, was away on safari. Shahid, her eighteen-year-old, was working and would remain in the house on his own. The local butcher's son, Mohammed Rafik, had promised to give them all a lift in his van to the bus stop on Race Course Road in the city. He went daily to collect slaughtered goats and sheep from the slaughterhouse early in the morning.

Sabra, as usual, got up before the alarm clock sounded. She woke

Shaira, who, after dressing in her travelling suit, started calling her siblings and cousins to get up. Though very excited about the journey the previous evening, none of them was willing to get up so early. Shaira had to shake and pull the pillows from under their heads. Huma, who was plump and chubby with a head of curly hair, rose first, grumbling and whining, and then the others too rubbed their eyes and scrambled out of their beds.

What a commotion! The young ones rushed to the bathroom, screaming "Lete maji moto!" at Mwangi for more hot water. Mwangi had heated the water in an empty kerosene tin on a three-stone jiko in the backyard and placed two bucketsful in the small bathroom. The boys pulled the beaker from one another to fill the basin and all three tried to grab the towel to wipe their faces. Amidst Shaira's calls to hurry up because breakfast was ready, they finally managed to sit at the table, though in their excitement about the journey and irritation at getting up early they did not do justice to the breakfast as they normally would have.

Mwangi had packed the safari lunch and flasks of tea and drinking water in bottles. Sabra checked and rechecked everything. She made sure everybody was wearing laced-up shoes and socks and had warm jerseys on.

Mohammed Rafik and his van arrived dead on time. As it was a closed van for carting slaughtered carcasses, it had no windows. Huma absolutely refused to sit at the back with her brother and cousins. "I won't be able to look outside and I'll suffocate when the back door is shut. I'm not a mbuzi or kondoo," she wailed.

"Well, then, you can foot it, dear daughter," Sabra told her. The boys all laughed and Mohammed Rafik said he would keep the door half open. Fresh air would come in freely. The ride to town was not long, no one would suffocate, he assured them.

The boys climbed in and settled on the sisal mattress that Mohammed Rafik had spread on the floor, as the vehicle did not have seats.

"Huma, you can take my place in front with Ami. I'll sit with the boys."

Like a shot Huma jumped into the front of the van lest Shaira change her mind or her mother order her otherwise.

Shahid came out of the house to help Mwangi load the luggage and to see the family off.

"Ha, Mohammed Rafik, what funny goats and sheep you have today!" he teased, peeping into the van as he helped his sister Shaira get in. At eighteen Shahid already had sideburns and a thick moustache, which gave him such a serious look that Mwangi had nicknamed him kihoro, or the "serious one."

"Kwaheri, Mwangi! Mimi ta bring kikwa for you," chirped Huma from the van.

"Asante Huma. Fika salama." Mwangi wished her a safe journey.

"Bye, Manjala Bhai." Huma waved to Shahid and the others too wished Mwangi and Shahid farewell.

Mohammed Rafik started the engine and the van set off, the children waving vigorously and Sabra giving last-minute instructions to Shahid and Mwangi.

3

The Township

STROLLING ALONG THE main street of the Nyeri township, Mussavir found it, as always on a Saturday, bustling with activity. European farmers dressed in casual clothes with wide-brimmed hats, wearing bushy moustaches and sideburns, were buying liquor from Rattansey Store. Their wives and womenfolk, clothed in dresses and farm trousers with loose pullovers, were busy doing their weekly shopping at the main Indian stores run by the Rattansey, Somji, Bhimji, and Vellani families. Outside the shops, transport lorries from Nairobi were off-loading goods. African men in bare feet, dressed in shabby garments, almost bent under the weight on their backs, carried sacks of produce, ghee and kerosene oil tins, soft drinks, beer and liquor crates, and other items which the merchants had ordered from the city and abroad. Some men lugged the loads on their backs, others dragged them over the damp grass, and still others wheeled the crates on wheelbarrows to the storage rooms behind the shops.

Lorry drivers who had already off-loaded and refilled were having refreshments from a tea house opposite Rattansey Store. Most of the transporters were Hindu Punjabis, Meman Muslims, or Sikhs. From there they often drove to the godowns and warehouses to load the farm produce for their return journey in the evening. The drivers who were still off-loading stood in groups talking in loud voices and laughing with the shopkeepers, perhaps updating them on the latest gossip from Nairobi and the Northern Frontier.

An Indian restaurant called The Cosy Tea Room, and nicknamed The Greasy Spoon, was run by a Hindu. It was the meeting place of the Asian drivers and transporters, a grimy yellow room full of pictures of Indian Devtas and Devis with many hands that stared down at the diners. The men sat on wooden chairs at bare tables to enjoy the spicy Indian sweetmeats and snacks, bhajia, dhoklas, and farsan, which they washed down with steaming spicy Indian tea boiled with milk and sugar. The proprietor, Purshotam Lal, wearing a white dhoti and shirt, poured the tea into cups from a white enamel kettle. He wore a yellow and red mark on his forehead, sign of a devout Hindu. The aroma of frying and spices was all pervasive.

Walking past the tea room, Mussavir called a greeting to the old Hindu proprietor, who replied with a wide grin.

Right across from this duka, the African drivers munched yellow buns and drank steaming trungi in a thatch-roofed, shedlike, ramshackle structure called a hoteli. They ate the refreshments on a shabby wooden table while seated on long wooden benches. The sufuria, full of trungi, simmered slowly for hours over a charcoal brazier kept in the open. Some ate ugali and urio, maize flour cooked with beans. The African man who served them poured the tea into mugs from a black kettle with a big spout. He wore shabby old clothes with an equally tattered sweater to keep warm. Mussavir waved jambo to the men on the tables and they responded, "Asante, Bwana Daktari," smiling wide white smiles.

Mussavir had often heard from the shopkeepers who delivered the foodstuffs and beverages to the European clubs and hotels that the Europeans, mostly white settlers and coffee and maize farmers, after shopping all drove to the Nyeri Club or hotels exclusively for Europeans. There, it was rumoured, they would have their elevenses or prelunch drinks in the verandas of the white-walled, green-roofed buildings with beautiful gardens and an excellent view of the mountain peaks on clear days. African waiters in clean white khanzus with red or green sashes around the waist and green fezzes waited on them. It was common knowledge that farmers came to the clubs and hotels to celebrate their successes or to drown their sorrows through excessive drinking.

Mussavir was friendly with the sons of Rattansey and Vellani, proprietors, respectively, of the provision and fancy goods stores. He often stopped for a soft drink and a chat and loved to hear the current gossip after a walk through the township. He liked the bustling and active Asian business community. He admired their industry and hard work. The Asians had helped the British open up the country and some were third-generation East African. Starting as hawkers, they had already advanced to proper shops doing import and export business. They all lived behind the shops, with an Ismaili jamatkhana, a tiny Muslim mosque, two Hindu temples of different denominations, and a Sikh gurdwara all nearby in the township, in a sort of watertight existence along ethnic lines, strictly following the culture and norms of India.

That morning Mussavir stopped at Vellani Store. He greeted the old man, and his friend Badru, the son, offered him a chair. While Mussavir was chatting with the old man, Badru's mother peeped out from the back door. A short, fat, middle-aged woman, she wore a long loose dress of printed material with a blue pachedi on her shoulders. In her nose she sported a glittering five-stone ring of the sort popularly worn by well-to-do Ismaili women. Mussavir stood up and bowed, saying, "Salaam, Masi Maan." She gave him a broad smile and replied, "Sahib Salamat, Bapa. Kem cho?" Mussavir told her he was well and brought greetings from his mother.

"Kem cho, Bhabi?" he said to Badru's wife, Shirin, when he went in with Badru and greeted his sisters Khursan and Doulat. The womenfolk were all sitting in the back veranda on low stools with trays in their laps, cleaning rice and grains. Khursan, who was plump and fair and dressed in a green dress, was peeling potatoes. Doulat, sitting on a wooden mbuzi, was scraping coconuts onto a round aluminum tray. The white and fluffy shredded coconut was piled up in a heap. A Kikuyu man was grinding some wheat between a two-stone grinder called a chakki by moving the handle of the upper stone with one hand and putting a fistful of whole wheat into the space in the middle of it. Cracked wheat was falling off the sides of the chakki onto the reed mat under it.

Badru's mother, sitting on the big rocking jhoola—a wooden seat hanging from the roof of the veranda—was peeling garlic, and the place reeked with the smell. A lot of white sheets and linen and other clothes hung on the washline in the sun. The cement floor of the courtyard was swept clean but the smell of sewage wafted in from the open drains. In the kitchen someone was cooking.

Mussavir and his hosts chatted for a while about his going to the war front, a subject Mussavir tried to avoid discussing but which was topical and often surfaced. Badru's wife said some of their relatives, business people in Addis Ababa and Mogadishu, were sending their women and children to Kenya. There was a lot of unrest there and it was not safe. Mussavir asked Badru's wife about her parents, whom he knew and who lived in Thika. He did not stay long. Taking a present of freshly cracked wheat from Badru's mother, he departed.

At the entrance of the shop he bumped into Major Saddler, an English farmer from Naro Moro whose wife had been Dr Bashir's patient for a while; Mussavir had accompanied his father on one of his visits there. Major Saddler was a huge man with a big paunch. He wore a small goatee with a droopy moustache. He was in his riding breeches and carried his whip in his hand.

"Good morning, Major," Mussavir said and moved out to let him pass.

"Oh . . . morning, my boy. A very good morning to you. So you're still here?" he glowered but in good humour.

"Yes, Major," Mussavir added and quickly asked, "How is Mrs Saddler?"

"Pretty good, thank you. She hopes to start her clinic on the farm soon."

"Good for her. Do give her my jambos, Major, and tell her I enjoyed reading the book she lent me about Adowa. I have a better picture of Abyssinia now."

"I shall, and good luck to you if I don't see you again. I mean before you leave." He flashed a smile and gave Mussavir a heavy thump on the shoulder as if to say, "Well done." Before going into the shop, Major Saddler walked back to the edge of the veranda and looked towards the car park. He waved his arm and shouted, "You there . . . where the hell are you?" He scowled at an African man who was lugging a crate of empty beer bottles and slowly waddling towards him. Mussavir had crossed the road, but on hearing the major's shout he stopped, as did many passersby and the people having tea in the hoteli.

"You . . . pumbafu, idiot . . . you listen to me. When I ask you to kuja to Vellani Store you bloody well kuj. Don't start chattering with your friends like a nugu. Come on, chop-chop. We don't have the whole day."

Some of the trungi drinkers started laughing loudly, while the passersby who had stopped spat on the ground and walked away. Mussavir started to walk up the slope, surprised at Major Saddler. He was friendly and kind one minute and the next he could flare up at his poor native farm worker, who was lugging a heavy load but could not help stopping to exchange a greeting with a fellow native. What the major had said to the worker was laughable. He had not learnt Swahili properly, not even the settler version in which expressions like "please" and "thank you" didn't exist. He had pruned "kuja," a crude version of "come," into the meaningless "kuj." Many settlers were like that. They bellowed orders in their own version of Swahili cum Kikuyu and expected the workers to understand and respond. They could be such bullies. But this seemed the order of the day. Even the Indian shopkeepers were like that. They called the natives "kallio" and "gollio," meaning "blacko" and "slave." They behaved as if it were their divine right to bully the weak. The natives quite rightly either laughed at their stupidity or ignored it. Mussavir had once witnessed the same major bring a worker injured at his farm to hospital, practically carrying him in his arms and very concerned about the man. He was very sympathetic towards the Abyssinians and detested the Italians for invading Ethiopia. He told Mussavir that had he been a younger man he would have offered to go and fight the Fascists.

What his mother had told him was on Mussavir's mind. He found his father already home for lunch, a bit earlier than usual. His sisters had finished their homework too. He stopped near the kitchen door. Ayesha, sitting on a low stool, was baking chapattis on a black iron griddle for lunch. Mugro, busy washing the family's clothes under the outside water tap in a small tin tub, was whistling.

Tall, thin, and full bearded with a broad forehead, Dr Bashir always removed his black jacket and trousers immediately on coming home. Under his trousers he wore a pair of white calico pyjamas tucked in his knee-length grey socks, kept in place with rubber garters, giving the pyjamas a breecheslike look over his black slippers. He rolled up his long sleeves to perform his wudu from an iron samovar kept in the back veranda not far from the kitchen. He was a neat, clean, fair-complexioned man. A good practising Muslim, he kept all his fasts and performed his prayers five times a day, and gave to all the required charities, which resulted in his being tight fisted at home. Apart from spending on his sons' education in India, he had saved enough to buy a house in India for his retirement. He did not smoke or take liquor, unlike many of the men his age in East Africa.

Mussavir was of a different generation. He was not a bad Muslim but could not adhere strictly to all the tenets of the faith. He had started smoking when in college and had also ventured to taste alcoholic drinks, absolutely forbidden by Islam. Not only had he tasted them, he still indulged in an occasional bottle of beer when he had the chance. All, of course, on the quiet. He did not regularly say all the daily prayers, but if near a mosque he would make it a point to attend the obligatory Friday prayers with the congregation. Often he made fun of a lot of religious teachings and disliked fanatical religious people, their hypocrisy and dogma, but made this known only to his mother and sisters or good friends. Ayesha seemed less serious than Mohammed Bashir. She had a good sense of humour and could laugh at herself and things in general. She seemed to enjoy her son's jokes and often said how proud she felt because he had inherited that trait from her side of the family.

Mussavir greeted his father and asked if there was any mail for him. There was none. Dr Bashir said he had received a letter from Ta'Ha, his youngest son. "He has absconded from college again and is staying with your mother's cousin in Hoshiarpur; he wants to come back."

"Really, Abu? That's bad. Leaving his studies halfway. I had thought he had settled." Ta'Ha had only a year and a half to go before qualifying for his BA. He was not studious and had run away from college once before. "Abu, you should put your foot down and make him at least finish his BA," Mussavir advised.

"It's no use forcing him back. He'll not pass. I am sure of it now," Dr Bashir stated calmly. "It's best to get him out and put him on a job in Kenya. He can work as a clerk in the bank or railways."

They ate their lunch in silence. Then Dr Bashir got up to perform his afternoon prayers before going back to work. Mussavir and his sisters went to the front veranda where later their mother joined them.

"It's a great pity Ta'Ha does not want to finish his studies," said Ayesha. "He could have got a good job in the secondary boys' school here after his BT degree."

"Abu should make him do it. Threaten him he'll remain a junior clerk all his life. Abu is lenient with him. Not at all firm as he was with Zahir and me."

"Your father is a practical man, son. He feels he cannot waste any more money on him. When we next go on leave, Hibba has to be married. That will consume quite a bit of our savings. Zahir still has two years to finish his master's. Pity Ta'Ha never settled in college after his FA. When forced back, he promised he would stay on till the end. He is bound to regret it later." Ayesha sighed and looked at the mountain.

Mussavir had an idea why his youngest brother did that, but could not reveal it to his mother. She would not understand how rough it could be in the hostels and men's institutions. Ta'Ha, a handsome lad, fair and gentle, sensitive and weak, became an easy prey for older tougher boys. All young boys went through that stage in a male institution. If tough, you could make it. Sometimes if you attached yourself to one boy, he would protect you from the others.

Aloud he said, "Maybe Abu is right. He might settle down here if he can get his teeth into something that interests him, and being nearer home might help."

"I think he should get married," Ayesha said, still looking towards the mountain.

"Get married? Mama, you want him to get married before he has even trained or got a job? For goodness sake, he's only eighteen. You're in a mighty hurry about marriage for everybody, aren't you?"

"It's the best way to settle down and become responsible," Ayesha replied calmly.

"Mama, I'm sorry, but you are living very much behind the times." Mussavir gave a small chuckle and added, "Have you got another thirteen-year-old girl tucked up somewhere for him too, or are you going to marry him to this Shaira?"

"No, and Shaira is for you. Ta'Ha will need an older girl, more his age, or even a year or two older." Ayesha was serious.

"Older girl! Why?" Mussavir felt his mother was full of surprises.

"He needs some mothering still."

"Mama, I really can't understand your logic and reasoning. Mothering! Older girl . . ." He laughed again and asked, "Why do you think he runs away?"

"To seek the company of older women."

Mussavir was taken aback by his mother's frankness, but touched; she was speaking with great concern, in sadness and not in anger, and was not joking either.

"You don't think he is running away from older boys and even men?" he almost whispered.

"That could be true too, my son. Morals are at their lowest ebb these days and these things happen. It's better, therefore, that Ta'Ha get married."

"Will he remain in India until then?"

"No, your father wants him to come out straightaway and work here. I shall bring a girl out for him later."

"And you think he'll agree to that?" Mussavir sat up and clasped his hands in front of him, his eyes glued to his mother's face.

"Why will he not agree?" Ayesha was sharp. "He'll have to agree. He can't let us down in every way."

Hibba came in with her embroidery basket and sat opposite her mother on another cane chair.

"Mama," she said, "I have decided to embroider with another shade."

"Why another shade?" questioned Ayesha irritably before Hibba had even finished explaining. "You have written to Shaira to bring some, haven't you?"

"Yes, but I am not sure if my letter will reach her before they leave," she said and put down her work, waiting for her mother's decision.

"No, don't use another colour. When Shaira comes, try and learn from her how to do the Kashmiri stitch, it takes far less thread than the satin stitch you are doing."

"But one doesn't mix the two stitches, Mama," Hibba said, raising her eyebrows.

"They can be toned in, Beti. The bigger leaves can be worked in the Kashmiri stitch and the smaller ones in the satin stitch. It does look nice. I saw the tablecloth Shaira embroidered last time."

Mussavir, sitting quietly, his hands now behind his head, was amused how his mother scored another point in favour of Shaira. But he also noticed that Hibba was not too impressed. "I'll leave the green out altogether for the time being and do the rest," she said, resigned.

Farida came in with her jigsaw puzzle box in hand and asked, "When are the guests from Nairobi coming, Mama?"

"Next week," replied her mother.

"Is Shaira Baji coming too?"

"But of course."

"Jolly good," said Farida happily as she spread the jigsaw pieces on the small table on the veranda.

"Why are you so happy about the guests coming from Nairobi, Farida?" Mussavir asked.

"I like Shaira, Baji. She reads interesting stories from her English books to us. When she combs my hair she does not pull and it does not pain." She cast a glance at Hibba and smiled timidly.

"Go and live with her then," said Hibba, who looked up from her work, glared at her sister, then made a face at her.

Farida made no reply, went on looking at her jigsaw pieces. Ayesha got up to go inside and said, "No need to be so sharp, Hibba. You seem to be on edge today. I am going in for my prayers. Farida, can you come in for a while? I want you to do something for me."

"What are you embroidering, Hibba?" Mussavir asked.
"A bedsheet."
"It looks like silk to me."
"Yes. It's Fuji silk."
"You like embroidery?"
"It's all right, Bhaijan," Hibba said, shrugging her shoulders.
"And this friend of yours, Shaira, why don't you like her?"
"I didn't say I didn't like her. She was my friend before even Farida knew her."
"And she is not your friend now?"
"Of course she is. I like her but . . ." Hibba stopped and, sticking the needle into the piece in the round frame, scratched her head. Her hair, parted in the middle, was plaited in a single braid down her back. She wore a pink cotton shalwar kamiz with black borders on the kamiz.
"But what, Hibba?" Mussavir was curious.
"Well, Abu and Mama praise Shaira so much. I know she is clever and all that, even younger than me. She goes to an English-medium school and I have not even been to an Indian school or any school, Bhaijan. I can't be like her." Hibba pouted and went back to the embroidery
"Has Mama told you she wants you to be like Shaira?"
"No, she hasn't, but in her heart I know she wants me to be like her. She likes her very much. Even Abu talks to her more than he does to all of us." Hibba looked up.
"But, Hibba, that doesn't mean they don't like us. Both Abu and Mama love us. Look how they have spent years in small places all by themselves, often with no friends, working hard for us." Mussavir paused and added, "I don't think Mama wants you to be like Shaira. She likes Shaira maybe for other reasons."
"What other reasons, Bhaijan?" Hibba's eyes widened.
Mussavir glanced around. No one else was about. "Can you keep a secret, Hibba?"
Hibba nodded.
"Mama and Abu want me to be engaged to Shaira."
"Really, Bhaijan?" Her eyes lit up. She left her work and leaned forward.

In the Shadow of Kirinyaga

"Are you going to? I hope you will. She's really nice, very pretty and fair. If she becomes our sister-in-law that would be super."

Mussavir was astonished at the quick about-turn. "But Mama says she is only thirteen, even younger than you."

"Yes, but she looks much older, Bhaijan. She is grown up. But she wants to study. Are you sure you'll be able to marry her?"

"I haven't decided. I have not seen or met her."

"Ah yes, you've come after such a long time. She must have been small when you last came to Kenya."

"Who looks after them? I hear she has no father."

"She has two older brothers. They work in Nairobi. Her mother is a teacher."

"Where do her brothers work?"

"The eldest, Zaffer Bhai, works for a car firm as a salesman, and the younger, Shahid, works with RO Hamilton, also in Nairobi."

"How old are they?"

"Zaffer Bhai must be your age and Shahid could be as old as Sinjla Bhai." She meant her third brother, Ta'Ha.

"Any sisters?"

"One. The youngest in the family. Her name is Humaira but she is called Huma. Their youngest brother, Hannan, is called Honey. He's older than Huma."

"What a collection of classical names." Mussavir smiled and asked, "How old are Huma and Honey?"

"Huma is eight, Honey must be ten."

"You seem to know them all."

"We've stayed with them so many times. I don't like Shahid Bhai though. He's sour and always grumbling, not very friendly. Zaffer Bhai is nice and can be jolly and tell jokes and funny stories."

"What's their mother like?"

"Khala Sabra? She's all right. I like her. Everyone says she was very good looking once."

"What's wrong with her now?" Mussavir said, laughing, "she can't be too old."

27

"She's younger than Mama but very grey, thin and old looking. But, Bhaijan, you are soon going to this war, when will you get married?" Hibba looked worried.

"Certainly not before I go. Maybe after I come back."

"I wish you weren't going. I get so worried. I really do." Hibba furrowed her forehead "I don't know why Abu wants you to go. Aren't you afraid, Bhaijan?" she asked. Before Mussavir could reply, she added, "Maybe because you are a man, you are not scared."

"What makes you think men are not frightened, Hibba?" Mussavir said, smiling affectionately.

"Are you also frightened then?"

"Sometimes."

"And you still want to go?"

"It'll be an experience, Hibba."

"I can't understand why the Italians want to come all the way to Africa to fight the poor Abyssinians."

"They are angry with the Abyssinians."

"Why?"

"A long time ago in the last century they suffered a humiliating defeat when fighting with the Abyssinians. The Italians have not forgotten what it was like to be the first European power to be defeated by a black country. They also want an empire." Mussavir shrugged his shoulders.

"But they have colonies in the Italian Somaliland, haven't they?"

"They want more. Abyssinia has rich and unexplored minerals. They want to explore them and enrich themselves and also give jobs to their own countrymen by using the cheap labour of the natives, as the British do here by growing cash crops for Europe and the world."

"But that would help the natives too, I suppose." Hibba shrugged her shoulders. It was all complicated and difficult to fathom, so she said, "I hope Abu is right. He told Mama the British subjects would be well protected. She was dead set against you going there."

"The British themselves need protection. Major Saddler told me they have got a Sikh regiment from India to guard their legion."

Hibba was thoughtful for a moment, then said, "I'll say special prayers for your safe return." And she smiled widely.

"Thank you, Hibba. And another thing, I hope you'll keep what I have told you to yourself. Don't tell Mama I talked to you and certainly not your friend who is coming next week."

"No, Bhaijan, I promise I won't tell anyone. But what if Shaira knows already?"

"How would she know? Mama and Abu have not asked for her hand yet. They want to know what I think of her first and whether I like her. I shall decide after I meet her."

"But supposing she does purdah from you? She wears a burqa."

"Mama told me that. She might not wear it while she is here. It's difficult to observe purdah in a small house. Mama is certainly expecting me to see her."

"I've promised not to say anything to Shaira, but I'd have loved to tell Shaira something she doesn't know. She always knows everything." Hibba smiled, more in amusement now. She seemed cheerful too.

Mussavir smiled too and decided to warn his mother not to compare Hibba too much with Shaira. His sister was very sensitive and could develop an inferiority complex.

4

The Journey

MOHAMMED RAFIK WAS a fast driver. Once they hit the main tarmac road, the van zoomed along Juja Road, slowing down only to turn onto Park Road, and raced towards Ngara passing the railway quarters on the right and the sweetmeat seller Chirra's shop on the left. Sabra had ordered some mithai to take to Nyeri. While Mohammed Rafik was collecting the package, the Mombasa cousins, who had been chatting nonstop, wanted to know why the shop was named after a bird. "Chirra" was the Punjabi word for a male sparrow! Huma, sitting between her mother and Mohammed Rafik, lifted the cellophane flap and told her cousins that Chirra was actually the nickname of Labbo's father, because of his beaklike nose.

"And is Labbo's mother known as Chirri? A she-bird?" Salim the younger cousin asked Shaira.

"She's fat, and round-round and short," Honey told him, making a gesture with his hands.

"And what does Labbo's ma do?" asked Majid. "Help her husband make sweets?"

"No. She runs a small fabric store in one of her bedrooms. Women come from all over Nairobi to buy materials from her and mithai from her husband," Shaira told him.

Mohammed Rafik brought some pipis and chewing gum as their farewell gift, and handed the packet to Shaira. The boys greedily put out their hands to grab the goodies, and Huma demanded her share. There was a chorus of thanks.

The van drove down the valley and up Race Course Road, turned left, and braked to a halt in front of the bus depot, which, despite the early hour, was already bustling with activity, mostly indigenous African travellers and their relatives who had come in great numbers to see them off. A few Asians stood around the buses parked in rows. Many people had already boarded the buses and were talking to their relatives or friends from the windows. Here and there African vendors were selling vitumbua and bananas to the passengers.

The young people jumped off the van and Shaira began organizing the group, ordering them not to move away. Sabra handed Mohammed Rafik the money to buy one full ticket and four half-tickets. Salim, the youngest, could go free as he was under six. Mohammed Rafik suggested Majid could go as an under-six too.

"Oh no, Majid is too fat to pass for an under-six. And it is a matter of saving only a shilling. You'd better get a half-ticket for him too," Sabra insisted.

Mohammed Rafik got the tickets and the family all trooped to their bus. The driver placed their luggage on the roof without bashing it about while they carried their hand luggage with them. The conductor checked the tickets and allowed them to keep the food basket and fruit and vegetables at their feet. Shaira sat on one of the front seats with Salim, Huma with her mother sat behind them, and Majid and Honey sat right at the back.

Mohammed Rafik, after seating them all safely off, took his leave, promising to meet them on their return, then went to pick up his slaughtered goats and sheep. The children waved vigorously as if they would never see him again.

A Sikh couple with a young son about Honey's age and a Gujerati couple with three small children boarded the bus and sat at the back. The bus began filling up with the local Africans. The driver, with the help of the conductor, covered the luggage on the roof with a tarpaulin and, after closing the doors, climbed onto his seat, put on his peaked cap, and peered into the bus from the opening behind his seat to check if all was set. Because of the cold it took time to start the engine, and when it ignited, the driver pressed the accelerator hard, making a loud burring noise. A similar noise drooled from several other buses that were warming up before leaving. Fumes of petrol and oil were all pervasive. Passengers' friends and relatives began to leave, still chattering and calling good wishes, and the bus to Nyeri crept out of the bus stop and onto the main road.

The day was misty and cloudy. The shops along the road were still closed as opening time was 8 a.m. but people were already moving about, mainly Africans and Asians of all sects and colours. A few Indian girls' religious and private schools were located in that area. There was the Muslim Girls School behind the bus station in the area known as Gian Singh's Shamba. And on the opposite side of Race Course Road, where it joined Duke Street, was the Sanatan Dharam Girls School, as well as the Sanatan Dharam Temple. Behind that stood the Sikh Girls School as well as the huge imposing Singh Sabha Gurdwara with its grand round dome in black and gold. The Arya Samaj Girls School and the Arya Samaj itself were also not too far from there.

The early pupils, all girls escorted by fathers and brothers, headed to their various institutions. Their saris and trouser suits made a spate of colour: the white suits and yellow chunnis of the Sikh girls, the colourful turbans of their fathers and brothers, the pink saris of the Sanatan girls, and the deeper yellow saris of the Arya Samaj girls intermingled.

There were no religious or private schools for boys. They all attended the Government Indian Boys Primary and Secondary Schools, which were at the other end near the main railway station.

African workers rushed on in long and short khaki or black trousers and coats, some wearing shoes, others wearing sandals made out of old tires, and still others in bare feet. All headed swiftly to their workplaces in the shops, small factories in the industrial area, bakeries and butchery shops, as well as the offices. On the roads there was the usual morning traffic of cars, lorries, buses, hand carts, and bicycles whirring along.

The bus to Nyeri with its passengers arrived at the Race Course Road bridge and, passing it, forked left and up the hill to Park Road, passing the dhobi ghat on the left. The grey washing slabs looked greyer in the mist.

The washermen in white dhotis were bashing white linen against the stone slabs. The bus picked up speed and raced along till it reached the Swahili town of Pangani, a lively settlement of mud huts with roofs made out of old petrol and kerosene tins beaten up and hammered flat. Over the years rainwater and sun had caused the tin to rust into various colours.

Here again one could see lots of pupils, now mostly boys, as well as men going towards Ngara and City Centre. Many men from that area went to work in the city and the buses were full.

After passing the Pangani outskirts the bus went down Forthall Road and up towards Muthaiga. The children settled in their seats and chattered away. Sabra, not being a good traveller, closed her eyes and, wrapped in her white burqa, sat back on the seat. Shaira looked out of the window, enjoying the morning breeze and scenic beauty of the area. The bus passed through an avenue of Nandi flame trees in bloom. The orange flowers blazed against the dark green foliage. The road up to Muthaiga was lined with these tall trees on the left and jacaranda on the right, also in bloom, showering purple petals on the lawns of the newly built bungalows in the Fairview Estate above the Mathare Valley. The Nairobi River flowed down through the city park towards Eastleigh and Dondora.

Shaira liked this estate very much. The family had lived there when Shaira's father was alive. She had been very attached to him and missed him a lot. Now life had changed completely. At the height of the Depression Sabra had had to sell the family home as well as the car and move to a cheaper rented house. She had also had to work as a teacher. Shaira's brothers were still studying then. She always hoped one day the family would return to live in the same area again.

The Sikh boy had moved next to Majid and Honey and they all seemed friendly already. The Sardarji, the boy's father, occasionally talked to the boys and Huma, asking where the family was heading and for how long. He said he and his wife were from Nyeri and were going back to their home after a family visit to Nairobi. Both father and son wore blue turbans. They talked to the Gujeratis, who told them they were going to Thika. The Gujerati man addressed the Sikh as "Masterji," which implied the Sardarji was a teacher.

After climbing the hill, from where the road branched off to Kiambu, the bus turned towards Ruarka and Thika beyond. They passed the coffee plantations of the Kamiti Estate on both sides of the road and some papyrus swamps near a small river. The road became dusty and corrugated and the bus slowed down. Shaira got out a book and started to read it under her veil, though the bumps hindered concentration.

The bus stopped at Ruiru to pick up passengers and drop off others.

"Shaira Api, when will we pass the Ruiru Falls?" Huma asked.

"Not far now. We have to go a few miles more," Shaira replied without looking back.

"Are they big falls?" asked young Salim.

"Not as big as the Thika Falls," Honey told him.

"Will we pass the Thika Falls?" asked Majid.

"Oh yes, but much later," offered the Sikh boy.

"Have you got waterfalls in Mombasa?" Huma asked her cousins.

"We have the sea, the Indian Ocean," Majid said, and gave a small chuckle. "You don't have waterfalls and the sea together."

"It's very big. And very blue at times. Big ships and dhows come from far away," Salim offered with wide eyes.

"But there must be waterfalls outside Mombasa. I know for sure there are rivers," Huma insisted.

"There is the big Tana River. Our teacher told us in the geography class," said the Sikh boy as the driver climbed onto his seat and started the vehicle.

The road was rough, the soil red as copper. When the bus was passing the Ruiru Falls, the Sardarji, who by now had established a good chatting relationship with the children, told them all about the falls as well as the dam and how it was the source of the electricity supply to Nairobi. The children were all ears and listened to him with interest and fascination, and asked many questions. After travelling for about five miles the bus stopped again. The driver got down and went round the bus looking at the tires.

"Ati rey rey!" he shouted to the turnboy. There was a puncture, the wheel would have to be changed.

Many people got down, some yawning, others grumbling that the bus would be delayed. The children, including Huma, all under the wing of the Sardarji, descended to watch the wheel change, some male passengers helping as the wheel was a big one. Others stretched their legs and walked along the road.

After watching the change all the boys crossed the rainwater drains on the side of the road and disappeared into the long grass and bushes. There they stood in a line and, putting their small chests out, started to pee. Each strained to see who peed the farthest, chatting and eyeing one another's streams.

Huma and Shaira went further into the thickets where Huma wanted Shaira to stand in front of her while she squatted so that no one could see her. "Get on. There's no one here to see you," Shaira scolded.

"The snakes and centipedes might come crawling," Huma moaned. "The boys are lucky, they can do it standing."

"If you didn't moan and groan you'd be finished by now," Shaira said. A frog croaked from a nearby pool.

Huma jumped from the squatting position and pulled up her shalwar. "What's the noise?" she asked. Taking long strides, she ran without waiting for Shaira, who laughed loudly, saying, "What a coward you are, my little sister. It's only a small choora!"

The bus then went steadily on, bumping on the rough and corrugated road, passing maize and millet fields on both sides, the latter quite high and in cobs. Here and there down in the valley stood round thatched mud huts surrounded by thick hedges.

Near the approach to Thika township more people emerged, women carrying heavy loads of produce or firewood on their backs as well as babies in their arms, their shaved heads shining in the sun.

The bus reached Thika before noon, drove into the market, and stopped at the depot. The driver informed the passengers there would be an hour's stop. They could walk about, have their lunch, but under no circumstances were they to move away from the market or delay the bus.

The market was bustling with activity. The rural women, wearing muddy brown leather aprons and lots of colourful beaded wire coils in their distended earlobes and round their necks, sat on the ground with their wares spread in front of them. Some older men sat a little distance away from the women and sold boiled mealie cobs, sweet potatoes, and roasted arrowroot kikwa. The women sold arrowroot yams, potatoes, spinach, tomatoes, and pumpkins, as well as raw bananas. The younger men, dressed in colourful blankets and shukas and holding long staffs, stood around chatting and laughing gaily.

The Sardarji's wife and Sabra, who by now had introduced themselves, got off the bus together. The Sardarji's wife spread out the mikeka she was holding in one hand under a shady pepper tree not far from the bus depot and invited Sabra to share it with her.

The Sikh boy, whose name was Tarlochen but who was called Tochi, came rushing to his mother and asked for a towel. "Father has found a water tap. He's washing his hands and face." His mother pulled out a towel from the basket she had placed near the mat. Huma too descended, all excited, her hands and face damp. She had used her small pink dupatta for wiping away the dust. Perhaps her cousins had used it too as it looked like a brown rag.

"You silly nut, why didn't you wait for a towel? It's in the basket," Shaira said crossly and went to fish the towel out.

"Everybody started using it before I could come," Huma justified.

"You must have started using it or how else would the others know they could use it," grimaced Shaira.

"Never mind, Bibi, the chunni will soon dry." The Sardarji's wife backed Huma. "She is only a balak, such a sweet child."

Shaira pulled the stole from Huma and spread it on the grass.

The Sardarji came back carrying green ripe bananas, boiled sweet potatoes, roasted maize cobs, and kikwa bought from the old men in the market. He advised them all to go and wash and freshen themselves, then come back to eat. He put all the food down on the mat while the ladies got up and ambled towards the water tap. When they returned they were surprised to see the Sardarji, with Honey's and Tochi's help, had spread the lunch brought by both the families on newspapers like at a picnic.

The children, who were now ravenously hungry, wolfed down everything. During the picnic lunch the two families exchanged confidences.

Sabra said she felt much better after the lunch and braced herself for the next leg of the journey, and the bus moved from the Thika market to the main road to Muranga and Embu. It passed the small Thika Falls without stopping. At the famous Channia Falls, it slowed down and crawled slowly over the bridge so the passengers could get a good view. The Mombasa cousins were surprised at the force of the water but said the sea was much bigger. Shaira enjoyed looking at the green coffee plantations and masses of banana trees with bushy green fronds on the ridges and small hills, the maize and millet fields in the valleys, and the few baobab, cypress, and juniper trees dotted all over. The bus moved on slowly and steadily, only stopping at Muranga to fill with petrol.

The passengers again got down to stretch their limbs, and the children, accompanied by Shaira and the Sardarji, strolled towards the Indian dukas. These shops served the peasant farmers from the ridges and the valley with coloured beads, knives with wooden handles, pangas, jembes, tobacco coils, keraies and sufurias in all sizes, and hurricane lamps. The big store sold sweets and chocolates, sodas, imported biscuits in packets, and tins of Nice and Marie biscuits made by Huntley and Palmers of England.

The Sardarji bought some sweets, Shaira a packet of biscuits. Huma admired the tinsmith making small dewa lamps—karaboi, from old milk and cigarette cans. He also cut empty kerosene oil tins in half and fixed covers on them to make containers for grains and spices.

It was almost dusk when they left Muranga and moved on, heading for their destination in the foothills of the great Kirinyaga, the sacred Kikuyu mountain.

5

The Meeting

MUSSAVIR WOKE UP to the noise of cackling chickens and a heavy smell of baking. His mother was up and already busy with her cake-making. Apart from the squawking of chickens, Mussavir could hear Mugro's shrill laughter as well as his mother arguing with someone. Mussavir edged out of bed and moved to the window. The chicken seller had come and Ayesha was buying chickens. They were arguing over the price.

"They are tiny, I tell you, changa sana, for a shilling each, Mzee," Ayesha told the old man as she inspected the birds, all held by him in one hand by their feet. They were squawking their little guts out.

The kuku seller insisted they were all young cockerels and not old hens. The price should have been one shilling and fifty cents. "Kweli Mama, yote jogoo hapana jike," he repeated. "You are my regular customer so I am prepared to sell you for a shilling each. Not a cent less."

The chicken seller, though a middle-aged Kikuyu, looked much older. He wore an old army overcoat, a remnant from the Great War, handed down to him perhaps by his father or some army officer his father had worked for. On his head he wore a khaki woollen cap and his baki snuff box stuck in his distended earlobe. A shining silver ring adorned his other ear and a small round cigarette tin, tied to a leather thong, hung from his neck.

He wanted to sell all ten chickens but Ayesha said she would only buy six. She did not have enough room to keep them all. The man hummed and hawed, saying he had walked from across the three ridges without breakfast and this was his first sale of the day. He needed the money to pay the kodi tax.

"Kweli?" asked Ayesha.

"Absolutely true Mama, haki ya Mu . . ." He raised his right hand but had not finished his sentence when Mussavir, standing at the window, completed the man's sentence: "haki ya mzungu?" Mugro and Ayesha burst out laughing. The old man looked at the window and laughed loudly, then wiped his eyes with his free hand and said, "Haki ya Mungu. Hapana mzungu!" I swear by God, not the Europeans, as you jest!

They all laughed. Asians and Africans, when not telling the truth, sometimes used the Swahili word for European instead of God when affirming or swearing.

"All right, Mzee, you have made me laugh so early in the morning. I'll buy all your chickens and you can have a mug of hot tea."

Mussavir asked Mugro to bring inside the bucket of water which was heating on a wood fire in the backyard. When shaved, bathed, and dressed, he came out to the kitchen to get his breakfast.

"Mussavir Beta, when you finish breakfast could you please slaughter three chickens," Ayesha requested after replying to Mussavir's greetings.

"Oh Mama! Not so early in the morning."

"I thought you were a surgeon. And butchering time does not matter." She smiled widely.

"Even a surgeon does not like to slaughter on an empty stomach. Can't Mugro do it?"

"Mugro? He's not a Muslim or even a Jew. And your father is not at home."

"We should teach Mugro to recite the prayer and slaughter the kukus. They'll be halal." Mussavir then quickly asked, "Who slaughters them when no Muslim male is around?"

"I have had to slaughter sometimes."

"Really Mama? You poor dear. You are brave," he said, smiling. "When are the guests expected?"

"Not till the evening. Buses are erratic and it also depends on the road and vehicle."

"There is the whole day then. How many people are you expecting, Mama?"

"Well, Sabra, her two daughters, Shaira and Huma, her son Honey and her two nephews on holiday from Mombasa."

"Six!" exclaimed Mussavir. "Quite a number, almost a regiment. And all under thirteen I suppose. It'll be quite a houseful. Where are you putting them? On Mohammedi bistras?"

"Only the boys will have to sleep on the floor. Sabra's in Hibba's bed. Farida and Huma are on the second bed. Shaira and Hibba will have to put up camp beds in the dining room."

"The boys will be cramped, won't they?"

"I was thinking of putting one of them in your room, but it would not be wise because of your smoking."

"Would they tell on me? . . . I don't think so," Mussavir said, answering his own question. "Let them sleep in my room. It's all right." Mussavir did not smoke in his father's presence.

"We shall see how it goes," Ayesha said and handed him the pot of tea with some freshly baked rolls.

Mussavir slaughtered the three chickens and handed them to Mugro, who shoved them in a basin and, picking up the kettle from the jiko, poured some boiling water on them. Then, sitting on the ground with his feet stretched out in front of him, he began plucking the birds as fast as he could. He whistled a Kikuyu folk tune while he worked, as if this was a most enjoyable job.

Dr Bashir returned from work in the late afternoon. After a brief rest he puttered about in the garden. Ayesha and the girls, having finished the extra cooking and arranging the rooms, waited on the front veranda watching the sunset. The bus stop was down the road at the back of the house, visible from the side window. The evening being clear, Mount Kenya was visible too.

Mussavir had gone to the Government Indian Boys School, the only place where Asian boys and men could play games of volleyball, tennis, or soccer. He promised to return before supper. He decided to be away when the guests came, not sure whether he was trying to delay meeting this thirteen-year-old Shaira or whether he was really nervous. He did not want his family to know that he was nervous and he also did not want to seem too enthusiastic so felt it was best to get away for a while.

It was already dark when he came back, in fact it was nearer eight. He slowly walked up the path leading to the back entrance. The house lights were on and he could hear voices and see activity in the kitchen. As he approached he saw a young girl come out the back door. She could not see Mussavir as he was in the darker part of the yard, but he could see her clearly. She walked towards the kitchen and had a towel wrapped around her head like his sisters did after washing their hair. She was slim and tall, fairer than his sisters in colour. Opening the back door, she went in.

Mussavir stopped where he was for a few minutes. Was she Shaira? It could not be her mother or sister. She certainly did not look thirteen. Fully developed and grown up, she could easily pass for sixteen or seventeen. He was surprised his mother was right. She looked attractive even with the towel turban on her head. His mother's voice from the kitchen interrupted his thoughts. He quickly moved towards the covered passage between the kitchen and the back entrance to the house and stepped onto the cement floor. His sister Hibba was helping his mother.

"Hey, are they all here?" he asked.

"Yes, Bhaijan, the bus was late. They arrived all dusty and tired and have just finished having their baths." Hibba stood up from her squatting position. Then, looking at him, she asked, "You are late. Did you have a good game?"

"I gave you more time to welcome your friends," Mussavir said, smiling.

"If you want to have a wash, Beta," his mother called, "hurry up. I am about to bring out supper."

"Sorry to delay you all. Is the bathroom free now?"

"It's quite free, Bhaijan," Hibba said, coming out of the kitchen with a jug of water. As she and Mussavir were about to go in, the girl he had seen earlier came out, this time without the turban; she was wearing a light blue dupatta, her hair combed and falling on her shoulders.

On seeing Mussavir she stopped at the door. She quickly tried to cover her head with the stolelike dupatta.

"Oh, Shaira, meet my eldest brother," Hibba called cheerfully.

Greetings exchanged, Mussavir inquired about the journey. Shaira replied slowly that it was fine but too many punctures and stops on the way had caused delays. She then went towards the kitchen, saying, "Let me help, Taijan," to Ayesha.

"I don't need any help now, Beti. The food is all heated up. Please go in all of you and get the others to come to the dining room."

Mussavir and Hibba went on, followed by Shaira. The children, all washed and bathed and in their nightclothes and with their hair combed, were already sitting around the table. Hibba came forward and made the introductions.

Shaira went past them on to the bedroom.

"You must be Huma then," Mussavir said, looking at the chubby-faced girl who turned and gave him a wide smile as well as her pudgy hand in greeting.

"What have you done to your tooth? Don't tell me the rat pulled it out?" he exclaimed, taking her hand.

"Rats don't pull anyone's teeth. It has just fallen off. It was my milk tooth."

"I'm sorry, so stupid of me really." Mussavir smiled back, patting her curly head.

"It's all right," replied Huma seriously, as if accepting his apology, but added, "But you are a doctor, you should have known." And she gave a chuckle.

"You are *absolutely* right, Huma. I certainly should have."

They were a precocious family, thought Mussavir. After greeting and talking to Honey and his two cousins, Mussavir moved towards the drawing room where Shaira's mother was seated chatting with his father. As he entered and saw Sabra, she looked familiar, as if he had met her before. He salaamed her in the Muslim way by bowing and touching his forehead with his right hand. She got up with a beaming smile and patted him on his shoulder saying, "Mashallah! By Allah's grace, you have grown up and are already a doctor. Congratulations, Beta."

"Thank you, Khala Sabra. When did you last see me?"

"Oh, it's many years now. You came to our home with your parents, I remember, when we lived in Gian Singh's Shamba. It must have been in 1928, or was it 1929, Bhai Bashir?" she asked, looking at Mussavir's father, who was seated in an easy chair near the fireplace.

Before Dr Bashir could tell her, Mussavir asked, "Was it a wooden house raised on stilts, blue or green?"

"Exactly," she exclaimed. "And the first in that row." Sabra seemed surprised.

"And you had a motorcycle with a sidecar?" Mussavir asked next.

"Yes, you really have a good memory, Beta."

"I am beginning to remember a bit. When Mama talked about you, I could not place you, but seeing you it has all come back like a picture. We even saw the first aeroplane flying in the sky from your house."

"How amazing, Beta. You must have been only ten or eleven years old then," she mused.

"A bit older than that, Khala Sabra." He smiled and leaned against the wall. "There were two boys in your house and they even let me sit on the motorcycle when we played outside."

"They must have been my son Zaffer and my nephew." Looking at Dr Bashir, she added, "Your son has a terrific memory."

"Yes. I remember that was the year when the Prince of Wales came to Nairobi—1928. We were in Kibos near Kisumu and had come to Nairobi for Idd and to see the Prince."

"I hear you had a rough journey with so many punctures," Mussavir remarked.

"Oh yes." Pointing to a chair near her she asked, "Why don't you sit down, Beta?"

"I must go and have a wash. Mama is dishing up the supper. I've already delayed everybody. You must all be famished." He excused himself and walked away.

When Mussavir came back to the dining room the children were already being served. They were seated cross-legged on a mat laid out on the floor and covered with a printed dastar khwan, the Indian hand-woven tablecloth. Shaira was handing the plates of rice and curry which Ayesha dished out. "Not too much, Taijan," she kept repeating, "they'll not be able to finish it all. They really stuffed themselves on the way."

"Oh, that was long ago," Ayesha said and smiled. "They must be very hungry now."

"I'm very hungry," Majid said. "I didn't like the dal paratha the Sardarji's wife gave me. It had a lot of ginger in it." He made a face.

"What about our parathas? You ate some and boiled eggs, guachi, bananas and so many maize cobs too!" said a surprised Huma. Majid looked sheepish but did not respond to Huma's taunt.

Mussavir stood for a while watching, holding on to the back of a chair. He could see Shaira clearly. She moved with ease and grace, was not rushed, and handed the food down quickly, instructing her brother, sister, and cousins to eat cleanly and slowly. He noticed she had put on a blue chador. It was loosely draped around her shoulders and chest. She was fairer than all the others and stood out in the group of young people.

Dr Bashir, Sabra, and Ayesha were seated around the table and there were enough chairs for Mussavir, Hibba, and Shaira too at the table. Shaira said she would sit on the floor, Farida could sit at the table in her place. She could keep an eye on the younger ones then. Dr Bashir laughed and said there were no babies around. "The young ones are capable of looking after themselves." He wanted Shaira to come and sit by him and have her supper in peace.

"You must have done enough looking after on the way here," he said to Shaira.

"It was easy for me this time, Tayajan. The Sardarji was a great help. I even managed to read my book!"

Shaira sat down next to Dr Bashir. Hibba was on his other side. Mussavir sat between Hibba and Sabra.

"What time did you leave Nairobi?" Mussavir asked Shaira.

Before Shaira could reply, her mother said they left Nairobi a little before seven in the morning. Apart from the punctures the bus was slowed down because of curves and bends on the steep road. Shaira, looking at

Dr Bashir, added that the road was also slippery at times and narrow.

"You were lucky it was not the rainy season or you'd have arrived much later," said Dr Bashir. "They often have to use chains from Forthall."

"Oh, I would never have come in the rainy season, Bhai Bashir. It's bad enough in Nairobi when it rains, and travelling is out of the question."

"Who was this Sardarji?" Mussavir asked.

"He is the son of Kishen Singh, the herbal medicine seller in Nairobi. He teaches in Nyeri," Dr Bashir added.

When Hibba brought out the mithai with the dessert, Dr Bashir expressed his delight and said he was looking forward to eating the kalakand. He asked if it was made by the corner shop at Ngara or River Road. Huma spoke from the floor, "Tayajan, we got it from Chirra's shop."

"Oh, did you now? I did not know he was still there."

"He is very much there, Bhai Bashir," added Sabra. "In fact, his kalakand is much better than the River Road one. He makes it from solidified milk without adding any flour to it."

"Why is he called Chirra?" asked Mussavir, smiling. A number of voices from the floor replied and repeated the history of poor Chirra the sweetmeat seller.

After supper the younger children sat around Farida and talked for a while before Shaira and Hibba, having cleared the table, came and ushered them to their beds. When bidding them good night, Ayesha stressed that they should wear their shoes and socks otherwise they could pick up a lot of jiggers, and Nyeri jiggers could be real nasty and even dangerous. Shaira told her she had already warned her two cousins who, coming from Mombasa, were used to walking barefoot. She said they had both picked up jiggers in Nairobi and Salim's went in quite deep and near the root of the nail and multiplied themselves. She had pulled them out with some difficulty.

"I hope you applied some spirit to the affected part on the toe afterwards," Dr Bashir cautioned.

"I applied some kerosene oil with cotton wool, Tayajan."

"And did you burn the needle before using it?" asked Mussavir, who was quite amused.

"Yes, I did that with a lighted matchstick."

"You must be quite an expert at pulling them out."

"I don't know. I don't like pulling out creepy and messy jiggers from dirty toes but I have no choice. No one else wants to remove them." Shaira made a wry face.

"They really give you all the tough jobs, don't they?" Dr Bashir said and laughed.

The grown-ups went back to the sitting room while Hibba and Shaira moved the chairs and started making their beds in the dining room. Sabra, after a cup of tea with her hosts, felt she must retire. Ayesha puttered about giving the houseboy instructions for the next morning. Mussavir and his father were left alone in the living room. They talked for a while about an operation Dr Bashir had performed that morning on a very sick patient whose condition was still critical. He was on call and would have to go to the hospital again. Mussavir offered to go with him but Dr Bashir did not think that was necessary. The hospital orderly would come for him and bring him back too.

Mussavir also told his father that at the boys' school he had heard King George's Silver Jubilee would be celebrated in May. "The school authorities have been ordered to make preparations for the celebrations."

"I heard about it a couple of days back from Dr Sergeant. His children were coming out for holidays but he has instructed they come after the Jubilee celebrations in England." Dr Bashir expressed surprise that it was already twenty-five years since King George V was crowned. He had been a young man then with plans to come out to Kenya. They chatted for a while and then Mussavir, wishing his father good night, went to his own room.

He lay on top of his bed with his feet stretched out and smoked a cigarette. The thirteen-year-old Shaira was on his mind. He was irritated to be thinking of her. He had hoped to find her childish and giggly like all teenagers but was surprised to find his mother was right. Shaira was young but not too young to look at, a reasonably good-looking girl too who seemed to have a pleasant nature. Compared to her, his own sister Hibba, who was a year older, was still childish. He also noticed Shaira commanded respect and radiated warmth. The younger sister, who was cheeky and sweet, and the brother obeyed her without question. Their mother, though a warm person to others, seemed impatient with her elder daughter. Every time he asked Shaira a question, the mother butted in and replied before Shaira could, and one got the impression the mother did not want Shaira to talk. He also thought the mother was somewhat demanding. However, it was only the first evening. He would have several more days to watch and observe her, and he was certainly going to talk to her and find out more about her if she was to become his life partner.

Mussavir then thought of what his mother had said. She was keen their nikah be performed before he left. He himself was not so sure whether that was a good thing. It was all right to be engaged and betrothed to a fifteen- or sixteen-year-old girl, but he did not want to be a laughingstock among his friends, being engaged to a thirteen-year-old. He had told his mother it could wait till his return, but now he was not sure, and that too irritated him. However, he got up and changed into his pyjamas and went to bed.

6

Morning with the Guests

THE NEXT MORNING Mussavir was surprised to find much less activity and commotion than he had expected, despite a house full of guests. Either they were all still slumbering or had gone out. When he eventually surfaced from his room, he heard his mother's and Sabra's voices. His sisters were busy at their lessons. No holiday for the poor girls even to enjoy their visitors. Dr Bashir was a real slave driver where lessons were concerned. No one knew that more than Mussavir. He asked where everybody was. Farida told him the boys were in the backyard and the women in the kitchen.

As he walked through the dining room to the kitchen, he saw a blue hardcover book on the table. It was an English book titled *The Heroes*, by Charles Kingsley. Opening it, Mussavir leafed through a few pages. There were three stories listed in the contents page: "Perseus," "The Argonauts," and "Theseus." All tales from Greek mythology. On the right at the top of the page the name "Shaira" was written neatly with a line underneath. Mussavir raised his eyebrows. Shaira was already reading Greek mythology! In India he had started with Hindu mythology when he was in Grade Six.

Leaving the book where it was, he headed towards the kitchen. His mother, standing near the door, was helping a Kikuyu woman off-load the heavy bundle of firewood she carried on her back. The poor woman was half bent. She slowly straightened herself and stood up straight, almost challenging. Like all Kikuyu peasant women, her head was shaved and she was wearing a muddy brown leather apron. She wore several bead necklaces round her neck and ornaments made with twisted iron on her arms. In her ears she wore several circular bead earrings. She held in her hand the leather thong which had made a deep mark on her forehead.

Shaira, squatting on the floor, seemed to be counting something in a basin full of water. Her mother, placidly seated on a piri nearby, was picking up and sorting out spinach leaves from a basket in her lap and placing the sorted ones in an enamel bowl.

On seeing Mussavir, Shaira looked up, then quickly threw her dupatta upwards to cover her head and stood up, saying, "They are twenty in here and all seem to be good, Taijan."

"Let's get another twenty, Shaira Beti. But the basin won't hold forty, so please remove the counted ones first."

"What will the basin not hold?" asked Mussavir. Coming nearer, he exclaimed, "Oh, eggs. A lot of them. How much are they?"

"Forty for a shilling," his mother replied.

"They are certainly better than in Nairobi. Eggs and chickens seem cheap here," said Sabra.

"How much would they be in Nairobi, Khala Sabra?" asked Mussavir, bending down to look at the eggs which Shaira was placing in the water.

"We get about thirty now. The price varies from time to time. In the 1920s we could get fifty for a shilling," said Sabra, laughing.

"But these are much cheaper than you would get in India. Why did you put them all in the water, Shaira? They don't look dirty."

"To check if they are fresh and good. Those that stay at the bottom are supposed to be good. Those that float on top are bad," she told him.

"A better method, I must say. In India you look at the egg against the light or sun."

"But in India lots of people don't buy that many eggs," Ayesha said. "There are many other goodies to eat for breakfast."

"That reminds me, I haven't had my breakfast!" Mussavir looked at his mother, saying, "Sorry, Mama. I'll get up early tomorrow and have breakfast with you all."

"That would be helpful, my son."

The Kikuyu woman who had been washing her hands at the tap and chatting to Mugro wiped her hands with her leather apron and came to Ayesha for her money for the load of firewood and eggs. Mussavir asked his mother how much she owed the woman and, shoving his hand in his trouser pocket, pulled out his wallet. The Kikuyu woman came forward and said, "Shillingi igre na kingotre tisa."

"Hapana. Kingotre saba tu," Ayesha argued, and she asked Mussavir to pay her two shillings for the eggs and seventy cents for the firewood.

"Mama, let the poor woman have what she wants. It's not much considering how far she has come." Mussavir handed her three shillings instead of two-ninety. The woman put her hand out and grabbed the money, flashing him a white smile. She picked up her woven bag from the floor and was ready to go.

Mussavir went inside for his breakfast. Ayesha handed Shaira the teapot and a small jug of hot milk in a small tray, saying, "Shaira Beti, could you please take these to the dining room for Mussavir and ask him if he wants fried eggs."

Shaira hesitated, then, getting a nod from her mother, she took the tray and went in. Mussavir was eating a slice of pawpaw. Shaira put the tray down, picked up the teapot, and placed it on the rack. She then put the small jug of milk on the table near the sugar bowl.

"Oh, thank you, Shaira, I should have brought the tray myself. I thought Mama was still making it."

"Taijan asks whether you'd like fried eggs."

"No thanks, I'll just have some tea and toast."

Shaira was about to go out when she heard Mussavir say, "Why don't you join me for breakfast, Shaira?"

"I had mine long ago."

"A cup of tea then? You could manage that, couldn't you?"

She was making up her mind when he said, "Ask Khala Sabra if she'd like some too."

"All right."

Shaira went to tell Ayesha her son did not want fried eggs, then to her own mother she said, "Ami, Mussavir Bhaijan wants you and me to have tea with him."

"Oh, I had two cups this morning. I can't take a lot of tea." Sabra did not say if Shaira could.

Ayesha said instead of her, "Beti, you go and have tea with Mussavir. I usually join him but I am busy now."

"May I, Ami?" Shaira asked her mother.

"All right, if you want to have more tea." Sabra nodded her assent and added, "Then come back and help your taijan."

Shaira picked up an empty cup and saucer and went in.

"Good, come and sit here. I'll pour it out for you," Mussavir said and picked up the teapot.

"I'll only have half a cup Bhaijan . . ." She had not completed her sentence when Mussavir asked, "With a lot of milk and sugar?"

"Oh no." She smiled and said, "Only a little milk and sugar." Coming forward she took the cup of tea, but she did not sit very near him. She kept two chairs away.

"Sure you don't want toast?" he asked again.

"No thanks. It's nearly lunchtime." She looked at her book, realizing she had forgotten to put it away.

"I was looking at your book," said Mussavir, thinking it a safe subject to talk about. "Is it a storybook?"

"Well, not exactly, although there are three stories in it. It is my textbook for next year."

"I hear you are preparing for some overseas examinations soon."

"Yes, I am sitting for my Preliminary Cambridge."

"Is it like standard ten?"

"No. We sit for this examination after standard seven, so it could be like standard eight and is the first of the three overseas examinations."

"And what are the others then?" Mussavir asked, buttering his toast.

"Did you not study in East Africa at all, Bhaijan?" Shaira replied instead.

"Only up to standard five, then I went to school in India. In our day the last overseas examination used to be the London Matric. Because we lived in very small districts where there were no schools even for boys, Abu taught us at home."

"Is that so? Well, after PC we sit for Junior Cambridge after one year, then in two more years we do Senior Cambridge."

"There is also something called School Certificate, when does one do that?"

"That is the same thing as Senior Cambridge, really."

"Do you plan to study further after that?" Mussavir asked, pouring another cup of tea for himself.

"I'd love to go for further studies, but I don't think that's possible," she said sadly. "As you know, we don't have a university in East Africa and now my father . . . not being alive, no one will send me overseas."

"What would you like to study? English? Or mythology—which I see you have started studying already."

"I'd like to do a BA or become a doctor . . . like you," she said slowly, "but I know that will never be possible. I shall be lucky if I can even go up to Senior Cambridge."

"You want to be a doctor, Shaira? Really?"

"You think it's not possible for women to study medicine?"

"Oh, it's possible all right, and many women are becoming doctors in India and even elsewhere. But it's difficult and a long course. I am surprised you think like that at such a young age."

"I am going to be fourteen next birthday and I am not frightened of working hard. In fact, I love my studies."

Mussavir stared at her for a moment or two, then asked, "When is your next birthday?"

"In May on the seventh."

"Nearly five months from now." He smiled and went on. "You are only thirteen and a half now. It's still young to be thinking of doing medicine. And you'll have to go to India, won't you?"

"That is the problem. Being young does not pose any difficulty because girls are getting married at fourteen and fifteen and that is a bigger responsibility than even studying, I think."

Mussavir was even more surprised to hear that. He smiled, then laughed quietly. "I agree that marriage is a greater responsibility than studies. But what do your mother and brothers think about it? I hear you have two elder brothers."

"Oh, my elder brother Zaffer and Ami would not mind or object if there was a university in Nairobi. But my brother Shahid does not even like me to go to the new school. He would like me to stop studying now." She looked towards the door to see if her mother had decided to come in. She had been warned not to talk freely to Mussavir, and here she was not only doing exactly that but also revealing family secrets.

"Why do you have to go to a new school?" Mussavir's question interrupted her thoughts.

"This is the last class and last year in the present school."

"I understand you were in the English-medium school. Why did you leave that?"

"The authorities would not allow me to go in Punjabi clothes or even a sari and certainly not a burqa. Also, Ami felt I should start learning Urdu now."

"But surely you must know Urdu?" Mussavir asked with surprise.

"I can speak Urdu and even understand it, but I can't read or write. I am working hard to learn it, though. I have to do a paper in Urdu for my PC exam."

"You think you'd be ready to do a paper set by an overseas body?" asked Mussavir with eyes wide open.

"It's not difficult really. I mean the paper. I have seen some old ones. The translation passages are very simple. It's the essay that is a bit tricky. I find it difficult to write straight in Urdu. In my last paper I wrote in English. Then translated it. But the time was not enough. I could not finish it."

"That is quite interesting, Shaira. You have to be very good to do that."

Before Shaira could reply, her mother came in. Shaira got up and began removing the breakfast things. Mussavir helped her take the cups to the kitchen. He asked Sabra where Huma and the boys were. She told him their Singh friends had come so they had gone out to play with them.

When Mussavir walked out to the back entrance and on to the yard he saw Huma coming into the house. She salaamed him and asked, "Mussavir Bhaijan, you have got up now?" Her little forehead had a furrow on it.

"Yes, Huma, I'm a very lazy man."

"You certainly are." Huma, as if fully agreeing with him, added, "If you had to go to school you'd never make it in time. Has Farida Baji finished with her lessons?"

"She might have by now."

"Good. I want to show her my dolls, especially my new one," she said happily.

"Have you brought the dolls with you?"

"Of course. I always take them with me when we go out—they would be so lonely otherwise."

"How can dolls be lonely? They can't feel or think."

She shrugged her shoulders. "I pretend that they do."

"Will you show them to me too?"

"If you want me to."

Mussavir smiled as she ran inside. He strolled on towards the backyard thinking what a delightfully natural and sweet child Huma was. The elder sister seemed somewhat serious, in fact too serious for a thirteen- or fourteen-year-old. Mussavir saw the boys playing gulli danda very seriously. The game was going on between Honey, Majid, and Tochi, the Sikh boy. Salim and another little Sikh boy were sitting on the grass at a distance, playing with marbles.

Honey had lifted and struck the pointed gulli away. The others, having missed catching it in the air, were counting the score. Honey was ready to hit again from another angle. As the ground was uneven he was pushing away the grass and anything lying just under the points of the gulli with his hand. Majid shouted that that was cheating but Tochi said that it was allowed if playing on the grass.

Mussavir was amused to see the young boys so intense. He was reminded of his own days when he used to play with his brothers Zahir and Ta'Ha and their other friends while at school in India. Mussavir was still some distance away when Honey managed to hit the gulli hard with the danda and away it flew into the air. This time Tochi ran and caught it. Honey was out. The boys, all excited, walked back to the starting point and it was Tochi's turn to hit.

"You hit very well, Honey. You are a good shot."

"But Bhaijan, this is not a very good ground and the gulli is not too pointed," Honey answered.

"There is nothing wrong with the gulli," said Majid. "You take such a long time to hit."

Mussavir watched the boys playing and even joined in but he was soon out, caught by Honey on his second hit. The boys seemed amused, even happy, to have got him out. Mussavir told them he'd teach them kabbadi during their stay in Nyeri, and after watching them for a few more minutes he walked away towards the front garden and then on to the veranda, where his sister Farida and Huma were busy chatting. They had spread a reed mat on the floor and were sitting with their dolls. Farida was also playing with her geetas, the game of five pebbles—spreading them on the ground, then picking them up in twos and threes after throwing one pebble in the air. On seeing Mussavir, Huma said, "Bhaijan, you wanted to see my dolls, they are here now."

"Oh, thank you, Huma." He went up the two steps and sat on the ledge under the honeysuckle vine that was hanging from the roof with clusters of orange flowers. Huma was very serious about her dolls. She picked up one and said, "This is my new doll," and handed it to Mussavir. Then she turned to pick up the other. Mussavir held the doll and inspected it.

"She is very nice, Huma. Where did you get her from?"

"My Zaffer Bhaijan got it from Whiteways, that big shop with mirrors on the roof, near the statue of the war askaris." She added hurriedly, "He got it for my birthday."

"What is she called?"

"June," said Huma, now holding the other doll.

"June? But that's the name of a month."

"Shaira Api wanted me to call her either Iris or June. June can be a girl's name too."

"Is that so?" Mussavir asked, amused that Shaira was applying her mythology to everyday life. "Why did you not call her Zohra or Mumtaz?"

"Mussavir Bhaijan, she is an English doll. How can she be called Zohra or Mumtaz? It'd be funny." Huma pouted.

"I see!" Mussavir remarked, then asked, "And what about the other one, what is she called?" He took the cloth doll stuffed with cotton wool in his hand. Its eyes, mouth, and nose were marked in black and red thread. Strands of black wool were stitched on its head with a middle parting. The doll was wearing Punjabi clothes.

"And where did you get this one, Huma?" he asked.

"Oh, that is a gurria, a friend of my mother made it," Huma said.

"Has she got a name?"

"Cloth dolls don't have names. You just call them gurria or guddi," Huma explained, showing her surprise at Mussavir asking such an obvious question.

"But why can't they have names? They are dolls like the others. One could call them Fatma, Salma, Uma Devi, and even Ram Pyari."

Farida, who had been quiet so far, guffawed, and Huma, seeming to have lost all patience with Mussavir, said in a sharp voice, "They can't be named, Mussavir Bhaijan, because they are not real like the others."

"Why is June real and not this poor gurria?"

"Well, June can open and shut her eyes and her arms and feet can also move. She squeaks if you turn her upside down."

"I see," said Mussavir, smiling. "How interesting."

He sat with them for a while and watched Farida and Huma play with the pebbles. Farida was very good at them and could throw and catch them in many different ways. He had watched her do that on her own many times.

Ayesha came out, followed by Sabra. They looked at the dolls, and then Sabra sat with the girls and began cleaning the rice in a wicker tray, while Ayesha went back to the kitchen. Sabra began a conversation with Mussavir.

Much later, when Mussavir went inside, he saw his sister Hibba laying the table for lunch. He asked her why her friend was not helping her.

"She likes helping Mama because Mama likes to talk with her at the same time," Hibba replied.

"Let me help you then."

"I don't need much help in laying the table, Bhaijan. I am almost done."

"Then I'll go and see what they are talking about."

Hibba seemed amused that her brother was beginning to be interested in Shaira.

7

The Geet Ceremony and the Snake Drama

SOON AFTER LUNCH Ayesha, together with her daughters and guests, all dolled up in their finery, headed to the small town of Nyeri to partake in the singing ceremony of the Ghai girl's marriage. They plodded up the hill and arrived home at dusk to find Dr Bashir and Mussavir sitting in the garden, enjoying the sunset.

"What was the geet ceremony like?" Dr Bashir asked Huma when she plonked herself on the grass near him. Clad in a red satin Punjabi suit, her rosy cheeks glowed in the twilight.

"Oh, Tayajan, they sang the funniest Punjabi song I've ever heard. I laughed so much."

"Who sang it?" asked Mussavir.

"The old, old ladies. All out of tune. Absolutely out of tune. They sang loudly, pounding at the drums and clapping their hands. But the words were so funny really. All about the bridegroom. His preferences and demands." Huma began to chuckle again.

"But what were the words?" Dr Bashir asked.

"Well, they said the bridegroom loves to eat lentils, especially the moongi dal, and wants more and more of it." Huma finished the last words in imitation of the old ladies.

"The song about Sham Lala was not bad," said Hibba and Shaira agreed.

But Huma insisted that it was funny too! She started singing it.

"Shayam Lala! Oh Shayam Lala! Peeli teri pagri gulabi shamla. Sham Lala! Oh Sham Lala! Your turban is yellow. And its tail is pink!"

"Beti, these are folk songs to tease the bridegroom about the colour scheme of his turban," Ayesha told Huma.

"They are jolly nice songs with a lot of rhythm," said Mussavir, and Dr Bashir said he liked them especially when Huma sang them.

"Did any of you join in the singing?" Mussavir asked.

"No, Bhaijan, we only sat and listened and sometimes clapped to be polite." Huma sighed and shrugged her shoulders as if singing had been a big burden.

"You certainly listened well!" exclaimed Mussavir. "You almost know the songs."

"I wish she'd learn her lessons that way too," said Sabra.

The next morning Mussavir got up early as he had promised and had breakfast with his family and the guests. He then announced that he was going to the post office to mail some letters and a registered parcel to his brother Zahir. After he left, Hibba and Farida got busy with their homework in the living room.

The young guests puttered around in the garden for a while and then Shaira, Huma, and the boys, together with Tochi and his brother, who had arrived earlier, trotted down to the river. It was calm and not full at that time of the year. The boys wanted to know if they could cross the river to the other side. Mussavir told them they could, but only from places where the river was not too deep, and they must not venture too far across as there were native shambas and they might not like visitors!

When Mussavir returned after finishing his tasks in the town, he stopped for a few minutes near the kitchen. His sisters had finished their homework. Mussavir was about to go in when Farida, who kept looking out of the veranda towards the valley and river, called him.

"Bhaijan, I see some children—African totos—running towards the river," she told Mussavir and added, "I wonder if anything is wrong."

"Why?" Mussavir asked.

In the Shadow of Kirinyaga

"Shaira Baji and the others all went down some time ago. They've not come back. May I go down and see?" She looked worried.

"Is Hibba going with you?"

"No. Apa has just gone to the bathroom to wash her hair."

Mussavir came out and stood in the veranda with her. He could discern some commotion and noise, then he saw an African woman rush down towards the river. He went down the veranda steps and raced to the edge of the hedge, Farida following on his heels. They began descending the slope. As they neared the riverbank they saw a group of women, men, and children shouting, "Piga mawe! Lete mawe! Hit it with a stone, bring a big stone!" in Swahili and then talking to one another in Kikuyu, "Nyamo! Nyamo, nyamo."

"Lo! Nyamo kinene. A huge snake," one woman was saying.

"Nduira? Is it a Python?" asked another.

"Mararu kinwe kinen," one man said with a laugh. "A big fat python perhaps."

Mussavir hurried down to reach the group. Huma, Honey, Salim, and Tochi were all huddled together and looking intently across the river. There, Majid was perched on a small rock and Shaira was standing near him with one arm around him.

"What's the matter?" asked Mussavir, addressing Honey and Huma. The crowd of men and women and the big and small totos moved apart on seeing Mussavir arrive.

"Oh, Mussavir Bhaijan, Api and Majid are stuck on the other side and there is a big snake on the rock below them. It's a very big snake—it could be a spitting cobra or a mamba." Huma moaned and made gestures with her arms.

"Snake! What snake? Where is it?" Mussavir asked as he went nearer the bank to have a better look at Shaira and Majid. At first he could not see anything, due to the glare of the sun. Then one of the women pointed at it and he saw a long shining object lying on the rock below, on which Shaira and Majid would have to step to cross back. That was the only shallow part of the river. They could not move back as the slope seemed not only steep, but mossy and slippery too. Huma told Mussavir that Shaira was waiting for the snake to move, but the creature seemed relaxed and still, perhaps basking in the sun.

"Bhaijan, one mama threw a stone but it did not reach the snake," Huma told Mussavir.

Mussavir rolled up his trousers and, pulling a heavy stone embedded on the edge of the riverbank, stepped onto the path, which was formed by a row of small rocks. He proceeded halfway towards the rock on which the snake was lying. He heard Shaira's voice above the river: "Don't come too near, Bhaijan. It's a very big snake. Only half of it is on the rock, the rest of it is still in between the other rocks. Be careful, please don't come too near."

Mussavir could now see the snake. It was big and grey with dark brown spots. He turned and asked Honey to run home and ask the gardener to bring a big stick, or a panga. In the meantime an African man came along down the slope wearing an old kabuti and a wide-rimmed hat. In his hand he held a rungu, a fat-headed club which most African men carry when going through the bushes. The mamas and children shouted, "Nyoka kuba sana! Nduira kinene." Mussavir tried to aim the stone at the snake's head from some distance away.

"Aebu ngoja Bwana! Wait a minute, Mister," the man in the kabuti said to Mussavir. Then, jumping into the river in his bare feet, he stepped towards Mussavir holding his club high. With his free hand he made a sign for Mussavir to stop, and, creeping nearer to the rock, brought down his rungu hard on the head of the snake. He hit again and again. The snake wriggled and hissed but the man brought the rungu down in full force once again and it was still. The man laughed loudly, then turning round he told the people on the bank and Mussavir, "Nimeponda kichwa, I've smashed the head," and he chuckled again. Then he looked properly at the still snake, moved his head from side to side, and exclaimed, "Ah-ah-ah—nyoka kubwa kweli! A big snake really. Nduira kinene!" He then made the distinctive Kikuyu sound: "Eee-eee-eee!"

There were shouts of laughter and some said, "Asante, asante sana."

Mussavir shook the man's hand and thanked him profusely. "It's dead now," he said, looking at Majid. "Don't worry, Majid, we'll get you over here soon."

In the Shadow of Kirinyaga

The old man moved towards the other rock and picked the snake up by its tail, and pulled hard. It was quite dead. The man brought the snake, almost a metre in length, dangling from his hand as if it were a long fish. He threw it down on the grass and it fell with a heavy thud. Some women and children screamed and moved away. Others stopped, came nearer to have a good look at the slimy creature, and praised the man for killing it. The man in the kabuti went up to the river and started washing the snake's blood off the head of his club. Just then Honey and the shamba man arrived armed with jembes and rakes and appeared very disappointed to find the snake already killed. Huma told them the man had smashed its head to a pulp, and she made hitting gestures with her arms and hands.

During this commotion at the riverbank, Mussavir told Shaira and Majid to come down slowly. Shaira did not move but gently pushed Majid towards Mussavir and asked him to take Mussavir's hand. Majid at first was hesitant, drained of colour, so Mussavir said, "Come along, pehlwan, there's nothing to fear now. The snake is dead."

Shaira pushed him further, holding onto one of his hands until Mussavir had got hold of the other. She then let go and Mussavir helped Majid onto the stones which formed a path in the river. He told Shaira to wait, he would come back for her. Depositing the terrified Majid on the bank, Mussavir went back to the rock on which the snake had been killed. He looked up at Shaira. She was standing exactly where he had left her and looked pale. When she made no move even after he came nearer, he coaxed, "Come along, Shaira, it's all right now. The creature is gone. Don't be like Majid." He smiled. She neither replied nor moved, only looked at her feet in a peculiar way. Mussavir was impatient. He did not like standing at the slippery and mossy spot and did not want to remain there long. What a silly madam, he thought. And why was she there in the first place? The child in her had come to the fore. "Shaira, while you're making up your mind another snake might appear. You know some snakes go in pairs." He smiled again.

She looked up. Covering her face with her hands, she crouched on her haunches, saying, "Oh, Mussavir Bhaijan! I can't . . . can't move." And she burst into tears.

Very surprised, Mussavir coaxed gently, "Get up Shaira, don't be afraid. I'm sorry, I shouldn't have mentioned another snake. I was only joking."

"I really can't move my foot . . . It feels numb and jammed and stuck. I feel sick."

Mussavir crept a bit further up and with the support of the next boulder jumped to the place where Shaira, crouched, was shivering uncontrollably. He stood very near her and said, "Try to get up please. It's all right now. You don't have to fear. I'll help you across."

She looked up wiping her eyes and pleaded, "My ami is going to be really angry with me. Please don't tell her you had to come up here to help me. Please!"

"Why should your ami get angry? You have been very brave."

"Oh, she'll be livid. You don't know her. Please promise you won't tell her," Shaira pleaded.

Mussavir looked hard at her as if about to lose his patience. Then he said slowly and gently, "I won't tell her, I promise. Come, get up now. I shall not let her get angry with you. Ever." He surprised himself by saying that.

She looked at him again in a pitiful way, tried to get up, but sat back again. Mussavir took her shoulders and raised her to her feet. Still keeping his hands on her shoulders, he asked her to take a step and try to move. She still could not. He then bent down and rubbed her calves with both hands.

"Mussavir Bhaijan, please don't do that. I'll try again."

He kept rubbing and rubbing and asked her to hold on to his shoulder and to try to raise her foot. She did so, and took a step, then another and another. He got up and patted her shoulder and said, "Well done, Shabash! That's good. Very good. Go on."

Mussavir held her hand and stepped down first, then asked her to follow slowly as the rock was slippery with moss. She was still shaking but did what he told her. They were now on the rock on which the snake had been killed. He put his arms around her shoulders and helped her step down to the stone below in the flowing river and the stone after that and did not leave her hand until he had brought her safely to the other side.

In the Shadow of Kirinyaga

The crowd started to disperse, but the children continued talking with excitement as they watched Shaira and Mussavir cross the river. Shaira, though still somewhat shaky, could now walk on her own. She pulled her hand from Mussavir's and said, "Thank you very much, Bhaijan. I'm really sorry and ashamed to cause all the trouble. I wouldn't have climbed the rock but Majid was frightened to come down. I went to help him."

"Bhaijan, it's all Singla Bhai Honey's fault," said Huma. "He dared Majid to go to that side. He said Majid was too fat and a coward and would never go."

"Well, never mind now," said Mussavir. "It's all done. Let's all forget about it."

Shaira started to say something but hesitated and then said, "I am very frightened of snakes, even dead ones. I never ever look at them. And I had to look at this horrible one for so long. My feet became stiff."

"When we get to the house I'll give you some tablets," said Mussavir, then he looked at the man who had killed the snake. "Let me go thank the old man."

The man was standing admiring his kill and deciding whether to take away the snake for its skin or give it to the people standing around. He asked Mussavir's advice. Mussavir told him he was welcome to it with everyone's best wishes. The man grinned widely and also accepted the baksheesh that Mussavir handed him.

As they headed towards home, they saw Hibba and Sabra hurrying down—Honey had told them about the snake. Mussavir walked faster and reaching Sabra said, "It's all right now, Khala Sabra. Shaira has had a nasty shock, please don't scold her. She was almost at the point of collapsing when I reached there."

"The silly girl should not have gone across in any case," Sabra bellowed, despite Mussavir's request. "There was no need to follow the boys."

Mussavir emphasized Shaira had not merely followed the boys for the sake of it. "Honey dared Majid to go across. Majid took up the challenge, was too frightened to come back, and Shaira went to help him."

Just then Shaira reached her mother. "I'm very sorry, Ami. I shouldn't have let Majid go in the first place."

"The snake would have crept back to its hole as snakes always do," said Sabra. "You can't avoid snakes in rocky places along the rivers. They are harmless if one does not irritate them." She then looked around and asked, "Where is that khabis, Honey? The rascal. Why did he dare Majid to go across? I shall not allow anyone to come near the river again." She glared at Shaira and said, "You run along now. Your Taijan needs help."

Shaira looked at Mussavir, who was standing not too far from her. Their eyes met for a few seconds. Then Shaira looked away and slowly went up towards the house. Ayesha and Mugro had also by now come out. Mugro wanted to know all about the snake and who killed it. The children gathered around him and with arm gestures began telling him about the adventure. They told him the snake was still on the grass near the riverbank. Grinning, Mugro rushed down the slope to see the dead snake. Ayesha took Shaira in her arms and hugged her, saying, "My poor child, how awful. Come and sit down."

Mussavir, without saying anything to Ayesha, rushed into the house and brought out some tablets for Shaira. Ayesha patted Shaira, then took her inside to lie on Farida's bed and instructed Hibba to stay with her.

When Dr Bashir arrived, Mussavir told him about Shaira's shock and the temporary numbness in her feet. Dr Bashir went in to see her straight-away.

"How are you, my dear? I hear you had an adventurous morning."

"It was silly of me, Tayajan, really. But then it became awful. I'm so ashamed I was so frightened."

"There is nothing to be ashamed of, Beti. Snakes are not everybody's favourites. They can be scary, even nasty. You were lucky not to have been on the same rock."

"I still feel shivery and have funny sensations in my legs."

"You'll get over it. You've taken the tablets Mussavir gave you?" he asked, and she nodded. "Take two more later on."

"Thank you, Tayajan."

Shaira did not come out for lunch. Both Dr Bashir and Mussavir felt it was good for her to sleep it off. Majid, however, seemed all right and even had a hearty meal.

In the Shadow of Kirinyaga

After lunch Dr Bashir as usual left for work. The children, surprisingly, sat at their lessons or read. No one showed any interest in going out. Mussavir joined his mother and Sabra for tea in the veranda but then got up abruptly and, gathering the newspaper from the table, disappeared to his room. For a while he sat on his bed and scanned the paper. Then, throwing it on the floor, he stretched himself across his bed with his hands behind his head and looked up at the ceiling. Was he disturbed by the incident at the river, he asked himself. Of course not. He was a doctor. Nothing really earth-shattering had taken place except for the appearance of a snake. And no one was bitten. And yet, he was not himself. And all because of this thirteen-year-old Shaira.

He was amazed at how frightened Shaira had been of her mother's wrath on finding out that he had gone and helped her. How extraordinary. Such fear at that tender age. He now felt sorry for being sharp at her and began reliving the crossing on the river—how protective he felt towards her, and so close. He could not forget her frightened eyes when she told him not to tell her mother he had to come fetch her. But the look she gave him after coming face to face with her mother—she was no child of thirteen then.

Mussavir paced in his narrow room for a while, then sat down. He did not like the state he was in. This thirteen-year-old was getting under his skin. He wished his mother had not told him about the proposed match with her. It would have been better to meet her normally like a guest. He wondered if he'd have felt the same in that case. He was not an emotional person; he never dreamt he could become emotionally involved with a girl in only three days. He decided he should go to Nairobi and stay with his cousin Latif to cool off before proceeding to Abyssinia. He decided to tackle his mother about it.

When he came out of his room he bumped into Hibba, emerging from the room where Shaira was supposed to be resting. "How is your friend, Hibba?" he asked.

"My friend?" Hibba seemed surprised, then smiling she said, "Oh, Shaira. She's sleeping."

"Were you with her?"

"Yes. For a while after lunch."

"Did she eat?"

"No. But she drank some juice and lots of water. I think . . ."

"Yes, what do you think?"

"I am not sure, but I suspect Khala Sabra has been scolding her again. Her eyes were red. When I asked why, she said she had been crying because of shame that you had to rescue her."

"Oh, poor girl."

"I consoled her and told her you did not mind. You were a doctor. It was the natural thing to do."

"Khala Sabra seems a bitter sort of a woman at times. She blows hot and cold in no time."

"Yes, she does. But Bhaijan, aren't all mothers like that?" Hibba said, rushing out at the call of her mother.

While the family and guests were having tea on the veranda the Vellani family suddenly arrived in a van whose noisy exhaust pipe belched out smoke. The men jumped out and helped the ladies and their old mother. The women were all dressed in their finery, shining black hair combed in scallops and fixed with kirby grips and clips. They were the owners of the big goods store next to the Rattanseys'.

Ayesha welcomed them and they all sat on garden chairs on the lawn. Whilst having tea the visitors related the arrangements the Ghais were making for receiving the guests who were to descend on Nyeri from Nairobi and elsewhere. They said all the neighbours had offered a room or two each in their homes to help out. The Ghai family had hired a hall for the festive lunch. The marriage ceremony would be in their backyard, and the Ghais had also rented a big house for the duration of the stay. An Indian cook and his helpers were expected soon. They'd be cooking throughout the three or four days the guests were expected to stay. The Ghai home was being decorated with coloured bunting and lights. The pundit who would perform the marriage was expected on the night before the wedding day.

When they had relayed all the news about the forthcoming marriage,

Badru Vellani said he was going to Nairobi for two days to collect some spare parts and machinery for the coffee-curing machines. He planned to leave on Monday and would be back on Thursday. He asked Mussavir if he'd like to accompany him, and Mussavir agreed to join him. Mussavir told his parents he could stay with Latif and find out more about his departure for Abyssinia. His mother kept quiet, not liking the idea, but Dr Bashir approved. Mussavir had spent only one night in Nairobi on his way to Nyeri. Badru agreed to pick him up on Monday morning at daybreak.

Shaira came out as the Vellanis were leaving. Ayesha, walking in with Mussavir, called and asked if she wanted tea.

"I'll make some, Taijan. Please don't worry. I am all right now."

After supper and coffee, as Mussavir went to his bedroom his mother accompanied him. She had told him earlier she wanted to talk to him. In the small room Ayesha sat on the easy chair while Mussavir plunked himself down on his bed and began removing his shoes and socks. He shoved the socks into the shoes and pushed them under the bed, then raised his feet onto the bed, grabbed a pillow, stood it lengthwise against the head of the bed, and leaned back.

"Well, my son, it's time we had another chat about the shauri we talked about the other day. But first I want to know why you have suddenly decided to go to Nairobi. Was it on the spur of the moment or were you planning to do that and took advantage of the offer?"

"I've been thinking of going, Mama. In fact, I made up my mind this afternoon and providentially the offer of a lift came along so I jumped at it."

"Are you bored waiting here or do you really have something to do in Nairobi?" she asked.

"No, Mama. I'm not bored. Having the guests has not been uninteresting. But . . . I feel a bit restless and even stifled. I don't know why."

"Do you like Shaira, then?"

"I don't dislike her. She's a sweet girl despite being somewhat serious. But I must say I am not so keen on her mother. She bullies the poor girl."

"That's not difficult to understand, son. Widowed at a young age, she had to support so many children. Her sons were young and started working much later. She had to be both mother and father to her children. And that is no joke. She's not very secure and feels overprotective towards her children, especially the girls."

"But, Mama, she does not have to be a bully. They all obey her without question. The younger ones get their way with her, but that poor girl can't take a step without her mother's permission. She's so cold towards her."

"She's not demonstrative, Mussavir. People are made differently. I'm sure she loves Shaira very much, son."

"She has a funny way of showing it."

"I like your concern for her. That's a good sign."

"That doesn't mean that I want to marry her, Mama. Please don't jump to conclusions."

"All I want to know is whether you like her and would have no objection if we ask for her hand in marriage for you."

"But Mama, she's only thirteen."

"Does she look or behave thirteen?"

"No. She does not. In fact, today I was so angry that I wanted to marry her straightaway and leave her with you when I go. I want her to be free and not be frightened. But then I realized I could not do that. It was then that I decided to go away for a few days and get my thoughts sorted out."

"You are already in love, my son. Go, by all means, and get your thoughts sorted out. Leave the rest to us." Ayesha smiled widely and rose from her seat to let him rest and dream.

8

The Ghai Girl's Wedding

THERE WAS QUITE a commotion at the Bashir home. The girls were dolling up for the festive occasion. They bumped into one another moving from one room to the other, borrowing a comb or a brush and asking for the use of the only long mirror in the house. Huma was ready before the others. In her tariwalla orange satin suit, she wore silver jewellery and a pair of anklets that jingled when she walked. Dr Bashir and Mussavir, wearing dark suits, were waiting on the veranda. They both admired Huma's clothes and the jingling anklets in particular.

"I'm sure you are going to be better dressed than the bride, Huma," Mussavir complimented her.

"Oh no, Bhaijan, she'll be dressed far more grandly. This," she said, pointing at her suit, "is not that new. I've worn it many times."

Farida appeared just then in a pale yellow suit with a gota border and Hibba followed in a sunflower-pattern outfit with black and silver embroidery. Mussavir admired his sisters' attire and remarked that Farida was growing fast. She was almost as tall as Hibba. The boys all wore their long grey trousers and green sweaters with long sleeves. Looking spic and span, they trooped into the veranda. Ayesha and Sabra joined the group wearing raw-silk shalwar kamizes with muslin dupattas. Ayesha wore gold earrings and bangles. Sabra had stopped wearing jewellery since she became a widow.

"Where is Shaira?" Dr Bashir asked.

"She must be putting away the clothes left all over the place by the others," Mussavir said to all in general. He was proved right, for Hibba confirmed it but added Shaira was almost ready.

Eventually Shaira surfaced gracefully, apologizing for delaying everybody. She was wearing a pink shalwar kamiz and dupatta with golden embroidery on the cuffs and borders. A delicate gold necklace and a pair of earrings studded with ruby-coloured stones adorned her neck and ears. Mussavir couldn't keep his eyes off her. Her own kohl-lined eyes, he thought, looked even more liquid than usual. The pink of her clothes matched her rosy complexion. He was pleased that she was not wearing her drab shawl. But he was surprised that she was carrying her burqa on her arm instead.

"You don't have to wear a veil at this time, Shaira," said Dr Bashir. "By the time we reach there it will be pitch dark."

Shaira looked at her mother. Ayesha said her husband was right, there was no need for veils. She was not wearing hers either. Sabra reluctantly allowed Shaira to leave hers behind.

They all walked in procession down the narrow road in double file towards the Ghai home in downtown Nyeri, behind the main street, where the Ghai family had a produce business. As the family and guests came out of the grounds of the Bashir home, they could see coloured lights. When they turned the corner, the sight of the Ghai home all lit up like a Christmas tree dazzled their eyes. The whole place was illuminated with red, green, and yellow lights and decorated with coloured bunting that gave it added glamour. The arched gate was decorated with fresh green banana fronds. Men dressed in suits and gala headgear and women in a spate of colourful saris and suits all stood around the gate.

The baraat, the bridegroom's party, had just come and the welcome ceremonies were being performed. As the Bashir party reached the gate, the bride, a bundle of red and gold escorted by her friends, met the bridegroom on the threshold of the house. The bride's mother handed her daughter a garland of fresh marigolds and a few pink carnations with greenery, which the bride placed around the groom's neck. She moved back into the house while the bridegroom along with his party moved inside the courtyard. Those standing around, family members and all invited guests, slowly moved to their seats escorted by the bride's relatives.

The mandap on which the marriage ceremony was to take place had a square-shaped platform made from banana trees cut at the roots and fixed to the ground at the corners. Between the four banana trees, strings of flowers and greenery were tied up with tinsel and other decorations that shone like lights. The floor was decorated with gala designs. A white tin container with a burning fire lay in the centre. Facing the fire stood two cushioned seats for the bride and groom to sit on during the wedding ceremony. On their left was a low seat for the pundit, who, in a white dhoti and shirt with an orange stole thrown over his shoulders, was already chanting loudly some mantras in Sanskrit and ladling ghee and incense onto the fire with a copper ladle from a tin container. The fire blazed with orange tongues of flame. The pundit wore an orange turban on his head and had a red and yellow mark in the middle of his forehead. He was quite obese but moved about with ease.

Along the sides of the mandap lay small cushions for the bride's and the groom's parents and brothers. Invited guests and other relatives as well as members of the baraat were seated in two groups facing the mandap, women and children on one side and men on the other. The men were seated on chairs, the women and children on the floor, which was covered with mats and rugs. Dr Bashir and his entourage and other non-Hindu guests, among whom were two British administrators, some English farmers, and their wives, were warmly welcomed by the hosts and escorted to their seats in the front row near the bridegroom and his party.

The bridegroom, wearing a three-piece blue suit and orange turban with a flower sehra tied on his forehead and a garland of flowers around his neck, was seated on the front row flanked on one side by his father. On the other sat his young nephew, dressed in a scaled-down version of the bridegroom's clothes. He was the sarbala.

Shaira and Hibba together with Ayesha, Sabra, Farida, and Huma sat with the women on the floor. Huma pushed her way to the front to watch the ceremony. Many women were already singing and chanting in the background and beating the dolki. There was laughter and joking and generally an atmosphere of joy and festivity.

The pundit stopped chanting and, facing the audience, announced that the ceremonies were about to start. But before starting he wanted to explain the concept of a Hindu marriage for the benefit of those who did not understand Sanskrit mantras. All became silent. The pundit spoke in Hindi, but what he said was translated into English by the Sikh Sardarji schoolteacher who had travelled with Sabra and her family from Nairobi.

The pundit said the ceremony had started with the milni, the bride's family welcoming the groom and his family. The bride had welcomed and garlanded her groom as required. Now the groom would offer prayers to Lord Ganesh, the provider of peace, for the internal peace and tranquillity necessary for proceeding with the ceremony.

The bridegroom was then led to the mandap and made to sit on one of the raised seats on the right. The pundit anointed the bridegroom's forehead with some liquid, presumably holy water, from a bowl with one finger. He then poured a ladleful of ghee and a handful of incense onto the fire while chanting the mantras. Now and again he walked up and down the small square holding a brass pot called a gardwi in his hand, and he passed it in a circular motion over the bridegroom's head whenever he was near him.

The pundit then asked who was giving away the bride, the kanya dan. The bride's parents answered that they agreed to give their daughter to the groom.

After repeating the same ritual once again, the pundit asked the bride's brother to fetch the bride, who, all dressed up in her wedding clothes of red and gold and wearing golden jewellery, her hands and feet dyed in henna, sat quietly among her female friends in the back row. The friends got up and escorted her towards the mandap and stopped at the entrance from where they handed her over to her brother, who was to carry her in his arms and deposit her on the seat. Her own brother was very young and unable to pick her up in his arms, so a cousin from her father's side came forward and carried the bride in his arms and made her stand near the seat to the left of the bridegroom. At the pundit's bidding the bridegroom rose from his seat. The bride and groom then sat down. The pundit anointed the bride's forehead with the same liquid he had used for the bridegroom and went on chanting, only louder.

The bride's father, wearing a pink turban, and her mother, in a pink sari, sat side by side. The cousin who had carried her stood behind the bride's parents. He wore a pink turban too. The bridegroom's parents and brother sat on the opposite side.

The pundit, still chanting the mantras, asked the bride's parents to join the couple's hands as the couple declared that their hearts had been united. They vowed to remain entirely devoted to each other. They also vowed to always remember the divine; always be loving, compassionate, and empathetic towards each other; help each other in all good deeds; keep their minds virtuous and pure; be righteous and strong; be affectionate towards their parents, sisters, brothers, and other family members; bring up their children to be strong in mind and body; and always welcome and respect their guests.

Pouring another ladleful of ghee and incense on the fire, the pundit asked the bridegroom's brother to lift the groom's flower sehra. He then placed a mouthful of parshad into the groom's mouth. Likewise, he asked the bride's mother to give the holy sweet to her daughter. The bride and groom held hands while the pundit again paced the square with the gandwi and circled it over the couple's heads. The relatives recited prayers and blessings and showered flower petals, signifying fertility and abundance, while the couple offered prayers to Agni, the holy fire, which is an element of life symbolizing God and thus serves as a couple's witness when the two are joined in marriage. All present watched the ceremony quietly as the couple walked seven paces together, reciting the following hymn that expressed their principal duties:

Let us take the first step, vowing to keep a pure diet.
Let us take the second step, vowing to develop mental, physical, and spiritual powers.
Let us increase our wealth by righteous means.
Let us acquire knowledge, happiness, and harmony by mutual love and trust.

Let us take the fifth step, so that we are blessed with virtuous, strong, and heroic children.
Let us take this step for self-restraint and longevity
Finally, let us be true companions and remain lifelong partners.

During the ceremony Mussavir could not help comparing the Hindu marriage ceremony and rituals to Muslim practices. He always found the Muslim rituals had a sense of sombreness about them. No fun or glamour, or even colour. A Muslim marriage was a straightforward civil contract. The consent and signatures of the parties concerned were all that was required plus a small sermon by a male or a maulvi to announce and enumerate the rules and conditions as prescribed in the Holy Book about the mehr. Even the presence of the bride was not necessary. Her father or brother could act on her behalf and give consent. At its conclusion, there was silent prayer and a distribution of dry dates and candy to the congregation. The Hindu marriage was different, with chanting and processing round the fire. Incense and ghee and water were all symbols of significance. Certain commitments were made and it was necessary for the bride to be given to the bridegroom and for them both to walk in procession around the fire with her groom four or seven times.

On and off during the ceremony Mussavir, in his mind's eye, kept replacing the bride with Shaira. He imagined her going through all the Hindu rituals with him. He could picture her looking like a goddess. Then he remembered the scene when he helped her back from the rock in the river, and he only came back to reality when the pundit was tying a knot to the stoles worn by the bride and groom before they proceeded around the fire.

The bride and groom, the stoles on their shoulders tied together, started their first circuit around the fire with the groom's brother walking alongside carrying a red earthen pitcher full of water. The pundit was chanting and ladling the ghee and incense. The couple took four rounds in all. On the last round the bride led and the groom followed. That completed the ceremony. They were husband and wife.

People sang songs of rejoicing and congratulation while the bride and groom were escorted by the bride's friends to the interior of the house. Huma followed on their heels, her anklets jingling. She managed to watch the ceremonies inside.

The bride's cousin asked the invited guests and members of the bridegroom's party to proceed to the back of the house where a marquee had been erected for dinner. People strolled out and went to their respective tables, men on one side and the women and children on the other.

After a while the bridegroom emerged, smiling. He had removed his headgear after the ceremonies inside. He joined the men when dinner was served. All the food was vegetarian, consisting of saffron-coloured laddus coated in silver, shining brown gulabjamuns in rich cardamom-flavoured syrup, and snow-white pieces of barfi coated in pistachio nut shavings. Fluffy puris and vegetable curries formed the main courses: cauliflower with potatoes, spinach with cottage cheese, rice cooked with peas and flavoured with cumin seeds, and lentil curry garnished with coriander leaves. Mango and lime pickles and chutney and dahi warras in spicy yogurt were served as condiments. The serving men kept bringing steaming hot and fluffy puris in silver trays from the small banda set up as a temporary kitchen where the halwai from Nairobi and his helpers were preparing the food.

After dinner the guests returned to their seats near the mandap. The Sardarji and his wife met Sabra and the Bashir family like lifelong pals and invited them to their home for tea the following Tuesday. Ayesha and Sabra accepted the invitation. Mussavir and his father mingled with the men and spoke to the groom and his father. Dr Bashir introduced Mussavir to the administrative officers and farmers, most of whom were his patients and knew Mussavir was heading to Abyssinia. The European wives all admired the bride's clothes and jewellery and later went inside the house to congratulate her.

Back in the courtyard it was announced there was to be a program of folk dancing and singing. Two young boys dressed as villagers from India, wearing colourful dhotis lehnga-style, with long shirts hanging over their dhotis and blue turbans on their heads, performed a bhangra dance. This dance is supposed to depict the drunken state of the dancers after

Sophia Mustafa

Bisakhi, the spring festival of harvest. Another young man, similarly dressed, beat the dolki and moved around dancing to the drumbeats. The dance began slowly with the dancers depicting how the bhang is planted. Then followed the various growing stages, from when it is ankle high, then knee high, to the last stages, when the crop is harvested, then how the leaves are ground on stone slabs with a stone mortar and lastly the liquid is prepared. The ceremonial serving and the tempo of the music quickened when they came to the drinking and drunken stages. The dance became very vigorous, the audience joined in the clapping. The dancers seemed to have lost all inhibitions and danced with complete abandon. People who were watching laughed and clapped. Even the groom, who was supposed to behave solemnly, laughed uproariously.

9

The Proposal

"HOW MANY EGGS shall I use for the fruitcake, Taijan?" Shaira asked Ayesha as she was creaming the sugar and butter in a cake bowl on the veranda. Hibba was busy kneading the dough with ghee and spices for the savoury scones nearby. They had both risen early to help Ayesha with the baking and frying.

"The eggs are not very big, so six should be ample, Beti," Ayesha called from where she sat near the kitchen door on the webbed piri frying shakkar paras. "Break one at a time and don't forget to add a tablespoon of flour while mixing the egg into the creamed butter."

Then she called to Hibba to pass her some rolled-out mathees. She would fry the savoury scones in the same oil. All the goodies, including mathees and shakkar paras, were to be sent to Latif with Mussavir, who was leaving the following morning. Shaira and Hibba were helping Ayesha with the rolling and kneading of the various doughs and Sabra was helping with the lunch. When Dr Bashir came home he laughed and said he could never understand why all the cake making was necessary when all the goodies were easily available in Nairobi. Ayesha justified the work this way: Latif was alone and far from home and she and her husband were the only family he had in East Africa, so he'd be happy to get home-cooked fare. Mussavir said that the females liked to create work even when there was no need to! He did not, however, refuse to cart the food to Nairobi.

Badru Vellani arrived on time at daybreak and stopped his van outside. He did not have to sound the horn as the van made enough noise not only to alert the Bashirs of his arrival, but also to wake up the patients in the hospital. Mussavir had finished his breakfast and was ready for the journey. His mother had risen early with him, and his father saw him off as he was already up for his morning prayers. Shaira woke up when she heard movement in the house, but did not get out of bed. She heard the van come and leave. She did not sleep after that but kept thinking of Mussavir. She could not understand why she so often thought of him. At the wedding the previous day she had been stealing glances at him more than she ought to have. In fact, since the snake incident at the river, a change had come over her. She felt bashful and nervous if he appeared suddenly. At the wedding she kept seeing him in place of the bridegroom and had to hush herself. She hoped he would come back safely and even said a prayer for him. She got up when Sabra called her and said it was time for morning prayers.

While Mussavir was away the boys visited Tochi and his friends in town. Tochi's father took them all to an Indian movie at the only cinema in Nyeri that showed silent movies from India. They came home and related the story of the movie to Huma with great excitement and exaggeration, telling her how much they had enjoyed the film *Do Rangi Dunya*, or "The Two-coloured World." They told her about the hero with admiration for his bravery—how he had overcome so many people single-handed in a fight, with a gun that had a long barrel; and before a fight how he would pour out grains of channa from the gun's barrel and eat them. This would give him all the necessary strength. Huma at first listened with wide eyes and moaned missing such a movie. But then she suddenly said she did not believe the film was real.

"Why not?" Majid asked.

"Channas can't come out of gun barrels, even if they are stored there in the first place! They would be poisoned with gunpowder."

The boys all laughed and Honey said, "Grapes are sour!"

The family visited a coffee farm owned by a European who had a young Asian man called Amin in his employ as an accountant. Amin lived with his wife, Hamida, and two children in an outhouse not far from the coffee-curing factory. Amin's father was a friend of Dr Bashir and lived in Mombasa. The young family had no other friends nearby, so once in a while they visited Dr Bashir at his home when the farm van went into town. Ayesha had promised to visit Hamida with her guests.

Amin met them at the depot and walked them down through the coffee bushes to his small home. The children seemed surprised to see the big farm with coffee plantations spread over many hills and ridges in neat rows. The three-foot-high green bushes were laden with coffee berries of green, yellow, and red. The red berries were ready for picking. Kikuyu women with leather aprons tied around their waists and bare heads, shaved and shining, were picking the beans into empty kerosene oil tins called debes. A number of round earrings made with coloured beads hung from their distended earlobes. They also wore lots of coloured bead ornaments around their necks and their arms. As the coffee bushes were grown quite close to one another, the women could chat or listen to others relating juicy gossip and then laugh loudly.

Amin told the visitors how each woman got a ticket or metal coin for each debe she hand-picked and emptied into a big pen near the machine. Later the tickets and coins were exchanged for money at the cashier's office.

After leaving Sabra and the older girls with Hamida, Amin walked down towards the factory with Huma, Farida, and the boys, who were bursting with excitement to watch the machines in action. African men sorted and picked leaves and twigs from the beans in the pens, then opened the hatches to allow the beans to roll onto another pen, where, mixed with a lot of water, the beans fell into a black round revolving drum with a lot of holes. The beans, crushed and separated from the skins, emptied onto long trays of wire mesh to drain. Two men picked up each tray and laid it out to dry in the sun. The crushed red skins and waste went through a pipe towards a big furrow.

The Mombasa cousins asked if tea was processed in the same way. Huma was quick to tell them tea was made from leaves, not beans. She related how she had been to a tea estate in Limuru with her elder brother and watched the women pick tea leaves and place them in the bags tied to their backs, then take the full bags to the factory.

"I saw the tea crushed like spinach and then kept in a big container for the chemical reaction to take place," she told her attentive cousins.

"What's a chemical reaction?" asked Salim.

"The tea changes its colour from deep green to brown and then a darker brown," Huma said, her eyes wide.

They were still discussing the drying processes of tea and coffee when they arrived at Amin's home.

Hamida, who was tall and slim and dressed in a printed cotton suit and dupatta, served tea with pakoras and cake.

While they were guzzling and praising the cake and the goodies, Hamida told of how she had learned to make the cake from her husband's employer's African cook on a Sunday when he was off duty. The cook, she said, was a very good breadmaker too.

Sabra asked if her husband's employers were friendly. Hamida answered that the wife was friendly and helpful. She was a nurse and ran a small clinic for the babies and children of the farm labourers. She had visited Hamida once to learn how to make curry, and occasionally sent Hamida vegetables from her kitchen garden. But the husband had a typical settler mentality. He worked very hard himself and expected the same from his workers. The employees were quite scared of him. He used the lash at times and so was nicknamed marira by the workers. The terms of service were strict. Mohammed Amin had one full day off per week. Friends could visit them in their small cottage, but they were not to wander beyond the factory or to the farmer's house and garden. Hamida said she missed her friends and family but was kept quite busy with her children and housework. European men and women from other farms came to visit the farmer and his wife on some weekends. And the employers threw big parties at times at which dancing continued till very late. But the Amins were never invited to these parties, or even to the house.

Before Mussavir returned from Nairobi, Dr Bashir and Ayesha broached the subject of Shaira and Mussavir's matrimony with Sabra one evening after supper, once the younger members of the household had gone to bed. Sabra did not seem surprised to receive the proposal; in fact, it appeared as if she had been expecting it, perhaps because the Bashirs had often hinted about it even before Mussavir's arrival in East Africa. She told them she was not only touched but grateful they liked Shaira. She considered Mussavir a suitable match for her daughter. He was already qualified as a doctor and had good prospects. He was likable and she was fond of him. She believed her daughter would be much liked and cared for in the Bashir household. But she felt Shaira was still young, and she was still studying. She and her sons desired Shaira to at least complete her secondary education before they gave her in marriage. She was therefore not very keen to have a formal engagement or nikah at this stage before Mussavir's departure. There was also the matter of consulting her husband's father and other relatives in India. And, of course, Shaira's consent was necessary. Sabra felt Shaira was emotionally immature and that she would not be able even to talk to her about it. In a couple of year's time, when she was fifteen, it would be easier and fairer to talk about it.

Ayesha and Bashir told Sabra they realized Shaira was young in age and they too felt the marriage should take place later, on Mussavir's return from Abyssinia. But they wished to confirm the matter in an engagement ceremony and exchange of rings before their son's departure. They felt this would give their son a sense of responsibility and something to look forward to.

Sabra insisted that had her husband been alive it would have been a different matter. There would then have been no need for the approval of those in India. Her eldest son, Zaffer, was now the head of the family and would act as guardian to his sisters in East Africa, but according to tradition and as a matter of courtesy it was necessary to consult the other relatives as well. That seemed reasonable to Dr Bashir, but Ayesha seemed disappointed. She remembered her last conversation with her son, but she knew she could not force the matter further.

So the Nairobi guests continued with their holiday, visiting other friends of the Bashirs and in return being visited by the Bashirs' friends. Shaira and Hibba helped in the house as well as in the kitchen. They worked at their sewing and knitting and needlework. Shaira read a number of books, but many a time she found her thoughts wandering and wondered how Mussavir was faring in Nairobi. Time did not seem to pass as fast as it had in the earlier week of their holiday. She secretly looked forward to Mussavir's return.

10

Latif Warns Mussavir

"HERE WE ARE at last, my friend!" said Badru Vellani to Mussavir as he braked his van with a loud screech of tires opposite the dispensary on River Road. "I've brought you in one piece despite the long and tedious journey."

"Thank you very much, Badru. I must say you're a jolly good driver. It's exactly five and before sunset as you promised. I hope my cousin is at home." He looked up towards the flat above, then asked, "Won't you come up and have a drink?"

"No thanks. I should push off or the family will leave for the mosque and I'll be locked out. I'm hot and dusty. I need a bath to shed this dust off." Badru smiled and added, "I'll pick you up on Thursday at the same time as I did this morning. Unless you want to stay on and enjoy the life in the big city?"

"Oh no. It'll be fine. I do want to go back. Definitely." Mussavir picked up his bag and the tin of goodies for Latif from the back of the van. Bidding Badru goodbye, he made for the side entrance and stairs leading up to Latif's apartment.

Latif lived downtown because he worked as a legal clerk with a Muslim lawyer who had his chambers not far away on River Road. Mussavir was five years younger than Latif but the two were good friends. Latif had come out to Kenya after his wife died giving birth to their first child, a son, who was being reared by Latif's parents in India. Dr Bashir had helped get him the job. After he'd been in Nairobi for two years, his parents persuaded him to agree to a proxy marriage whereby they would select a bride for him and send her out. The proxy marriage had already been performed in Nairobi with Dr Bashir acting as wali on behalf of the bride's father. Latif was waiting for his new wife's arrival.

When Mussavir lugged his belongings up the long staircase and banged at Latif's door, Kalingwa, the houseboy, a native of Ukambani, opened the door. "Karibu, Bwana! Karibu," he greeted Mussavir, showing his filed teeth. He then put out his hands to grab the suitcase and the tin.

"Jambo, Kalingwa," Mussavir responded, then looking around the hall-like room he asked, "Wapi Bwana?"

Kalingwa smiled widely and said Latif was still at work but would be coming shortly. He then inquired about Mussavir's parents and Nyeri. After dusting the luggage with a rag, Kalingwa took the bag to the spare bedroom. Then coming back he picked up the tin of goodies and asked Mussavir if he would like to have a bath or would he prefer a cup of tea first.

When Mussavir surfaced from the bathroom all clean and fresh, he asked Kalingwa if there was any beer in the house.

"There are a few bottles in the cupboard, Bwana. I'll get one for you." He went to the kitchen and came out carrying a bottle and a glass tumbler together with a bottle opener.

Mussavir had not had a beer for a long time so was pleased Latif had some in the house. He lit a cigarette as Kalingwa opened the bottle and slowly poured the frothing liquor into the tilted glass. Mussavir thanked him and picked up the copy of the *East African Standard* lying on the coffee table. Before he'd opened the paper there was a knock on the door and the turning of a key. Latif stepped in and stopped, as if not believing his eyes. "Oh! This *is* a pleasant surprise!" he exclaimed. Covering the distance in two long strides he greeted his cousin, asking, "Have you got your orders to go?"

"No, I've not heard from the authorities yet. I plan to find out tomorrow. Badru Vellani was coming to get some spare parts for their vehicles, so I came along for a couple of days." Mussavir put the paper aside. "Sorry to land on you unannounced like this. I hope it's all right."

"But of course. You know you are always welcome, my friend. Khala Sabra and her children must be in Nyeri."

"Yes. The house is bursting at its seams with guests."

"So, you had enough of them? And took to your heels?" Latif laughed as he removed his jacket and handed it to Kalingwa, who had come out of the kitchen to greet his employer.

"No, I just felt like being on my own for a few days to think and sort myself out."

"How are my uncle and aunt and the girls?"

"Oh, they are all well, thanks. They send you lots of love and Mama has sent you some home-cooked goodies. She spent the whole day baking and frying yesterday."

"Oh, that's sweet of Chachi Jee. Thanks for lugging it along."

"Mama and Abu are eagerly awaiting the news of your new wife's arrival. When is she expected?"

Latif stroked his hair and, looking at Mussavir, said, "It won't be for another two months or more. The family she was coming out with has delayed their return." He sat down on the small sofa next to Mussavir and stretched his legs in front of him.

"Oh, that's a shame. Did your parents send you her photo?"

"No," Latif replied slowly, looking down at his feet. "I did not ask for it."

"But why?"

"What difference would it make, yaar?" He again stroked his straight dark hair, which was combed with a side parting over a wide fair forehead. Latif had an aquiline nose and sported a thin moustache above his small mouth and lips.

"Supposing she is ugly. And fat. Aren't you concerned, man?"

"Maryam was my mother's choice. Was she ugly and fat?" Latif said smiling.

"No. You're right. She was a real smasher. The poor girl died so young! But you should have at least asked for a photo before you agreed to a proxy marriage."

"It's destiny, my friend. What will be will be." Latif gave a small sigh.

"I wish I could accept that attitude for myself."

"We are all made differently."

"How old is Jamila? That's what she is called, isn't she?"

"Jamila Bano. She's eighteen or nineteen I'm told. Why?" Latif looked up at Mussavir.

"That's better. At least you are not betrothed to a thirteen-year-old," Mussavir said, and picking up his tumbler he took a big drink.

Latif smiled. He had heard his aunt and uncle talk of Shaira as a suitable girl for Mussavir.

"But you are going away for two years. She won't be thirteen when you come back. And she is mature, grown up, handsome, and a wholesome girl. I'm sure you've also had a chance to meet and see her. So what's the moaning about?"

"Oh, she is quite grown up to look at. And, well, not bad looking, either. It's hard to believe she is thirteen. But whether she is ready for marriage mentally or emotionally, I'm not sure."

"By the time you come back she'll be all right. Don't tell me you are planning to get married before you go."

"Oh no. I couldn't do that even if I wanted to. She has to be sixteen before she can get married according to Kenyan law. You should know that."

"What's the worry then? Don't you like her?"

"I'm not sure." Mussavir furrowed his brow and took another big gulp from his tumbler.

He then told Latif about the conversation he had had with his mother about Shaira and his misgivings over her age and about his going to the war front. "But then something happened and brought a sudden change. I can't even believe it myself."

"Something happened to make you dislike her? What could that be? Don't talk in riddles, yaar," Latif said with a scowl.

"Oh no. It did not make me dislike her. Far from it. It's the opposite: I have begun to like her immensely. Not only that, I wish I could marry her before I go."

He then related the incident at the river with the snake, his discovery that Shaira was terrified of her mother and of his own reactions to her sensitivity.

"This sudden feeling of protection for her and wanting to marry her straightaway shows you have fallen madly in love! How romantic!" Latif laughed and sat back, looking more relaxed than when he was answering questions about himself.

"Do you think it's that? Or only sympathy for her?" Mussavir asked. Then he drained his tumbler and called Kalingwa to bring him another beer.

"Had it been only sympathy, you'd not have been affected so strongly as to make you bolt away."

Kalingwa asked if he could serve supper. Latif said he could and got up, excused himself, and walked to the washroom.

Kalingwa served kofta curry and rice, a dal curry, and some fried chicken with chutney and a bowl of fruit salad. The aroma of the rich curry and steaming rice made Mussavir realize how famished he was. The cousins ate and chatted about Nyeri and then about current happenings in Nairobi. Mussavir praised Kalingwa's cooking at such short notice. Kalingwa told him he had already cooked the koftas when Mussavir arrived, so the only addition was the chicken. During the meal Mussavir finished his second beer, which was a bit more than his usual intake. Latif said, "Mussavir, please take it easy on this thing." Pointing to the glass of beer he added, "You are going to the war front. You should have more control over yourself."

"Oh, it's all right, yaar. Don't be a real elder brother. I'm tired. And worried. I didn't touch a drop in Nyeri. And I am not at the war front yet."

"When you think rationally you'll be able to make the right decision," said Latif. "Please don't act in a hurry. Let your parents decide when you should get married. It's enough for the moment to tell them you like the girl and would not mind marrying her."

Mussavir did not reply, so Latif asked, "Have you met Shaira's brothers, Zaffer and Shahid?"

"I have a vague feeling I've met Zaffer. But I'd like to meet them now that I'm here," Mussavir replied. "I suppose you know them well."

"Fairly. Zaffer has been here a few times and asked me over to his home too. I'll ring him tomorrow. And invite them both to supper."

"A good idea, thanks."

They talked for a while over coffee and then Mussavir said, "I see from the paper they no longer have the silent movies. I used to watch Charlie Chaplin, Eddi Polo, and Douglas Fairbanks, and, aha! Miss Salochana Chatterji in Indian pictures!"

"English movies all have a sound track now. They show silent movies from India in the flea pit."

"Which is the flea pit?" laughed Mussavir.

"The Alexandra of course."

"But that used to be quite nice. The flea pit was the Majestic Cinema, the one behind the post office with the wooden seats and the funny screen. It was converted from a garage and was quite scruffy."

"That's closed now. There is instead one on Sixth Avenue called Theatre Royal and another on Harding Street."

"Let's go to the Alexandra then, it is nearby."

"Very well, but it won't start till after nine."

The next morning Mussavir, though awake, stayed in bed while Latif was getting ready to go to work. Latif had opened the tin of goodies. He came into Mussavir's room exclaiming, "Chachi Jee has really sent a lot of appetizing eatables. Thanks for carrying them. They look delicious."

"Hibba and Shaira helped her," Mussavir said and sat up in bed. "They were at it the whole day."

"I'm going to try some for my breakfast. Do you want yours now or later?"

"You can pour me a cup of tea now. I'll have my egg and toast later."

Latif handed Mussavir a cup of tea. After finishing his breakfast, he dressed in his black suit and tie and left for work.

Mussavir shaved, washed, then dressed in a casual grey suit. Over breakfast he chatted with Kalingwa. He asked him if the Kamba still filed their teeth. Kalingwa, who was dressed in a white shirt and shorts, smiled widely and said they certainly did. And worked at wood carvings, too.

"What about the dancing and high jumps?"

"Oh, they do that too, Bwana. When were you last in Ukambani?"

"A long time ago. We lived in Kamba country for nearly two years when I was a young boy."

"Which township?"

"My father was a doctor for the whole of Machakos District."

"Was he now?" Kalingwa grinned and said he was himself from that area.

"Two things I remember about Machakos," said Mussavir. "One, very sweet oranges and tangerines, and two, the snakes! Mingi sana. Nyoka of every kind and kabila. The snake charmer used to come and snake-proof the house and the garden around it with charms and potions. Though nobody believed it would work, the snakes did creep away. Even then my mother would not let us play outside."

Kalingwa grinned widely and said there were still snake charmers going around with their dawa and potions in small gourds, but the snake population had somehow gone down because of cultivation and land clearance.

Mussavir finished his breakfast, lit a cigarette, and walked over to the end of the room, where the windows faced the road outside. The shops had opened and he could see the colourful clothes and fancy goods arranged inside them. Outside on the covered pavements, African tailors and cobblers had set up their treadle machines, leather, and tools. They were already busy working at their various crafts. Colourful shirts and dresses on hangers were arranged on the wall for display. People, mostly Asian and African, were going up and down in the hustle and bustle of the morning rush. Cars, lorries loaded with bulging gunny sacks piled high, buses packed with people, bicycles, and motorcycles honking their horns and ringing their bells were rushing along. Some African pedestrians carried bundles on their heads and baskets in their arms. Others had small pushcarts on two wheels with sacks of produce for delivery.

Mussavir felt good watching humanity pass by, seeing the place teeming with life. He had slept like a log and got up relaxed, happy that he had come to Nairobi. His chat with Latif made him see things in perspective. He remembered Latif's warning about the beer. Latif was right. He had to curb his dependence on beer and other alcholic drinks when under strain—he was going away to a place which was not going to be free of stress. He had to avoid the risk of becoming addicted to alcohol at all costs.

He then thought of Shaira. In a way he missed her. He was surprised that in such a short time the girl had affected him so much. He had liked her presence in his parents' home and enjoyed watching her moving around the house, helping his mother and sisters as well as obeying her own mother's numerous commands. He admired her very affectionate but firm attitude towards her younger brother and sister. He was pleased he would be meeting her elder brothers in the evening. He wanted to know more about them all.

Towards midday he went out and walked alongside the High Court, which was only a stone's throw away and visible from the dispensary. Like all government offices it was housed in an old wooden building, painted dark brown and standing on cement stilts with a long veranda roaming its entire length. A roped fence surrounded the grounds and car park which faced Government Road. Policemen in uniform were moving about the grounds and the black prison van stood on one side. Two lawyers in their wigs, black robes flapping like bats' wings, were rushing up the wooden steps to the courtroom. As he crossed Government Road he walked along the row of shops where windows displayed fancy goods and European-type clothes and goods on models of white men and women. He walked on the clean cement pavement towards the headquarters of the Red Cross to visit the authorities responsible for his travel arrangements.

There he met one of the other doctors, Dr Tara Chand, who was to accompany him to Abyssinia, and together they went to see their third companion, Dr Gopalan. They all lunched at a small Indian restaurant near the big and imposing Aga Khan Mosque. Mussavir told them about the Major in Nyeri and the book the Major's wife had lent him about the Adowa war and the defeat of the Italians. Tara Chand said the Italians were going to be better prepared this time; their armies were sailing through the Suez Canal in great numbers with all the military hardware. One of his relatives, a transporter, had told him the Italians in Kenya were busy buying up all the donkeys, mules, and even lorries and road-making material in Kenya, to ship to Italian Somaliland.

"I am not surprised," said Mussavir. "The Major said they had done the same in Egypt and Aden. And their agents were sent to Tanganyika Masai areas to get as many donkeys and mules as they could get. In fact, they had even paid for pregnant donkeys and were collecting mule fodder from everywhere."

"What determination and sheer madness, to be fighting so far away from home in a mountainous place where there are hardly any roads," said Gopalan.

"The Major told me the Italians are very good road makers," said Mussavir. "They will start carting the stuff on mules and at the same time build roads as they go along. The tanks and lorries will then follow. They are determined to reach Addis Ababa come what may."

"We'll perhaps be expected to travel on mules. There is no shortage of them in Abyssinia," said Tara Chand. He asked Mussavir if he could ride a donkey or mule. Mussavir laughed and said he could if pushed to it. But he would be too tall to ride on a poor small donkey.

Later the trio strolled along to Indian Bazaar, stopping at one or two shops. After tea at a small tea house near the Jivanjee Gardens, Mussavir parted from his friends and walked back to Latif's home, where Kalingwa was busy cooking the evening meal. The aroma of frying and meat simmering in spices was pervasive.

Latif came home holding a pink envelope which he handed to Mussavir. Mussavir's heart missed a beat as it often did when a telegram came. "Who is it from, yaar?" he asked and quickly pulled out the single sheet from the opened envelope. His face lit up and he flashed a smile at Latif. "Oh! She's coming as originally planned?"

"It would seem so," Latif replied.

"But that's wonderful. I'll be able to meet her before I go. And Mama is really going to be happy."

"You can take the telegram back with you. My uncle and aunt can advise me what to do."

"What is there to do?" Mussavir asked in surprise. "You are an independent man. You need no one's advice, man! Go to Mombasa. Meet her at the docks. And bring her back with you."

"But..."

"But what?"

"That's not how it's done. There'll have to be a rukhstana of some sort and then the walima feast, even if only a small one."

"I am sure Mama will love to come and organize it all."

"That's why I think you should take this telegram to Nyeri."

They were still discussing the good news of Latif's wife's forthcoming arrival when Zaffer arrived. He apologized for Shahid not coming, saying he was working late. Zaffer had come straight from work and so was dressed in a striped tie, a tweed coat with brown rubber patches over the elbows, and grey trousers. His brownish hair was combed back with a side parting and he wore dark-rimmed glasses. Mussavir could see the resemblance between him and Shaira.

Latif made the introductions. Zaffer said he remembered Mussavir. "You have not changed much except your height. And you are a little older," he said laughing.

Mussavir said he could say the same about Zaffer, and they laughed and talked of the days of sidecars and motorcycles and rickshaws. Mussavir then asked Zaffer how he liked being a salesman.

"It's not bad, though I am not a full salesman yet. I am only an assistant. The full salesman is a mzungu, an Irishman. I travel with him, and I get a small commission and travelling allowance apart from my salary. Of course, a lot depends on sales."

"Has the Depression affected the sales ?"

"Oh yes. Though it's still early to say, the market is picking up."

"Khala Sabra said you have to travel a lot. It must be a lot of promotion work. The Sahib could not know the vernacular or Swahili. Or do you only sell to Europeans?" Mussavir asked.

"In a way, yes, but it's good to have the Irishman. He can speak some Swahili and knows a lot about cars, trucks, and even tractors, spare parts as well as machinery. I have learnt a lot from him. We go to Mombasa quite often to take deliveries. We supply cars and lorries to farms in

Tanganyika and Uganda, so we visit those territories too. In fact, I was in Kampala when my mother left for Nyeri. How are they enjoying their holiday, by the way?"

"They are liking Nyeri and its quiet countryside very much after the bustling city here and the boys have found friends. They are kept busy bashing away at gulli danda and I taught them kabaddi. Huma and Farida have their dolls and geetas. And Mama and Khala Sabra have not stopped talking!" He laughed. He did not mention Shaira.

"Marvellous. They all seem well occupied. I'm glad. They needed a change. It was jolly decent and kind of your parents to invite them."

"Mama and Abu are very pleased to have them. In fact, Huma, who is so sweet and so unspoilt, has livened the place up."

"Oh, Huma is the limb of an aflatoon. She can be quite a handful at times, and only Shaira can keep her under control." Zaffer laughed with a glow in his eyes.

"She is very observant and quick on the uptake." Mussavir told Zaffer about how she had picked up the Punjabi folk song at the wedding and sung it for his father.

While the two were chatting Latif went to the kitchen to give Kalingwa instructions for the dinner. When he came back they all moved to the sofas and seated themselves whilst Latif asked if they'd like something to drink. To Latif's surprise they both said they'd have a soda.

"There are a few bottles of beer," Latif teased. "You don't have to impress each other by having soda when you know you'd prefer beer."

Mussavir and Zaffer laughed sheepishly and agreed to have beer.

"How long do your parents think they'll remain in Nyeri?" Zaffer asked.

"They don't expect a change until their next tour at the end of next year," replied Mussavir.

"I hope they come to Nairobi. They have been in the countryside for a long time now."

"Yes. My father expects the next change to be for Nairobi."

Latif joined them and they discussed Indian politics for a few minutes and then the Italian-Abyssinian war. Zaffer said the British were helping Abyssinia by using the Red Cross in Kenya and East Africa. He said a small incident over the wells at Wal Wal had set all Europe aflame, so to speak. His Irish boss got the English papers and a lot of diplomatic activity was going on in Europe. But Mussolini was adamant. Mussavir agreed but soon changed the subject by telling Zaffer that Latif's wife was coming earlier than expected.

"Is that so? That's wonderful," Zaffer said. "I hope it will not mean this place will be out of bounds to bachelors like us?"

"I can't say what it will be like, until I see her myself," Latif said and smiled. "One thing I know will have to disappear and that is this occasional beer drinking."

"That you certainly will have to do, my dear cousin," Mussavir was quick to reply. "I'm jolly glad I shan't be here to disgrace you."

"Never mind the beer ban. I am glad your wife is coming. It's not good to be a bachelor for a long time," Zaffer offered.

"Look who's talking!" said Latif. "And what about you? You are older than all of us."

"I have lots of responsibilities yet. And I want to retain my freedom for a bit longer."

"Arey bakre ki maan kab tak kher manaeygi! How long will the lambkin's mother pray to God to save him from the knife!" Latif said and laughed.

"You have a point. My mother and relatives are already after me but I keep making excuses." He asked Latif when his wife was expected to arrive in Nairobi.

"The ship will dock in ten days' time."

"That is very soon. Will you go to Mombasa?"

"I don't know. The family she is coming out with are from Nairobi and plan to take the train to Nairobi the same day."

"There is no harm in your going to meet her," Mussavir added.

Before Latif could reply, Zaffer said, "Yours was a proxy marriage, the nikah has been performed. She could come straight here."

"That's true. But I am leaving it to my aunt and uncle to decide whether they want to take her to Nyeri first or let her stay here."

"She is coming to be your wife and to stay with you, not with your aunt and uncle in Nyeri for heaven's sake. You seem so uninterested," said

Mussavir irritably.

"She is going to be landed with me forever," Latif said with a smile. "No harm in letting her relax and get used to Africa with my relatives and cousins."

"I am sure Taijan and the girls will want to celebrate, so Latif is right to let them decide," Zaffer offered.

"The celebrations could all be arranged here too," said Mussavir. "Mama and Abu and the girls can come here and receive her. The poor girl should not have to travel by road after a long sea voyage and train journey. Have a heart, man."

"That's true, Latif. You are welcome to use our home and garden for the walima and other celebrations. The weather is fine these days."

"Thanks, Zaffer, but I think I'll let the elders decide on that," insisted Latif. "It's good Mussavir is going back the day after tomorrow. He can take the telegram to his parents."

Kalingwa announced supper, and the trio at the dining table talked about the movie Mussavir and Latif had seen the previous night.

"I was hoping to see an English movie but it turned out to be *Bhagata Soordas,* which I saw in Bombay," said Mussavir.

"They are showing *Congrilla* in the Theatre Royal," Latif said.

"That should be interesting. What about it, Latif? Are you capable of seeing another movie tonight?"

"You and Zaffer can go. I have to study some important files."

"Let it be my treat then, yaar. Latif, you have received good news so we should celebrate. You can read your files later."

Before leaving for the cinema Zaffer asked Latif if he'd cared to bring Mussavir to join him and Shahid for supper the next day. "My mother and sisters are away but our cook, Mwangi, can produce a good meal, too. It's cool and pleasant these days."

Mussavir liked Shaira's home in Eastleigh. The place was neat and tidy, though simple. The bungalow was quite large and not in a crowded area. It stood alone with a lot of open ground around it, a wooden house built on stilts. A covered veranda all around was divided into cubicles which were used as bedrooms. The entrance to the living room was on the side with a view of the lawn. A thick hibiscus hedge walled the four sides.

"It's a nice big house, and in a pleasant spot," Mussavir exclaimed.

"Yes," replied Zaffer. "But we occupy only half the house. The owner and his nephew live in the other half. They are away on holiday so we are allowed the use of the other side if we have guests. Latif, you can celebrate your walima here and your uncle and aunt and cousins can all be housed here."

"That's very nice of you, Zaffer. May I tell my mother about it?" Mussavir asked before Latif could say anything. "You can invite all your guests and have a jolly nice party in the garden."

"How many friends do I have?" Latif laughed. "But you are right, it is a lovely place and so quiet and peaceful."

"Not when all the dogs in the neighbourhood collect here some nights," Shahid offered. "It then becomes a battleground, especially if some unfortunate bitch is in heat."

"On moonlit nights the fisis end up here too! So it is safe and we have never had any thieves."

Shahid seemed a serious sort of a person for his age. Mussavir remembered his sister Hibba had said he was not particularly friendly. He did ask Mussavir about his parents, however, and once about Mussavir's expected journey to Abyssinia. He said a friend of his had relatives in Addis Ababa who had sent their women and children to Aden. People said it was going to be a very messy war. The feudalistic Abyssinians with their high-sounding titles of Duke and Prince always dressed in elaborate embroidered black robes and carried fancy swords and lethal daggers. They had no idea what they were up against. The Italians with their modern weapons, planes, and tanks and stronger army would defeat them in no time.

"Oh, I am sure they know what they are up against," Mussavir told Shahid. "They have engaged mercenaries and fighters from Austria and even Turkey. But you are right, they will not be as organized as the Italians this time."

After a good meal Mussavir and Latif took the last bus from St Teresa's

Mission in Eastleigh, which brought them straight to River Road, not far from Latif's flat. The next morning Mussavir left for Nyeri with Badru Vellani as planned.

11

The Telegram

MUSSAVIR RETURNED FROM Nairobi long after sunset on Thursday evening, dusty and tired. The children surrounded him and showered him with a chorus of greetings and began relating their visit to the coffee farm and the great movie they had seen while he was away. And most important of all, they had scored in the kabaddi and gulli danda. Mussavir responded to all the greetings and said he was happy to be back but the return journey was rough in that it had rained a lot between Thika and Forthall and the road was ever so slippery.

He handed Latif's telegram to his father, who read it and broke the good news to his wife and daughters.

Ayesha's face lit up. "Is Latif happy about it?"

"He did not jump or dance with joy, Mama, if that's what you mean by being happy. But he must be pleased, or relieved at least, that she is not delayed."

"Latif is *not* the type of person who'd jump and leap with joy when happy," replied Ayesha. "I'm so glad he will have company and a family again." Then, looking at Sabra, she added, "His first wife was a beautiful girl, sweet and good natured, and they were a happy couple. The poor girl died young and he came to Kenya soon after. I hope this Jamila will make him happy again."

"He's a decent boy and deserves happiness," said Sabra.

"What are his plans?" Dr Bashir asked Mussavir. "Is he going to Mombasa to meet her?"

"I advised him to do that, but he has left the decision to you and Mama. He insists you both are his elders here and should advise him."

"Now that *is* noble of him, to respect and uphold the family traditions," exclaimed Ayesha. "I hope we can rise to the occasion and do what is necessary," she said, eyeing her husband, who seemed deep in thought. "But I am afraid there seems very little time to arrange it all."

"Would you be required to organize elaborate ceremonies?" Sabra asked.

"We'll first have to be in Nairobi to receive her," Ayesha said. "And then give her away to Latif. There would have to be a small walima celebration."

"Why don't you come with us to Nairobi? We can then arrange it all. Our landlord is away and we have the use of his rooms. We have ample grounds and a nice garden."

"That's very sweet of you, Sabra, but it's not only going to Nairobi that I am thinking about," said Ayesha, furrowing her brow.

"Would you have to go to Mombasa?" Sabra asked.

"I don't think that would be necessary," Dr Bashir replied.

"Latif says the family she is coming out with are coming up to Nairobi. And Zaffer, too, suggested what Khala Sabra has advised," said Mussavir.

"Oh yes, Bashir Bhai," replied Sabra, "you can receive her and bring her to our home from the station. She can rest there till the evening and then Latif can take her to his home."

"Could the cooking for the feast be done in time?" Dr Bashir asked Sabra.

Before replying, Sabra asked if they would be inviting a lot of people. Ayesha told her only family and a few friends. Dr Bashir thought there would be at least thirty people altogether.

"In that case we could ask the nai to make half a deg of pilau, a small sufuria of zarda, and some mutton korma. That won't be difficult."

The girls, attentively listening to the conversation between the elders, were nudging one another as if wanting to ask something. Farida timidly asked if there would be mehndi. Huma's eyes lit up on hearing this and she could not help asking if there would be singing and dolki beating.

"We could have a small henna-applying ceremony on the evening before the bride's arrival with drums and singing," said Sabra.

"Are you sure it will not be a bother and too much work?" Dr Bashir asked Sabra.

"Oh no, it'll be such a pleasure to be of some use. You leave that part to me. We will invite a few young girls from the neighbourhood to sing. They can also come one afternoon and help clean masala and rice. The shopping could all be done in Eastleigh and we could ask Mohammed Rafik to get the meat all cut up and ready." Sabra detailed it all like the planning of a timetable for a class. Being a teacher, she was methodical and a clear thinker.

"You make it sound so easy," Dr Bashir said laughing, and he gratefully accepted Sabra's offer. He said his wife and daughters together with Mussavir could go with Sabra and her family, but he'd have to follow a couple of days later.

The girls all joined in, chatting about festive clothes and what to wear and the rituals at such occasions.

Mussavir, who had saved his own news for the end, told his parents what the authorities in Nairobi had advised the three doctors. They were to be ready to go in ten days' time and it would be preferable if they all stayed in or very near Nairobi.

The smile on Ayesha's face faded. She said she hoped he would not have to go before Latif's walima at least.

"Well, Mama, I might still be around, and if not, then it can't be helped." He smiled and shrugged his shoulders.

"I have a feeling you'll go after the walima."

"I hope you are right, Mama dear. You often are, you know." Mussavir put his arm around her shoulders.

Mussavir noticed that Shaira, though in the dining room, did not say much, except for agreeing with her mother occasionally about their being able to cope with the celebrations. In a way he was glad she did not express great excitement like his sisters and Huma: that showed a certain maturity, but on the other hand, he'd have liked some response from her. He thought she avoided his eyes, and that made him sad. However, he found her looking more radiant than he remembered. With her head covered, her dupatta and shawl thrown over her shoulders, he could not see her figure, but the chador did give her a certain grace too. And he did remember her very well on the day at the river when she was wearing only a red cardigan. It had clung to her body. She had looked ravishing on the day of the Ghai girl's wedding. He wished his nikah could be performed along with Latif's walima. He'd then be able to correspond with her freely.

Leaving the females still discussing Latif's walima feast, the details of the celebrations, and the trip to Nairobi, Mussavir went to sit with his father.

"I have written to Ta'Ha to come out immediately," Dr Bashir told him, "and even sent him the fare by telegraphic post."

"Then he should be out in the next boat!"

"I hope so. When he is in Nairobi, I shall approach some friends to see if he can get a job."

"I made some enquiries with my colleagues. They tell me clerical jobs in the post office, banks, and railways are still available."

"That's good." Dr Bashir seemed relieved.

Mussavir was quite tired after the journey, so he bid his father a good night and went to his room. He could hear his mother and Sabra and the girls excitedly discussing the forthcoming festive occasion. He was about to go to bed when his mother came in. She sat with him and first spoke about Latif and then told him about the talk with Sabra. She repeated the conversation between her husband, herself, and Sabra.

"It would have been wonderful if we could celebrate your engagement, too. But Sabra is quite adamant," Ayesha said sadly.

"I am disappointed, Mama. I was hoping against hope to ask for the rukhstana to be performed before I left. But I suppose I was asking for the impossible." He smiled and looked up, then added, "Maybe I'll feel different when I go away. I shall perhaps be so busy I'll not even have time to think about it."

"You have met her brothers. What did you think of them?"

"I like Zaffer. He seems a decent and pleasant sort of man, quite fond of and concerned about his mother, brothers and sisters. I could not make out much about Shahid—he is perhaps more like his mother!" Mussavir smiled.

Mother and son talked for a little longer and then Ayesha got up and Mussavir went to bed. He slept fitfully.

The next morning, the moment he entered the dining room his mother told him they had decided to go to Nairobi on Sunday, only two days away. Both Ayesha and Sabra were looking at some brightly coloured materials. Shaira was tacking a silver border onto some red material and his sister Hibba was involved in a similar exercise.

"I thought I had come for breakfast, but it looks more like a tailoring mart," he jibed.

The girls looked up and smiled. "Sabra is helping me decide which suit to take for Jamila," said Ayesha.

"How come, no homework?" Mussavir asked Hibba.

"Abu said we can help prepare our clothes for Nairobi," Hibba told him. "We have to wear red dupattas for the ceremonies, so Shaira is helping to tack the silver border."

"Mussavir Bhaijan, I shall wear my red satin suit with stars on it," said Huma, as always full of animation.

"Where is the suit?" he asked.

"In Nairobi, of course. We are all going on Sunday and you are going to stay at our home. We'll get a dolki from Masi Jantey and sing lots of songs, ha!"

"Mostly the lentil song?"

"Yes, and we shall sing: Latif Bhai wants more and more dal! Ha-ha!"

Ayesha told Mussavir his father was going to phone Latif at his office and give him the news about the family returning to Nairobi with Sabra.

Mussavir was amazed at the speed with which everything was being organized for Latif's wife's arrival and the festivities. He was sure there was going to be mad activity in Nairobi. When his mother and Sabra moved out of the room Mussavir went nearer to where Shaira was sitting.

She looked up, then quickly lowered her eyes to her work.

"Shaira, did you go to the river again?" he asked.

"Oh no," she said, looking up. "I don't want to go there again." And she lowered her head.

"You should, you know. It's not good to be frightened of a place just because a snake passed that way." Shaira let her sewing fall in her lap. He added, "I was going to suggest we go there again and cross the river and walk up to the hills. You get a wonderful view of the mountain there."

"We saw Mount Kenya from the coffee farm when you were away. It must be the same, surely," she said, her heart thumping loudly in Mussavir's presence.

"It's different from where I want you to see it."

She picked up her work and looked at it but made no reply.

"Will you come with me, Shaira? This afternoon?" he asked, lowering his voice.

"How can I come? My . . . my . . . I can't."

"Why can't you come? Wouldn't you like me to show you the mountain?"

"Ami will never allow me to." She looked at the door nervously.

"Would you come if there was no objection from her?"

She was quiet for a moment or two, then said in a low voice, "Yes, I'd like to."

"Your mother and Mama are going to town this afternoon. During lunch I shall tell them I am taking you all to see the mountain from across the river."

12

The Walk

DURING LUNCH THE females were still jabbering about the forthcoming festive event. Dr Bashir told Sabra that Latif had agreed to inform Zaffer and Shahid about their mother's arrival in Nairobi on Sunday together with Ayesha, Mussavir, and the girls. Latif had also confirmed that his bride would arrive in Nairobi Thursday morning. Dr Bashir had further asked him to issue the invitations to the few friends for the festive dinner on Friday evening. The cooking arrangements, he told Latif, would be done by the ladies on their arrival.

"Khala Sabra, will you and Mama be long in the town?" Mussavir asked Sabra.

"That will depend on your mother, Beta. She plans to go to a few shops."

"I want to take all of you across the river and a little further to view the mountain. If you don't come back by four I'll take the girls and Salim," Mussavir said to his mother loud enough for Sabra to hear. Sabra was about to respond but Ayesha nodded instead, to Mussavir's great relief.

The boys said they were going to Tochi's home. Salim did not want to go to Tochi's. He said he'd like to see the mountain instead.

Later in the afternoon when Sabra, Ayesha, and the older boys had left, Mussavir called Hibba to his room in order to hand over his clothes that needed mending. Mussavir told her about Sabra's resistance to his nikah with Shaira before his departure for Abyssinia. He also said he wanted her help.

"So you have decided to be engaged to Shaira then?" Hibba asked.

"Yes, Hibba, I have. I do like her."

Hibba looked happy but did not say anything, so Mussavir quickly asked, "You *are* happy about it? Aren't you?"

"But of course, Bhaijan, I'm so glad. I was only wondering how you want me to help you."

"Oh, that . . . Yes, we shall go across the river this afternoon. I want you to keep the young ones with you in front or take them ahead. I'll walk slowly with Shaira. I want to talk to her."

"It is not going to be easy to keep Huma away from you."

"Make her pick up pebbles from the river and tell her some Kikuyu folk tales about the mountain."

"I can try. And ask Farida to do that too. She knows far more stories than I."

Hibba was happy that her brother was confiding in her. They talked a bit more and then Hibba collected the clothes and left.

Mussavir came out of his room earlier than he had planned. "It might rain," he said, looking out the window. "It seems cloudy. We had better go across earlier."

"Then won't there be mist around the mountain peaks?" Shaira asked.

"I am sure it'll clear before we reach there."

"But . . . Ami and Taijan are not here," said Shaira.

"They are bound to be late," Mussavir said. He told the girls to wear strong shoes, Salim too. "There could be jiggers down by the river."

"I picked two from Salim's foot two days back," Shaira said.

"And Singla Bhai, too, had one," Huma called from the table and got up to get ready for the walk.

"Where is Hibba?" Mussavir said, looking around.

"Coming, Bhaijan!" came Hibba's voice from her room. Coming out she said, "I was packing some oranges and informing Mugro we are going out." She was carrying a small kikapu in her hand.

They all gathered in the veranda and then set out for the river. They walked through the garden, past the white wooden gate, and down the slope. Huma stopped to pick some yellow wildflowers. She walked past Hibba and Shaira and joined Mussavir. Farida walked faster and was soon down the hill. Shaira and Hibba walked slowly talking about the dupattas for the mehndi which Sabra had said could be dyed in Nairobi.

Salim began to throw pebbles into the river as they approached the bank. The river seemed to be flowing more slowly than on the last occasion. Shaira was not keen to cross it straightaway. She said she was not afraid but there was no need to cross it at that particular point. It was pleasant to walk along the wonderful leafy bank down the valley. Mussavir said for a really good view they would have to cross the river but it need not be at that point; they could walk further and then cross. They started threading their way in single file on the narrow path.

A Kikuyu woman approached them from the opposite direction carrying a heavy load of wood covered with green guachi leaves. She was almost doubled over beneath the enormous bundle that was strapped to her back with a leather thong. Her head was shaven and she wore bead ornaments in her ears and neck. The strollers had to make way for her to pass so they moved to one side. As she came nearer she called a greeting in Kikuyu and flashed a smile. Huma and Farida both replied to her greeting in Kikuyu and Mussavir said jambo to her. She said "Jambo sana" and smiled, revealing very white and even teeth.

"Poor women! Their lot has not changed," Mussavir said after she had passed. "I am surprised her back is not broken."

"Mussavir Bhaijan, I am glad I am not a Kikuyu girl. I would not be able to carry all that load. And I am scared and don't like the bad things they do to them." Huma placed her hand on her mouth as if she had said something she should not have said.

"You'd have to carry some weight if you were in India," her sister told her. "Women carry heavy loads there too!"

"Do they?" Huma asked, looking back at Mussavir.

"They don't carry that much wood, but as Shaira says, they carry pitchers and copper chattis and fill them from wells and ponds in the villages. In the cities the water carriers, all men, do that. In the villages women carry fodder for cattle on their heads. Water is carried on the hip."

Before Huma could comment, Salim asked, "What bad things do they do to the Kikuyu girls, Huma Baji?"

Both Huma and Farida smiled as if sharing a secret joke but neither told. Farida had described to Huma in great detail the female circumcision among the Kikuyu. Huma was perhaps referring to that. Salim did not probe, so they went on.

Mussavir slowed down and remained behind them all. Hibba went forward and asked Huma and Farida to follow her to the far tree that was visible above the riverbank. Salim wanted to follow them, but Shaira said he must not run. She was about to take his hand when Mussavir took it instead and said, "He is all right. He is a man. You must not frighten him. Let him go." He led Salim towards the girls and let go of his hand. Shaira started to walk faster in order to join the girls when Mussavir stopped her and asked her not to rush, saying he wanted to talk to her. They were walking besides clusters of African lilies, whose large white hanging flowers resembled bells. Above the ridge, masses of juniper, Nandi flame, and jacaranda trees in full bloom gave the valley a wild look. The foothills of the great mountain were also dotted with masses of pine and spruce.

Mussavir put the wicker basket down and lit a cigarette. Then, pointing to a stone, he asked Shaira to sit down. He said he'd like to finish his cigarette before crossing over. They could see the others now in the nearly shallow riverbed, looking for pebbles. Shaira was hesitant to sit, and so, still standing near the stone, she asked, "What did you want to tell me, Mussavir Bhaijan? I cannot sit here for long."

"Why not? What's the hurry? Your mother is not here now."

"Well, you know I am not to sit with you alone."

"Why not? I am not going to eat you up, am I?"

"No . . . but I am supposed to be in purdah." Her heart began to thump again so she sat down on the edge of the stone.

Mussavir, who was leaning against a tree, puffed at his cigarette and, blowing the smoke in the air, asked, "Is that the only reason?"

"I think the main reason."

"But aren't you supposed to be in purdah from all these men walking about?"

"There are no men here," she said, looking around in surprise.

"What about them?" Mussavir pointed to a group of African men standing in the fields as their goats grazed close by. There were also women tilling in the fields. Shaira looked up. "Oh, but they are Africans!" She flashed him an amused smile.

"That's true. But they are grown-up men nevertheless."

She laughed at the way he talked. Her tension eased a bit. "But that's different." She shrugged her shoulders.

"Why? Like me they have hands, feet, and even eyes. They can see you exactly like I do and I am absolutely sure they can think like me that you are a very beautiful girl."

"Oh, I don't know, somehow one thinks it is not necessary to observe purdah from them." Her comment sounded a bit stupid to her ears.

Mussavir chuckled and then said that if one was a good Muslim and believed in purdah then purdah should be observed from *all* men and not only a select few.

"But they are black and of a different race. One does not marry them," she said in justification.

"Islam does not say you should observe purdah from all men except black men, does it? You are supposed to observe purdah from all grown-up males with whom marriage is permissible. Black men can be Muslims, in which case marriage with them is allowed. Poor Shaira, my poetess, I am sorry to say you have been brainwashed and confused."

Shaira became thoughtful and after a moment or two said, "My Bhaijan Zaffer says that too. He thinks people make rules for their own convenience and according to their own prejudices."

"He's right," replied Mussavir, and added, "anyway, tell me, poetess, do you know why your mother wants you to avoid me?"

"I am supposed to be in purdah from you. Why do you call me poetess?" The girls and Salim had gone a little further with Hibba. Now and then their voices floated across to them. Shaira kept looking in their direction.

"Is that the only reason?" She heard Mussavir's voice again. He did not say why he called her poetess.

"Perhaps that is not the only reason. Why do you ask? You must know the reason yourself. I can only guess and I am not sure if I am right. My mother has not given me any reason other than your being a grown-up man and therefore one of those I have to observe purdah from." She was surprised she could say that.

"One would have thought Khala Sabra, being educated and a teacher herself, would have told you frankly that my parents are keen that you become their elder son's wife."

She went very quiet. After a moment she asked, "And I suppose you don't like me?" and immediately felt silly and uncomfortable.

"Oh no, it's not like that. Not at all." Mussavir was surprised at her quick assumption. "I like you very much."

Shaira became fidgety. She tightened her shawl around her shoulders and said, "It's not easy for my mother to talk of things like that when I am only thirteen."

"You may be thirteen years old but you are mature for your age. You *are* grown up. Aren't you?"

"Is it a crime to grow up? It's not my fault," she said wryly.

"Of course growing up is no crime and I am certainly not blaming you, Shaira. In fact, I am very happy to find you grown up." Then he added, gently, "Because I like you very much, Shaira, I'm not happy when you avoid me. I want to talk to you and be with you. I shall soon be going away and may not see you for a long time. Or, who knows, not at all."

She suddenly looked up and at him. Then she lowered her head and said, "But you will come back one day."

"Maybe, maybe not. I am going to a war, not a holiday."

"Then why do you want to go?" she said uneasily.

"It is not in my power now to stay back. I am committed."

"But you could have refused, said no. You are a man and already a doctor. You can make your own decisions, can't you?"

"Yes, I could have, but I don't want to annoy Abu. He is so proud that I have agreed. Also I feel I owe it to him."

"One of my teachers' father is a retired English colonel from India and is going with a team of doctors from Nairobi. She told us that Abyssinia is a feudal country, but the Emperor is a sophisticated, dignified man. He does not like the Italians at all. She says this war is causing a lot of tension in Europe too. Why is that?" Shaira was happy to talk about the war rather than herself.

"The European powers, especially Britain, France, and Belgium, tried to intervene and help settle the dispute, but Mussolini is in a warring mood and won't listen to anyone. In fact, he has intimated that he will go to war with any nation in Europe that stops him from invading Abyssinia."

"Would he really? Surely Britain is a much stronger nation than Italy."

"They are worried he will join up with Germany, who lost Tanganyika and their other colonies in the Great War."

She pulled at her shawl again as if feeling cold, but remained quiet.

"Why do you keep this shawl on when it is not even cold?" asked Mussavir. "You keep it on not only at home and outside but even on a walk." He smiled and crushed the butt of his cigarette into the ground.

"I have to wear it because I am not wearing a veil."

"But you wear it in the house too."

"Yes, because Ami says I must wear it and cover my head and . . . when *you* are around."

"I see!" he laughed. "A most peculiar attitude."

"It is according to custom and tradition."

"Very stupid custom, don't you think? For this day and age when people are going forward. If you and I are to be married one day, then we should know more about one another and be allowed to see one another even more. Don't you agree?"

In her heart she agreed with him, but she dared not tell him that openly. So she told him she did not know if it was absolutely necessary to know one another more or meet more often. It was not possible to do away with religious and age-old cultural customs.

"But don't you think it is wrong not to let us meet freely and talk freely?" he asked again.

"It does not matter how I feel or if things are wrong. One can't do anything about them."

"Some things don't concern us so we needn't bother, but I think marriage is very important."

She was thoughtful for a moment, then said, "Look at Latif Bhaijan. He has not met his wife. She is not even a relation, so she could not have seen him either."

"He does not mind, but I would not marry like that."

She started to get up. "I think we should join the others. They will wonder why we are sitting here and Salim or Huma might even tell Ami. Please let's go and join them. I am scared."

"Why are you so terrified of your mother, Shaira? We have to respect our parents, I know, and obey them, which you do more than all of us. But there is no need to be so frightened. Remember, the more frightened you are, the more your mother will bully you. You are a big girl and a person in your own right, so you should assert yourself and not let anyone bully you."

"It's easy for you to say that. You are a man."

"One more thing and we shall go. Khala Sabra is not agreeable to our nikah before I depart. She says she has to get permission from your relatives and that will not come in time."

"But relatives are not the only ones whose permission is needed. Everyone, including you, seems to forget that my own permission is needed too. I am not a piece of furniture, who can just be handed over to you because your parents want it and because you are suitable for me."

Mussavir could not believe his ears. He was surprised that she had started asserting herself. After the initial shock he began to feel pleased. That she had a high spirit, buried deep somewhere under her mother's domination and her own sense of duty, he now had no doubt. But it delighted him that he was able to provoke a quick response out of her.

"Bravo! Shaira, my poetess, how right you are. Your permission is most important. I was coming to it. But you have beaten me to it."

"You have been talking to me about needing the freedom to speak with me and about when the nikah should take place, but you have not even asked me if I like you." She looked towards the hills beyond the shrubs.

Mussavir moved from the tree he was leaning against and stepped towards her. She seemed ill at ease and sat down again with her hands in her lap. He moved nearer and put his hands on her shoulders and said, "Look at me, poetess, look at me and tell me honestly if you like me a little."

She did not look up at him but kept her head bent. "Please, let me go, Mussavir Bhaijan," she pleaded. "I am sorry, I should not have said what I said. I had no right to answer back."

"You had every right to say what you said. I am very happy you pointed it out in time. I'm sorry I have not been very considerate about your sensitivity. But I have to know if you like me. It's important, as I am going away. If you tell me you like me, I shall have something to be happy about, knowing that you are waiting for me."

She looked up and met his gaze. Then, looking away, she said, "I never said I did not like you. Before I came here I did not even in my wildest dreams think . . . about liking someone and marriage . . . and that you would be telling me about it. I have begun to like you and trust you, but it's your being in such a hurry that frightens me. It is all very strange for me. I don't want to do anything that will bring shame to our family."

"I most certainly don't want you to do anything that shames your family. How can you even think of that? If you told me you didn't like me at all, that would be the end of the matter. I'd ask my parents not to force your mother. I only brought in the matter of nikah because I feel we can write to one another and get to know each other during the period I am away."

"I don't think I'd be allowed to meet you on my own or to write to you even after the nikah is performed," Shaira said. "They say that is the most dangerous period. Moreover, I want to study. I really do. It's better this way."

"But Shaira, I have no intention of stopping you from studying further. I think it is very good. It may, however, not be possible for you to become a doctor, but you could go on studying even after marriage if you like. I don't even want you in purdah wearing that silly burqa. I want you to live a free life."

She looked up in surprise, but apparently not displeased about living a free life, for she said after a moment or two, "You must tell my mother that. I mean about studies, but not about purdah, please. At least not yet." She rose, saying, "Let's go see the mountain as you promised."

"All right. But don't run away. Be nearer to me, we'll talk again. I am not finished yet. And one thing more before we go down. Please stop calling me 'Bhaijan.' I am *not* your brother."

There was a faint smile on her face as she stepped down and Mussavir followed. They were soon with the others and near the river. Huma had a heap of pebbles in front of her and was engrossed in telling the others about fisis and hyenas as well as the yangaus, the scavengers.

"Salim does not even know the difference between a fisi and a yangau!" Huma exclaimed, as if that were the height of ignorance.

"And what is the difference? I don't know it either," Mussavir told her. Huma glowered at Mussavir, but before she said anything, Hibba said, "I think fisis are female hyenas and yangaus are the big male hyenas who grab everything from the others."

Huma continued with her story: "Maangi told us that all hyenas at first had four good legs. One day a yangau saw the full moon. It was very white. He thought it was a piece of meat from the tail of a lamb. He yearned for it, his mouth began to water. But he could not reach out and grab it all for himself. He thought for a while and then summoned all the fisis and showed them the meat in the sky. Their mouths began to water too. They all wanted to get at the meat but it was too far away. A meeting was called and hyenas from different holes in the hills and beyond the ridges came rushing. They sat and discussed for a long time. Finally it was decided the biggest yangau would stand under the meat and a fisi would climb on his back and another fisi would climb on the back of the one standing on the back of the yangau and so on until all the hyenas had climbed on the backs of one another until they reached the meat. All the fisis climbed on one another's backs but still they did not reach the moon. They began to feel unsteady. The big yangau was tired now with all the weight and he moved his leg slightly. That shook all the hyenas and they came tumbling down, falling and crushing one another. They fell on the big yangau, breaking their own hind legs and his too. Since that day all the fisis have only three good legs."

"Huma, when does Maangi tell you these stories?" Mussavir asked.

"Whenever I go to see his wife and play with his children."

"And when she partakes of ugali and urio with the family at their dinnertime," Shaira added.

They walked on until they reached a narrow bridge made from wooden planks. They crossed the bridge in single file and walked over a path with guachi vines on both sides. The dark green heart-shaped leaves were fresh and shining and covered the shamba like a sea of green hearts amidst long stems of millet and sorghum. A flock of bleating goats rushed out of the banana grove, across the leaves. Some of the goats wore bells which tinkled as they trotted along. The party tramped through the banana grove then filed along the leleshwa bush. A covey of partridges rose from the grass and flew to the sky.

"I wish I had my catapult," moaned Salim. "I would have shot at them."

"I didn't know you were so bloodthirsty. They look so nice as they are," said Huma.

The ground suddenly sloped sharply away, revealing the valley below. It was dotted with round huts surrounded by small shambas. Mount Kirinyaga stood in all its glory with just a hazy mist on both its peaks. The rugged edges of the peaks shone with snow.

They all sat on small granite stones embedded in the ground and feasted on the beauty and enormity of the mountain.

"We are now almost in the shadow of Kirinyaga—Kirinyaga ki goad mein," said Mussavir, translating into Urdu. The mountain looked close enough to touch.

Shaira agreed it was indeed the most beautiful view she had ever seen. She said there were many stories about Kirinyaga—or Mount Kenya—being sacred. She always wondered whether they were legends or really true.

"The Kikuyus believe it is sacred. It was the abode of their God and his wife Mumbi," said Mussavir. "They had nine daughters, from whom sprang the nine Kikuyu clans."

"Mugro told Farida the whole story," said Hibba.

Huma and Salim pressed Farida to tell the story, which she gladly did.

"Mogai, the God of Nature, sent for Gikao and told him to live on the mountain. He married him to Mumbi and they had nine daughters. When the daughters were old enough to marry, there were no men available. Gikao prayed to Mugai, who said, 'Sacrifice an animal under that fig tree!'

When he did, nine men suddenly appeared. That's why there are nine Kikuyu clans."

Salim wanted to know what were clans, so Huma tried to explain, while the others peeled and sucked on the oranges and sweets Hibba had brought in the small basket.

Shaira asked Mussavir if he had seen the Himalayas and Mount Everest in India.

"Only some of the smaller peaks like Nanda Devi and Kunchan Chunga from the Murree Hills," he told her. He said the mountains at Kangra were breathtaking too.

On their way back Huma, Salim, and Farida went ahead. Hibba, Shaira, and Mussavir followed. After a while Hibba moved on and joined the others. There was not much distance between them this time. They did not stop anywhere except the spot where the snake had been killed. Mussavir asked Shaira to see the place again and get her fear out of her system. They also stopped at the place where the snake had been thrown onto the ground before the old man took it away. Shaira and Mussavir stood for a few minutes and talked while the others began tackling the steep climb towards the house, Huma moaning that she was thirsty and famished. They all passed the white wooden gate into the garden as the sun was setting, and they watched the twilight from the veranda.

13

Shaira in a Dilemma

SHAIRA TOSSED AND turned in bed after Hibba went to sleep. The walk by the river and the talk with Mussavir were on her mind. She had deduced already that there had been some talk between her mother and Mussavir's parents about his marrying her. Ayesha had once even said to Sabra in Shaira's presence that she should consider Mussavir as one of her sons; she herself considered Shaira as her own daughter. These were indirect ways of indicating a matrimonial interest in each other's offspring. Shaira now understood why her mother was so adamant that she keep her distance from Mussavir. In such circumstances parents did not want their daughters to be considered too forward. They had to appear shy, modest, and reserved and keep in the background.

Shaira had of course known she would be married one day, but it had seemed very far away, something that would happen after she had finished her studies. Certainly not when she was only thirteen. How stupid of me not to understand, she thought. No wonder her mother was impatient at her slow-wittedness. If she had an elder sister or a sister-in-law, it would be her duty to tell Shaira about what was going on. She had neither. But she was surprised, that being the case, why her mother did not talk to her herself. Mussavir was right when he said her mother, being educated and a teacher, should not have found it difficult to communicate with her daughter. But Sabra was like that. She had never prepared Shaira for changes at puberty either. Shaira had come to know about them at school when she was eleven. Sabra expected her daughter to guess it all somehow.

Then she began to think about Mussavir. She had begun to like him since the incident of the snake at the river. He had been kind and protective and had even stood up to Sabra, and he had not treated her like a child. Since then she had felt warm towards him. This afternoon she was happy to learn he liked her. She was surprised she could talk to him easily. Not only talk, but also able to say things one would not say to a man one was going to marry. Somehow she had found the courage. He wanted her to assert herself and not be too frightened of her mother. She agreed with him, but it also made her feel disloyal to her mother. And that she did not like at all. She loved her mother.

On the way back, Mussavir had suggested she meet him in the living room after Hibba had gone to bed. He said Hibba was a heavy sleeper. There were family jokes about how she could sleep through lightning and thunder and even bugles if they were blowing full blast. Shaira liked to read before going to bed, but as there was no bedside lamp in the dining room she could not pursue her reading while on holiday. She talked to Hibba until she showed signs of sleep and they said good night to each other. Shaira waited for Hibba to sleep, and Hibba was asleep now, but Shaira was not sure whether she should do what Mussavir had asked. At the same time, lying in bed, tossing and turning, unable to sleep, she yearned to be near him. He had said he wanted to tell her a lot of things. He would not do anything to bring shame to her. She trusted him, but supposing someone got up and heard them talking or walked into the living room!

She edged out of bed slowly, wrapped herself, and walked barefoot to the window. It was pitch dark outside. She could hear the crickets chirping and the squeaking of other small night insects. In the distance the revolting cackles of hyenas could be heard. Perhaps they were drinking water at the riverbank. Nearer the house she could hear the rustling of the breeze and Hibba's light snores. She took a few steps towards the living room, paused, and started again. She stood still, transfixed on the spot. She crept back on tiptoe and lowered herself to the edge of the bed.

The next day was a busy one. She got up early. In fact, she had not slept much. She helped her mother pack up for the boys and Huma and later helped Ayesha with housework. She knew she would not be able to face Mussavir if she saw him. Luckily, he had risen early too and rushed to the hospital soon after breakfast to bid farewell to the doctor and assistants, and later he would walk to the town to say goodbye to the few people he knew, particularly Badru Vellani. The boys likewise all sauntered down to visit their Singh friends.

Next morning they all walked to the bus stop. Mugro and another worker from the hospital helped carry their luggage down the slope in two trips. The bus came on time and they all scrambled in and settled on the empty seats here and there. The bus drove slowly away from the shadow of Mount Kenya. The drive in the cool and misty morning was pleasant and not dusty. The foothills of the mountain, with the Kikuyu peoples' shambas and the dark green of the forest in the background, were clearly visible, though the area just below the snowy peaks was cloudy. People were already moving about, especially the women with their backs bent under heavy loads of guachi and potatoes of all kinds, arrowroot yams, bananas, and even firewood. They were heading towards the markets of Nyeri or further down to Karatina. Men wrapped in red and brown blankets, carrying their three-legged stools, were briskly walking along the main road. Some wore sandals made out of rubber tires, others were barefoot and clutched rungus and long staffs.

The bus stopped at the T-junction of the main road and a branch road going to the railway station at Karatina. Around it on both sides was a market. Women, their overloaded burdens of yams on their backs, and pots on their heads, holding live chickens and eggs in baskets, floated in from all sides. Those who had arrived earlier had already arranged their wares on the ground. The place looked colourful despite the misty morning. Shaira was amazed at the amount of weight the women could carry. Ayesha told her some of the women came at daybreak from as far as the Sagna River and even the ridges beyond.

Old men sat under the mbuyu trees on three-legged stools sniffing baki from leather pouches that hung around their necks on leather strips. Some of these old men placed a pinch of tobacco powder under their tongues. Now and then some spat and wiped their mouths with their shukas. Younger men surrounded the bus and peeped in and smiled at the passengers. Some laughed and passed remarks in their vernacular dialects. The passengers who got on the bus from Karatina wore coats and trousers, some quite tattered and patched, and old felt hats that looked muddy brown. They carried rungus and almost all of them had bead ornaments in their distended earlobes.

The boys all kept firing questions at Mussavir, who was sitting on the front seat. He answered, but only briefly. Shaira, who sat with her mother on the other side, was nearer to Ayesha. She could see him from under her veil. She was happy he could not see her. She would not be able to face him or talk to him freely. But she was in a happier frame of mind than when she had come to Nyeri. She could not read and all thoughts of lessons were wiped out from her mind.

After Karatina the bus picked up more passengers at Forthall in Muranga and then Embu and drove through a place where young men stood on the roadside selling bananas. The bus stopped and the passengers leaned out of the windows and bought some. They all grinned and seemed pleased and kept repeating the words "Eh muragwa! Muragwa!" The driver and the turnboy bought several huge bunches and placed them on the roof of the bus to take them to Nairobi. Mussavir bought a couple of hands and gave them to his mother and Hibba, who distributed them to the others to eat on the journey. Sabra asked him to buy a whole bunch for her to take home for Mwangi and his family as well as her sons. He did that and the driver allowed Mussavir to stand the bunch in the bus on the right-hand corner in front of his seat. The driver then started the bus and headed straight for Thika. The sun had come out and the bus dashed down the corrugated highway bumping the passengers against one another. Many transport lorries carrying gunny sacks full of produce and kerosene oil tins full of honey zoomed past the bus. Family members, women and children of the transporters in warm clothes and caps and scarves, had perched themselves on top of the bulging produce.

Sophia Mustafa

Mussavir and Shaira hardly talked during the long and tedious journey. They arrived in Nairobi at dusk.

Zaffer, Latif, and Mohammed Rafik with his van met them. Zaffer had hired a taxi too. On reaching Sabra's home in Eastleigh they all gathered on the lawn to greet one another with handshakes and jambos. Sabra was already at work on the cooking for the feast. As she came in, Mohammed Rafik carrying her small basket, she said, "Please tell Maaja Nai to come early, because after he gives us his list, we'll do the shopping in Eastleigh."

"Inshallah, Masi Jee, I'll do that first thing in the morning on my way to the slaughterhouse. I have to pass that way."

"Thanks, Beta. May Allah grant you a long life." Mohammed Rafik was a favourite and most helpful neighbour. Sabra told Ayesha she had already ordered a goat from Mohammed Rafik, who had also agreed to have it cut up at his butchery both for the pilau and the korma. She also told her how Mohammed Rafik had agreed to tell Maaja Nai, the Muslim barber who normally became a cook on festive occasions and who lived in the third section of Eastleigh, to call at Sabra's home the next morning.

"Would you like some liver and kidneys for the evening?" Mohammed Rafik asked as he was about to go.

"Good idea. Thanks."

He then bade good night to all and, saying "Khuda afiz," went his way.

Mwangi had heated water in several empty kerosene debes for the travellers to wash themselves. Ayesha and her daughters were installed in the part of the house belonging to the landlord, who was away. Mussavir could have stayed there too, but after his wash and supper he decided to go back to the city with Latif. During the meal they discussed jobs to be handled by the menfolk. Ayesha said she'd have to visit Latif's flat and organize it for the bride.

Latif had made a list of guests which he asked his aunt to check. After advice from Zaffer and Sabra some names were deleted and others added. It was also decided that Friday week would be fixed for the walima. As Friday was a working day, the feast would have to be a buffet dinner in the evening. Shahid and his friends would get the garden organized for that purpose. Shahid knew one neighbour who worked at the Electricity House; in fact, the family were known as bijli wallahs. One of their sons could fix electric wires and bulbs to light up the garden and lawn.

On the bus Mussavir and Latif had discussed how quickly the womenfolk had worked out the whole thing. Latif said he could not oppose his aunt, but he did not feel the need for rejoicing as this was his second marriage. There was no need of mehndi either. He said that he was, in fact, quite nervous. He repeated this sentiment again when they were at his flat.

"It's true this is your second marriage, my dear cousin, but what about Jamila?" Mussavir said. "She has to be welcomed and well received in a new country where she is coming among new people. She is not even a cousin. Mama therefore quite rightly feels she must be given a warm welcome."

"It's so generous of Khala Sabra and Zaffer to throw open their home and render so much help," Latif said.

"I don't think they mind. In fact, they seem more excited than any of us. Even Shahid has offered to help!" Mussavir said, "I wish they would be helpful to me too."

"What help do you want from them?"

"I wish they would agree to announce my engagement to Shaira before I leave."

"They are at least agreeable to the match, aren't they?"

"They have not said no outright, but neither have they said yes. Mama is going to talk to Zaffer during her stay here and see if she can persuade them."

"What about Shaira? Did you manage to see more of her or talk to her?"

"I was able to have small chats with her, at first outside the house and later inside as well."

"What does she think?"

"All I can say at this stage is that she does reciprocate my feelings to an extent. I don't think she would have any objections to a proper ceremony. She is naturally somewhat shy and cannot say very much, but the fact that I got her out of the dining room twice and we were on our own for a little while has convinced me she likes me too."

"How did you manage that? And right under the noses of everyone there. It could have been dangerous."

"The risk was there. But some risks are worth taking. I was surprised at myself, but I had to see and be sure that she was grown up."

"What do you mean? I hope you did not take any liberties with her. That would be disastrous, man."

"No, I have not slept with her, if that is what you mean," said Mussavir, smiling. "I have put a stop to her calling me 'Bhaijan' and she has agreed to write to me."

"Has she started using your name then?"

"No, she has not addressed me directly, but she has not used the word 'Brother' again. In fact, she has a sense of humour despite her serious manner. She asked me if I would like her to call me Dr Sahib."

Latif guffawed and then asked, "And how are you going to correspond with her?"

"Ah, that's where you come in. I shall need your help."

"My help? In what way?"

"You and Jamila will have to jointly help me. I plan to write to her care of your address. I'd like Jamila to be friendly with her."

"But we don't even know if Jamila is a friendly person or will join in our scheme."

"I'll know before I go."

"You seem to be so determined and full of this romance. I wonder if it is because of Nyeri and the sacred mountain."

"It could well be," Mussavir said, smiling widely.

14

In Nairobi

SOON AFTER BREAKFAST Huma and Farida trotted away gleefully to Masi Jantey's house to borrow a dolki. Sabra instructed them to visit Munni's mother and a few other neighbours on the way and invite the women and girls for the henna-applying ceremony, or mehndi, on Wednesday evening at 8 p.m. They were to ask some to come on Tuesday afternoon too, if possible, to help clean the rice and spices. It was common practice for neighbours to help out on festive occasions when necessary. The females were always ready to oblige as it was fun to get together and keep up with the latest gossip. And at a festive occasion women and girls had a chance to show off their gala clothes and jewellery.

Jannat Begum was universally known as Masi Jantey by the women and Auntie Paradise Begum by the males since "jannat" meant "paradise." Though small in stature she was strong and sturdy and worked and moved about quickly. She had lived in Eastleigh for more than twenty years in a farmhouse with a big garden and grounds full of fruit as well as other shady trees. But the fruit trees were old, perhaps planted by a pioneering Dutch farmer from the south, and did not bear a lot of fruit. The children of the neighbourhood, including of course Huma and Munni, always loved to visit the place in the hope of picking up a guava, a peach or two, or a pomegranate if lucky.

Masi Jantey and her husband also kept cows in their backyard and sold milk. She made her own butter, cream cheese, and ghee. Sitting on a low webbed stool with the red earthen mtungi in front of her, she churned the butter manually with a long wooden beater. She boiled and clarified some of the butter to make ghee for cooking, and during the warm weather the neighbours' servants and children came flocking for lassi, which she ladled out after she had removed the butter and safely put it away in a cooler. She was always helpful and lent her small dolki and supplied milk, butter, and cream cheese, as well as yoghurt on festive occasions, to the neighbours.

By the time Huma and her entourage came back within an hour, not only the whole neighborhood but also the African vegetable and fruit vendors had learnt of Latif's wedding celebrations at Sabra's home!

While Huma and Farida were away, Sabra asked Honey and Majid to go to Baba Fakir Mohammed's ration shop opposite the small mosque in Eastleigh Section One, about a ten minute walk from the house. They were to ask Baba Fakir Mohammed to send his son Rasheed to arrive at Sabra's home in an hour's time in order to take down the order for the ingredients for the dinner from Maaja Nai, who would have arrived by then. Rasheed arrived a bit earlier than the cook with his notepad in his hand and a pencil stuck behind his right ear. He was a tall, lanky lad with a long nose and bushy shining hair.

Maaja Nai, a barber by profession, lived in Eastleigh Section Three. He had come to Kenya with his family and two brothers from India after the Great War, and like the other few people of his tribe in Kenya, he also cooked the food at festivities for the Muslims in Nairobi. He was a middle-aged man but active and good at his work. On getting Sabra's message from Mohammed Rafik, he got his bicycle out and set out on the long dusty road pedalling his way towards Sabra's home. Inside the courtyard he stood his bicycle against the kitchen wall and first went to the garden tap to wash his hands. He wiped them with a white handkerchief from his coat pocket and passed his hands over his thick moustache. Then he touched his white turban with both hands to push it up, and lastly, pulling at his brown coat, he walked briskly up the steps of the veranda, as if all ready and prepared to face Sabra and her guest.

Rasheed, standing just inside the veranda, met him and greeted him with a bow and raised his right hand to touch his forehead as a sign of respect towards an elder. Sabra called a welcome from her seat, "Come in, come in, please, Bhai." She pointed to the empty chair near Ayesha. Maaja Nai thanked her and touched his white pugree and bowed and even congratulated Ayesha when Sabra introduced her. He arranged the pleats of his white shalwar and sat down. Sabra asked if he would like some tea. He said he would love a cup of tea if it was very hot. Sabra smiled and called Mwangi and asked him to bring a moto-moto scalding cup of tea for the guest.

When Mwangi presented the steaming tea in a cup and saucer on a small tray, Maaja Nai thanked him, smiling widely, "Asante sana! Hiyo ndiyo na chai mazuri! Hapana ya mazungu. Now that is what I call a good cup of tea. It's not like the English tea," and he winked at Mwangi. It was a common belief that the Europeans drank their tea lukewarm and weak, and not scalding hot and milky as it should be.

Mwangi gave him a broad smile and thanked him profusely, saying, "Asante, Bwana Kinyozi."

Maaja Nai then picked up his cup and poured some tea into the saucer and slurped it while blowing and puffing at it slowly. He joined in the women's conversation and asked how many people were expected for the feast. Ayesha told him the number would come up to thirty-five, including women and children. Maaja Nai calculated the amount of rice, ghee, oil, and spices as well as onions, garlic, and green ginger that would be needed. He dictated the order to Rasheed, who took it down on his notepad, squatting on one knee near the barber.

Maaja Nai said the amount of cooking required was small and would not take long. He asked, "Are you making any vegetarian food for the Hindu and Sikh guests?"

"Two Hindu doctors are invited and they eat meat," said Sabra. "But there are a few neighbours like Munni's ma and her family and another Brahmin family, Draupadi and her husband."

"But you know the Brahmins won't eat our food even if cooked by

Munni's ma," said Maaja Nai, surprised that Sabra should include them in the guest list.

"Yes. They will come after eating at home. And Mwangi can cook vegetables and puris for the few neighbours like Munni's family."

"I'll bring my own two helpers on Friday after the Juma prayers," said Maaja Nai to Sabra, and asked if there were any big stones around the house for making two stoves. "Six stones would be ample as the sweet rice could be cooked on a charcoal jiko."

"That will be no problem, Bhai," said Sabra, "there are some cement blocks behind Mwangi's outhouse. They could be picked up and used. There are lots of cut-up logs in the shed too."

"Very good. I'll bring my own sharp knives for chopping onions and ginger, but you will have to provide other utensils from the house."

"We'll collect what we have and borrow some from the neighbours. Mwangi will keep them ready," Sabra said.

Maaja Nai had now finished his tea. He placed the cup upside down on the saucer and handed it to Huma, who had just come up the steps and put the brown dolki down. Taking the cup, she asked, "Why have you put the cup upside down, Baba Jee?"

"Because I don't want any more tea, Beti."

"And you drank from the saucer!" she exclaimed.

"Yes. I like to drink from the saucer. It tastes better and cools quicker," he told her and grinned.

"But Mwangi said you wanted very hot tea," Huma continued, having not finished with him yet.

"That I certainly did. You should try drinking hot tea from the saucer," he said and chuckled.

"I'd love to sometimes but Api and Ami get very angry. They say the saucer is for holding the cup, not for drinking." Huma pouted as if she had been deprived of a wonderful practice.

"Now Huma, run along and put the dolki away for the moment," said Sabra. "And stop arguing with elders. It's a bad habit."

"I wasn't arguing Ami, I was only talking," moaned Huma, taking the cup in one hand and grabbing the dolki with the other.

Sabra told Maaja Nai the meat for the feast would be delivered on Friday morning. She would ask Mwangi to keep it in a cool place. Ayesha offered to pay Maaja Nai his cooking charges in advance, but he said he would take it all in the end. He would charge thirty shillings for the cooking and five shillings each for his helpers.

After lunch Shaira and Hibba made shakkar paras, namak paras, and mathees. Razia and another friend called Mumtaz came to help them. Rasheed kept his promise and delivered all the groceries—rice, masala, ghee, oil, onions, garlic, and ginger—by three o'clock in the afternoon.

Zaffer and Shahid came back from work towards the evening and Mussavir and Latif followed soon after. Shahid had seen his friend the electrician, who had promised to get the lights fixed. Shahid had also arranged for more chairs for the garden on the day of the feast. Sabra and Ayesha compared notes with them and everything seemed under control. The women decided to go to town the next morning for some shopping and later visit Latif's flat to see what was required to brighten up the place for the bride. Lastly they would visit Latif's boss's house to invite them all for celebration and walima.

Mussavir had visited his doctor colleagues, who told him they had been asked to be ready to leave within twenty-four hours as the order to depart was expected by the weekend, or even sooner. Mussavir had not told this to anyone except Latif. His mother was in a jovial mood. He did not want to dampen her spirits.

At Sabra's home Mussavir did not see Shaira. He wondered where she was. She did not appear even during supper as she had the previous evening with his sister Hibba to help serve the food. He had presumed the girls all ate separately and later. He asked his mother where his sister Hibba was. Ayesha told him the girls were all in the other part of the building, perhaps getting the dolki tightened.

After supper and before going back to Latif's flat, Mussavir came out through the veranda, on his way to the other part of the house. As he approached he could hear voices and laughter. He walked up to the steps which were not far from the huge round water tank that sat on a two-foot-high cement terrace to collect rainwater from the corrugated iron roof. As he was about to walk up the steps, the door opened and the first person to come out was Shaira. She was surprised to see Mussavir and stopped in the doorway, but did not say anything except to greet him.

"So, you are hiding here, Shaira? I was wondering where you were."

"We are tightening the drum," she said, and then hesitated and added, "There are some purdah girls inside."

"Does that mean I can't go inside?" he asked.

"I'm afraid not. Do you want something from the room?"

"Yes, I need some papers from my suitcase which I left behind."

"I'll call Hibba for you," she said and turned, but Mussavir stopped her.

"Wait, Shaira, don't call her yet," he said, then asked in a low voice, "Why have you not been around this evening during dinner?"

She pulled at her dupatta, arranged it on her shoulders, and said, "We have all been busy and people have been coming in and out of the house."

"You are again avoiding me, poetess," he complained.

"I'm not . . . not avoiding you deliberately."

"Have you been asked to keep away from me?" Shaira made no reply, so he said, "I have not told my mother, but I got news today that my orders to go are expected soon, in the next twenty-four or forty-eight hours. That's why I want to collect my papers and passport from my case."

"Oh . . . I see . . ." She looked down at her feet. "You won't be going before the wedding feast, will you?"

"I don't know. I could go on the day itself or the day after."

"I'm sorry. I . . . kept away . . . because . . . both my mother and my brother Shahid want me to."

"I suspected that. They will definitely be happy to see me go. Perhaps you too will be relieved."

"I can't help it. I have to obey my mother and brother."

"But Shaira, I want to see you and be with you as much as I can until I go. I told you that, didn't I?"

"It is not possible, really," she said sadly.

"Then we have to make it possible."

"How?"

"By meeting secretly."

"Secretly? How?"

"Like this." He nodded his head at the passage between the hedge and the water tank and said, "We must meet here and wherever we can."

He took her hand and she stepped down and walked with him to the place behind the tank. There was a border of red canna lilies between the narrow strip of the lawn and the thick hedge behind the tank. The broad green leaves looked dark in the moonlight. The small space was like a pocket and could not be seen from the door. They stood there for a few moments, Mussavir still holding both her hands. Then she tried to pull her hands away and said, "I must go now, really."

"Promise me you will meet me here tomorrow evening."

"I can't promise, it is difficult."

"I shall wait here. Please, Shaira, don't fail me," he pleaded.

"I'll try my best. I promise. Let's go back now. I'll get Hibba for you."

Still holding her hand, he walked her back to the entrance of the room. She came back with Hibba and left Mussavir and his sister there, then walked to the backyard and into the kitchen. She stayed there for a few minutes to get her bearings. When her heart stopped thumping she went into the room she shared with her mother. She was happy to have met Mussavir but sad to hear the news of his imminent departure. She had known he would be going, but she had somehow driven the thought from her mind. She could not help feeling sore with her mother and brother Shahid for restricting her movements even at home. Nobody bothered about strict purdah during marriages and festivities. People moved about freely. It was one of those occasions when strict purdah was not possible.

Her elder brother, Zaffer, had not said anything to her, but both Shahid and her mother, though careful not to say anything in Zaffer's presence, kept reminding her about it. They both felt Zaffer was soft with her and Huma. Shaira had felt like rebelling against their attitude since she came back from Nyeri. Mussavir made her feel important, did not treat her like a child, and seemed very fond of her. She had liked being with him in Nyeri even before she became a bit more familiar with him. She had felt elated ever since she met him. She felt emotions she had never experienced before. She had read about love in books but could never imagine it happening to herself. The experience of being kissed and being in a man's arms was novel, warm, and pleasant.

Deep in her mind, however, was a nagging fear of being found out. She would be in great trouble if discovered and would be classified among bad girls. Not even Hibba knew about her meetings with her brother. She hoped and prayed no one would find out about it in her home. She had a sort of intuitive feeling that Mussavir was not at all happy to go to Abyssinia. Maybe he was scared. Who would not be? Going to a war in the country of the Habshis, which was not even in one's own country or a British colony. But his father had pushed him into it. She hoped and prayed he would come back safely. She would keep praying for him while he was away. And she would make him happy and show him she cared in the next few days, even if it meant deceiving her mother and brother.

15

Catching the Thief

AYESHA AND SABRA, wrapped in their white tentlike burqas and walking shoes, were ready to go to town by the eight-thirty bus. Giving instructions to Shaira and Mwangi about the necessary chores, they hurried to the bus stop opposite St Teresa's Mission. Mussavir met them on the other end and took them to the jewellery shop on River Road. The goldsmith and proprietor, a Hindu Punjabi, invited them into one of the cubicles made out of plywood boards. They sat on chairs in front of a small table to inspect the jewels they wanted to buy as wedding presents for Jamila, the bride.

Ayesha asked to look at gold necklaces and Sabra wanted to buy a pair of round bali earrings. They eventually chose the pieces they liked and the man wrapped them in pink paper. Suddenly Ayesha said she would like to buy a ring. She asked Mussavir to choose it. At first he said he did not know anything about jewellery, but at his mother's insistence he pointed at a small one, studded with a ruby-coloured stone. Ayesha asked the man to put it in a small box.

Mussavir then went to the Red Cross headquarters and Ayesha and Sabra trotted among the shops on River Road, holding their burqas tight against the wind. They turned left to a side lane to hand over the material, which Ayesha had brought from Nyeri, to a tailor who would stitch it and tack gota ribbons on it. When they reached the shop the tailor was busy folding clothes for a customer. He gave Sabra a broad smile and said he would be with her in a few minutes. When he attended to them and learnt what they wanted him to do, he said there was very little time to get the suit ready for Friday. He had to meet other deadlines before. After some coaxing and arm-twisting by Sabra he agreed to work at home to finish the job by Friday.

The two ladies then crossed the road and walked to the Gulam Mohammed halva shop and ordered some Indian mithai and savouries for the henna-applying ceremony, or mehndi, the next evening. It was nearly lunchtime so they headed back to Latif's apartment. Kalingwa welcomed them and served them sodas. They checked the rooms and noted what was needed to make the place festive to welcome Jamila. Latif had informed Kalingwa to prepare lunch for them. After lunch the ladies caught a bus to Latif's boss's home in Ngara to invite the whole family for all the ceremonies and the walima feast.

The girls at Sabra's home in the meantime were busy dyeing their white muslin dupattas. They had mixed the pale orange dye with rice water in a large basin. They wet the dupattas under the tap and rinsed out the water. Then they slowly lowered the wet dupattas into the orange dye mix in the basin and soaked them in the liquid so that the colour would seep in evenly. Shaira soaked the dupattas and rinsed them and Hibba and the others spread them on the line to dry. When all the dyed dupattas were drying, Shaira blended dye powders of different colours in small bowls and mixed them with a little water. They were bright shades of green, indigo, yellow, blue, and red. Hibba and Huma rolled pieces of cotton strips into skeins. Each skein was dipped in the dye and pressed in criss-cross designs on the dupattas, which were folded lengthwise to the breadth of three inches and arranged on a table. They also made designs of crescents and stars. When the dupattas were unfolded, designs of the rainbow over the plain orange base were pleasing to the eye. Huma was very excited to see her own handiwork on her dupatta.

As the original orange dye was made with rice water, the dupattas were starched. These stiff dupattas were then folded lengthwise and twisted like pieces of rope. One girl held a foot length of the twisted material in both her hands, pulling it tight, while another curled the twisted ropelike dupatta with her thumbs and forefingers very finely into gathers. After the whole piece had been worked upon and opened, it was all pleated.

Several mboga sellers carrying huge wicker baskets full of vegetables called out, "Mboga! Mboga! Matra, carroti na binda. Viazi, turnipi na bringanya," the names of vegetables for sale descending periodically the whole day into Sabra's backyard. The vegetable vendors had learnt from neighbours about the festivities to be held at Sabra's home. This was their opportunity for earning extra money. And so they outdid one another in reducing their prices, each vendor insisting his vegetables and fruit were fresher than the others.

In the absence of her mother, Shaira had to get up again and again to go and bargain with the vendors. With Mwangi's help she managed to select and buy a few dozen eggs, potatoes, peas, carrots, cucumbers, lettuce, and tomatoes. Mwangi requested she buy some herbs, like coriander and dill, and limes and green chillies. In the afternoon a chicken seller rode in on his bicycle, ringing the bell, a basketful of live barnyard chickens of all colours cackling away with their tiny yellow beaks and red frills sticking out from the holes in the basket. Shaira asked Mwangi to select four and let them loose in the chicken coop behind the kitchen. Mwangi threw a handful of chenga inside the coop and also put some water in the tin tray.

After the chicken seller had gone, the women who had been asked to come and help clean the rice and masala began to arrive. Shaira asked Huma to bring an old bedsheet from the chest in the bedroom and spread it in the middle of the back veranda. Huma and Farida moved some chairs to the walls and laid the bedsheet on the wooden floor. The women removed their sandals and sat around the sheet, leaving the middle free for the rice. Mwangi emptied the small sack of rice onto the middle of the sheet. The women started to clean it, picking up tiny stones, husks, and bits of straw while Huma and her friends sat nearby beating the drum and singing. The women joined in the singing and rejoicing, which in the beginning was slow, but increased in tempo after a few songs when all had relaxed. When Sabra and Ayesha came back, they too joined the party and some of the girls got up and prepared tea and served it with the shakkar paras and other goodies made the previous day.

Suddenly, Honey, Majid, Salim, and a couple of other boys who had been playing in the next-door neighbour's backyard rushed in, looking excited. Honey, out of breath, asked Shaira where her old chappal was kept. When asked why he needed the chappal, he said Munni's mother (who had not come and was home) had asked for it.

"And why does Munni's ma want my old chappal?"

"To catch the thief," said Majid.

Just then Zaffer, Mussavir, and Latif arrived. They had heard Majid from the veranda.

"To catch a thief, did you say, pehlwan?" asked Mussavir.

"Someone has stolen money from Munni's father's coat."

The women and girls stopped playing the dolki and all ears were alert. They all looked at Honey and then Majid, and Mussavir asked again how the thief was going to be caught with an old chappal.

"They are first going to find out who has stolen it," said Honey, and he again asked Shaira where her old chappal was. Before Shaira could tell him, Huma got up like a flash saying she knew where the old sandal was and rushed out of the veranda and headed towards the bedrooms. She came out with the shoe and called the others, who all followed as she ran towards Munni's home.

"Haven't they got any old sandals in their own house?" Sabra asked Honey.

"Munni's ma said it has to be the shoe of a Muslim. Api's old shoe is suitable," he replied, and hearing Huma's call, he rushed out not wanting to be questioned again.

Zaffer looked at his mother and asked, "Ami, what is this chappal and thief business? I hope they are not serious about it. I don't like my brother and sister to grow up believing in superstitions. It must not be encouraged."

Before Sabra could respond, Zohra Begum, one of the neighbours, spoke from the floor: "Zaffer Beta, it is not superstition. The shoe really takes a full turn at the guilty person's name. It is because of the power and karamat of the Holy Quran."

The women and girls all started talking at the same time. Mussavir, taking a seat emptied by one of the girls, said: "I am still at sea. How, pray, does the Holy Quran come in?"

Latif and some of the others smiled as Sabra tried to explain that there was an old way of casting a faal in order to discover a thief.

"When some money or jewellery is lost," said Sabra, addressing all present, "you write the names of all the suspects on small pieces of paper and nail one piece at a time with a two- or three-inch nail through the middle of an old shoe or chappal. Two persons then lift up the shoe by their fingertips. They hold it still while the relevant sura from the Holy Quran is read. The shoe is supposed to turn around on the fingertips of the holders and fall down when the name on the piece of paper is that of the culprit."

"It is really a matter of faith," said another neighbour.

"You mean the shoe turns by some magic power?" asked Mussavir.

Some women started smiling. Others laughed. Zohra nodded. Sabra said, "It probably does, who knows?"

"What nonsense," said Zaffer. "The nail, my dear elders, in my humble opinion slips because by holding the darn thing up in the air until the recitation stops, the arm gets tired. I'm sure of that." He paused, then added, somewhat harshly, "I don't believe in all this bunk," shocked that his own mother believed in it.

"But I always thought shoes are never brought near the Holy Book," said Mussavir, smiling and trying to calm Zaffer, who really seemed upset.

"The Quran is kept away from the shoe. The reciter just recites from a distance where he or she sits," Zohra said, and she began to relate how they had always very successfully caught a thief this way many times.

"And they were of course always the poor African houseboys or ayahs," said Zaffer.

The sarcasm was lost on Zohra, who quickly said, "Not necessarily, Beta. There were other people involved too."

"I'm surprised that Munni's ma, a Hindu, believes in this faal," said Hibba.

"In India the faal is sometimes performed with a lota, a form of a pewter pot with a spout. I know lots of Hindus believe in it," Sabra said. "You'd be surprised how many people believe in it." She laughed and added, "Even Mwangi asked me once to get a faal cast for him when his money was stolen!" Then, looking at her first-born, she said, "Zaffer, Beta, you are right, though, about the children. It is not good to encourage them. But I think they are more excited seeing the shoe move. Look how the whole lot of them have disappeared. They have got enough sense not to believe in it," she added, to appease Zaffer.

"But when you bring in the Holy Book, it is bound to confuse them," Zaffer insisted.

The men started talking about white and black magic and the females who had now finished cleaning the rice and masala got up and put all the cleaned rice in a big sufuria and the packets of cleaned masala in a tray and began to get ready to leave.

Huma, Honey, Salim and Majid came back. Huma was quite breathless and excited. She sat down on the floor. "The shoe turned around twice on the same names," she said, raising her two fingers as demonstration. "They now know who stole the money. Everybody was quite frightened, Ami." And she moved closer to Sabra.

"And who is the thief?" Mussavir asked.

"The kitchen toto and Munni's own brother," Majid and Honey said in unison.

"Did the shoe move on both the names?" asked one of the women.

"Oh yes, Auntie, it did," said Huma, facing the woman with wide eyes.

"Huma, who read the Quran?" asked Mussavir.

"The Mswahili Malam from the mosque brought his own Quran and read it too."

"No! Did he really now?" Zaffer exclaimed, sounding horrified.

"Yes, Bhaijan, Munni's ma gave him three shillings and one cent!"

"It is more likely her son took the money for his cigarettes."

"Yes, Bhaijan, that's exactly what the kitchen toto said," Huma told her brother.

"Did he?" Zaffer now smiled. "It is interesting, very interesting. But I'm not surprised."

"Bhaijan, he said after he had bought the cigarettes, he gave the change to Munni's brother who gave him ten cents as baksheesh," said Majid. Zaffer began to guffaw and the others joined him. Zaffer then asked if Munni's mother was going to report her son to the police.

"Do you think she will, Bhaijan?" said Huma, getting up and going towards the dolki.

Zaffer took hold of Huma's hand and said, "Listen, Huma, and you too for that matter," he addressed Honey, who was standing with Majid. "I don't want you two to go to people's homes to help them cast a trap to catch a thief in this way. It's not a good thing. I shall be very angry if you do it again. Do you understand me?" Honey remained silent.

Huma argued: "But Bhaijan, everyone goes to see, it is fun to watch."

Zaffer repeated what he had said and more firmly this time. There was dead silence. "You and Honey are never to go again. Am I clear?"

Huma could not resist replying, "But, Bhaijan . . . can't we even go sometimes?"

"No. Not even sometimes. Now go along," He let go her hand. He winked at Mussavir and suppressed his laughter. Huma's quick retorts always amused him. Mussavir seemed amused, too, at Huma's disappointment, but he did not say anything or crack a joke as he agreed with Zaffer that such superstitions should not be encouraged. Huma and the others went inside the house and the women, now collecting their shoes and thanking the hosts and receiving thanks from Sabra and Ayesha for their help, started to leave. They were all reminded to return the following evening at 8 p.m.

Mohammed Rafik brought the livers, hearts, kidneys, and lungs and Mwangi received them and placed them in the cooler part of the meat safe.

After supper when the grown-ups were having tea and chatting, Shaira went and sat in her bedroom, which was not far from the front veranda. She could hear the voices of the grown-ups and also the young people's beating of the dolki. Zaffer came out of the veranda and passed through the bedroom where Shaira was sitting on her own.

"Why are you sitting here by yourself, Shaira?" he asked. "Are you unwell?"

"No, Bhaijan, I'm fine. I haven't anything to do in the kitchen and I don't feel like reading."

"Then why don't you join the others? They are all sitting in the veranda. Huma and Farida are beating the drum."

"Shahid Bhai says I am not to sit there."

"Oh, bother Shahid! Come along, why must you sit by yourself. It's a festive occasion. There is all the time later to be in purdah."

Zaffer put his arm around her shoulders and guided her to the sitting room. She then went to where the girls were sitting on the rug in the corner and joined them. Her mother saw her come in with Zaffer but did not say anything. Mussavir was happy to see her again. They had spent a few minutes together earlier on, near the tank. Mussavir had told her he was moving from Latif's flat the following day to be with his mother and sisters, and he hoped they would have occasion to meet.

16

Latif's Mehndi and Rukhstana

DR BASHIR ARRIVED in Nairobi on Wednesday in the late afternoon. Mussavir met him at the bus depot and brought him to Sabra's home in a taxi. On the way Mussavir told his father that he was expecting his orders any minute but had withheld the information from his mother. Dr Bashir agreed it was best not to tell her until the order actually came.

After a brief rest and a bath, Dr Bashir came to Sabra's side of the house and heard about the celebration arrangements in detail over a cup of tea. He was not only surprised but very impressed at the smooth way in which everything had been done. Mussavir, too, could not help being impressed and had to admit to himself that Sabra was a good organizer and not as scatterbrained as he had presumed her to be. He was surprised at how cheerful she appeared. Zaffer and Latif too arrived and welcomed Dr Bashir.

Supper consisted of curried kidneys and hearts and liver cooked with fenugreek leaves, garnished with fresh coriander. It was served with freshly baked nan, and eaten early, as the female guests were expected for the henna celebration.

By eight-thirty the place was cleared and ready, the girls all dressed in their party clothes, the dyed dupattas making a grand spate of colour. They all started to sing to the beat of the dolki. Zohra Begum had helped to soak the henna powder in a bowl with water and lemon juice to make the dye stronger. She put a little of the henna paste in a soup plate and decorated it with small coloured candles. These were to be lit when the henna was carried in a procession by young girls to the bridegroom.

All the invited guests arrived by nine. Latif's boss and his wife, their son and daughter-in-law Attia, plus their other children, had all come dressed in colourful garments fit for the occasion. Latif's boss, as he was generally called by the Bashir and Azim families, or "the muslim lawyer," as he was known by others, sat in the garden under the trees with Dr Bashir, Zaffer, Mussavir, and a few neighbours who had accompanied their wives.

Latif was summoned in by Ayesha and seated on a piri. Ayesha wore one of the dyed dupattas. The females began to sing, clap, and beat the dolki. The procession of the girls with the tray containing the candlelit henna started to move from the landlord's side of the house. Huma and Farida held the tray with the henna paste and candles and Hibba and Shaira carried the thalis containing sweets, nuts, and mithai covered with a red cloth. Zohra's daughter, and Munni, and her sister Shashi walked along with a matchbox to relight the candles in case they were extinguished by the wind. The procession moved slowly through the backyard to the front of the house. Mwangi and his children and a few houseworkers of the neighbours had all gathered in the yard to watch. Shaira had given Mama Wanjiro a dyed dupatta which she wore, and she joined the women inside, laughing loudly and clapping with them. Now and again she ululated. As the girls climbed the steps they were welcomed by other females singing folk songs. Those holding the candles and henna approached and stood in front of Latif, who was clad in a simple grey suit.

Ayesha came forward with some barfi from one of the trays and put it in Latif's mouth. Then, taking his right hand, she first placed a mulberry leaf, which she had earlier asked Huma to pluck from the tree in the garden, on his palm and put a little of the henna paste on the leaf with a tiny spoon. Seven married women, young and old, including Mama Wanjiro, each placed a little henna paste on Latif's palm. Four married women then stood holding the four sides of an orange dupatta, which had been dyed for that purpose, like a canopy over Latif. Ayesha dipped her finger in the small bowl of oil on the tray and applied it to Latif's hair, amidst singing and rejoicing. The songs indicated the bridegroom was being prepared with turmeric and oil for the next day. There was laughter when some women became naughty and put the oil over his forehead too. Poor Latif just bent his head and suffered in silence.

After the ceremony, Latif joined his uncle and cousin and other males outside in the garden. Tea and katlama were served. The young girls all started to dye their hands with henna paste. Some put a little paste on a piece of paper to apply it at home. It was not easy to walk back with wet hands and soiled clothes.

Dressed in her gala clothes and dyed dupatta, Huma was very excited. She sang her dal song many times using Latif's name. The females also sang the sehra song, which is sung for all bridegrooms, sometimes composed specially by some poetic relative. Latif went back in his boss's son's car and the singing continued after he left.

The next morning Latif arrived in a taxicab and his uncle, aunt, and Mussavir went with him to the Nairobi railway station to meet his bride. Sabra and the girls cleaned and dusted the living room and Shaira put freshly cut flowers and ferns from the garden in vases in the living room and veranda. Then they all dressed up and anxiously awaited the bride's arrival. Some neighbours like Zohra, Munni's mother, and Draupadi turned up too.

The taxi returned at eleven carrying the bride and groom, with Mussavir, Dr Bashir, and Ayesha. Latif, however, went back to town in the same taxi as he had to work for a few hours in order to be free the next day. His presence, in any case, was not necessary as at that stage the ceremonies to be performed were only for the bride.

Before the bride walked in, Sabra poured some water and oil on the steps for good luck and to ward off evil spirits. Women sang songs of welcome. Jamila, the bride, wore a light blue burqa which Ayesha helped her to remove before escorting her to the settee. She was an attractive girl, slim but not very tall. She had smooth golden skin and her kohl-lined eyes were big with long lashes. Her features were delicate. She wore a red and gold embroidered suit and a matching dupatta. Her hair, which was very long, was pleated in a single braid with a red three-tasseled silk peranda woven into it.

Ayesha introduced her to Sabra and the guests and her own daughters and Shaira. Huma and Farida sat beside her. All present congratulated her and welcomed her to Nairobi and Sabra's home. They asked about the sea voyage and the train journey. Tea and mithai were served to all present. After lunch Jamila was taken to Shaira's room to rest for a couple of hours. At five o'clock she was dressed in her gala clothes and made to wear all her jewellery, including a jhumar on her forehead. When ready she was again escorted to the settee in the living room. All the young girls seated around the room started singing and beating the dolki. The henna which the girls had applied to their hands the previous evening had taken well.

The men all sat in the garden on chairs which Shahid had got for the occasion. Shahid and his friends were fixing the electric bulbs onto the wires tied around the pepper trees. They were to be lit the next evening at the walima feast. Latif arrived dressed in a dark suit, and Mussavir placed a garland of flowers, which Latif's boss's son brought, around Latif's neck. He sat with the males for a while but was soon summoned inside by the females. Accompanied by Mussavir he was met on the doorstep by his two cousins, Mussavir's sisters Hibba and Farida, as well as Huma and Shaira. The other ladies all stood in the background with beaming smiles. Hibba and Farida held a bowl of raw gram dal in both hands. As Latif stood on the first step the girls started to sing "Waag Pakrai," a Punjabi song specially sung when the bridegroom goes to fetch his wife. Traditionally the groom is supposed to travel on horseback. His sisters look after his horse before the long journey, and he gives them a reward for that and for holding the reins. "Waag Pakrai" means holding the reins. The girls all sang the symbolic song:

Ki kutch dena aey vira waag pakrai?
Waag pakrai wey vira dana charai.

What do you propose to give me, brother
Dear brother? Not only for holding the reins

But also for feeding your horse.

The bridegroom's reply is sung by the other females:

Panj rupaye ni bebe waag pakrai
Waag pakrai ni bebe dana charai.

I shall give you five rupees, oh my sisters
Five full rupees for holding the reins
And feeding my horse.

Latif was allowed to enter the room after he had placed some money in the bowl of gram. Before he reached the settee, however, he was stopped again by a sister-in-law (Latif's boss's daughter-in-law acted as his sister-in-law for the occasion). She was holding a tiny silver container with antimony powder which was to be applied to his eyes to keep cool while travelling on horseback. The women all sang:

Ki kutch dena aey dewera surma puaai?
Surma puaai wey dewera surma puaai?

What do you propose to give me, oh brother of my husband
For applying surma to cool your eyes?

The women again sang Latif's reply, similar to the one to the sisters, except that they substituted "wife of my brother" for "sister."

Ayesha gave the present instead of Latif. After the song and present, Latif was at last escorted to the settee, where his bride sat with her head bent. When seated Ayesha brought out a note of five shillings and waved it around both Latif's and Jamila's heads five times and put it on a plate. This was to ward off evil spirits. Then all the females in turn waved a shilling or fifty cents around the heads of the pair to ward off more evil spirits and gave the bride a shilling or two for good luck. The money in the plate was to be given to charity. Sweet cardamom-flavoured milk garnished with almond shavings was given to the bride and groom to drink from the same glass. Lastly, Ayesha placed a coconut and some dried fruit in Jamila's lap. It was for fertility and wealth and good luck.

After refreshments and a chorus of congratulations and good wishes the pair were escorted to the car outside by Dr Bashir and his wife. All the others stood around and the girls threw rice and flower petals as they drove away in the car driven by Latif's boss's son. His wife, Attia, accompanied them to escort Jamila to Latif's apartment.

While waiting for the car to come back for Latif's boss and his family, the men sat and talked about the state of the economy and business in general. They also discussed the concern of the local European farmers in the country about Italy's attack on Abyssinia and the help that the British proposed to give that country through the Red Cross Society in the way of medical personnel and medicine. Latif's boss felt Dr Bashir was very brave to send his son to a war front.

"Dr Sahib, I really admire you. I would not have had the courage."

"And what about Mussavir? Is he not brave too?" said another neighbour.

Before Dr Bashir could reply the Muslim lawyer, pointing to Mussavir, said, "Oh, he is not only brave but also a very obedient son." All agreed.

Mussavir was about to say something when Zohra's husband, touching his bushy and droopy moustache, butted in, saying, "Personally, I don't think it is good for the British to involve themselves in somebody else's war."

"I think the British are *right* in giving help to the Abyssinians," said Dr Bashir. "They naturally don't want the fascist Italians to be installed at their doorstep. That would have very wide repercussions."

"But, Tayajan, the Italians are already installed there or nearby in Italian Somaliland," Zaffer said. "It is they who instigated the Somalis in the attack, even though the brawls were in the Abyssinian territory. What repercussions would there be?"

"Well, the Germans are already demanding the return of Tanganyika, which was their colony before the war and which the British have been burdened to administer now for more than fifteen years," replied Dr Bashir.

In the Shadow of Kirinyaga

The Muslim lawyer, who had been listening intently, smiled and said, "But, Doctor Sahib, Tanganyika has not been a liability or a burden. It is a potentially rich country and a ready-made market for British goods. It will be very useful in the coming days too. Don't forget."

"I don't think there is any real danger," said the neighbour who had spoken earlier. "The British are a clever and shrewd people and a great power. They will help quietly from the back door. They can't help openly as they don't want to annoy and irritate Italy. As the newspapers tell us, Mussolini is in an aggressive and belligerent mood already. He might join the Germans."

"That is true to some extent," argued the Muslim lawyer, "but let's look at the facts: would the Italians have dared to attack in the first place if they thought the Great Powers and the League of Nations were really going to help Abyssinia? Would they have attacked if they believed the threat of sanctions against them?"

"You are right, Uncle," said Zaffer. "It is obvious the poor Abyssinians would be no match for the Italians with their tanks and guns. In fact, the area where the fighting began is not significant strategically, just some small deserted camel wells called Wal Wal in the Ogaden under the Governor of Jigjiga, all miles away from Addis Ababa."

Mussavir, who had read about the wells, nodded in agreement, adding, "There were strict rules about the use of the wells. They are spread over a flat dry area, each well with a camp of nomad wanderers and their livestock. Wal Wal is one such place."

"I am told the actual event that ignited the conflict was petty, almost absurd," said the Muslim lawyer. "An Abyssinian flung a bone at a Somali. A fight broke out, escalated, and when the fighting was over, up to one hundred were dead, and many were injured."

"It was more than that, Uncle," said Zaffer. "Quite complicated too. It's a long story, in fact many stories—the Somalis have one version, the Abyssinians another, and of course the Italians have their own."

Zohra's husband, himself a transporter of goods to those areas, had been to Somaliland and Abyssinia many times over the years. He claimed there were over a thousand wells in the Ogaden and not just a few deserted ones. In Somaliland a well was invaluable property and not just a water hole in the ground. A group of families owned each well, and groups of wells were owned by a clan. Some wells never ran dry while others were seasonal. The former were more valuable. So, however small the incident at Wal Wal appeared, the territorial stakes were always high. Forces from Abyssinia and those from the former sultanate annexed by Italy both behaved like clans for control over the wells.

Zohra's husband said, "Omar Marjan, a fellow Somali transporter, told us a funny story—I am not sure if it is true. According to him, towards the end of November last year the wells at Wal Wal were occupied by both Somali and Abyssinian troops. There were about two hundred bande under a local Somali officer who had set up camp in the middle of the wells. The commander of the Abyssinian troops, an Englishman, put up his tents a few hundred yards away, parallel to the Somalis, and raised the Union Jack. That same day a junior Somali officer from the Abyssinian camp crossed the lines and deserted. The British commander sent a threatening letter demanding his return. The bande leader responded that he would like to send the deserter back, but could not because his men would prevent him, claiming that the soldier had taken refuge under the Italian flag. Even if it cost them all their lives, he declared, the deserter could not be returned to Abyssinia. Notes were exchanged back and forth; there was even an interview, which ended stormily. In one of the letters the Somali officer was referred to as the chief Shifta, a serious insult! The situation became extremely tense and finally exploded with the tossing of the bone that resulted in many Abyssinian deaths and injuries."

The men smiled wryly, some even chuckled.

"We have an Italian mechanic called Kartoni working in our garage," said Zaffer. "He is a jolly fellow, always making fun of the elite and rich in Italy, including the Pope. He happened to be in some Arab sultanate where he saw the rich and poor praying together on the same mat. He said this could never happen in Italy. The rich have their own pews and Kartoni, he always points to himself, sits in the last row. He laughed loudly telling us about it. We don't usually take him seriously, but he said something very pertinent the other day. He said the Abyssinians made a great mistake lodging a protest with the League of Nations and asking for arbitration in their conflict with Italy, when it was after all on Italy's recommendation that they were admitted to the League in the first place.

"The sorry state of affairs continued when the Italian counter-demand called for the Abyssinian minister to come to Wal Wal in person and formally present his apologies to the representative of the Italian government for the various insults that had fuelled the incident, while the Abyssinian detachment saluted the Italian flag. The Italians also wanted those responsible for the offence to be arrested, demoted, and made to salute the Italian flag. Obviously these terms were rejected, and war became inevitable. The Emperor is looking for help from wherever he can hire it."

"You are right," said the Muslim lawyer, "but though the incident at Wal Wal started everything, the fighting is not going to be restricted only to that area."

"Where are you actually going then?" one of the neighbours asked Mussavir.

"We haven't been told exactly where, but I suppose we shall first go to Addis and get our orders from there," Mussavir told him.

While the men were chatting, the females inside were making preparations for the next day, the festive feast in the evening. The world and its affairs were not on their agenda for the next few days.

When the car came back after dropping Latif and his wife in town, the Muslim lawyer and his family took their leave, receiving thanks for their help and requests to come the next day.

That evening Mussavir told his mother he was expecting his orders very soon, perhaps by the weekend. To his surprise, she took it better than he had thought. She tried to cheer him up and said time would soon pass and he would then look forward to his own marriage. She was persuading Sabra and Zaffer to formalize the engagement, at least by accepting a ring for Shaira and drinking the ceremonial milk. She hoped they would agree. In fact, she told him, that is why she had bought the little ring.

17

The Auspicious Day

"AMI, LUGGI'S WIFE has brought a gorgeous sehra made of leaves and flowers," chirped Huma, rushing in from the garden where she and Farida were picking flowers for the decorations. "She wants to hang it on our front door, Ami."

"Luggi's wife! She has come *all* the way from school?" Sabra seemed surprised, for the school was in the city and closed for the holidays. "The poor woman must have walked three miles." Turning to Ayesha, she told her Luggi was one of the few Hindu sweepers from India who worked at her school. He lived in a small wooden house in the school grounds. "I wonder who told her about the occasion."

"Masi Jantey met her husband at the market and told him."

"Oh well, let her come here, she must be tired and thirsty," said Sabra.

"But she wants a ladder to hang the chaplet first." Huma was in a hurry to go back.

"Tell Mwangi to take it to the front door then, I'll come and see her," Sabra said, and both she and Ayesha got up.

"Peri peniyan Ustani Jee. Salaam alaikum," was Luggi's wife's greeting to Sabra. She was dressed in a dark green sari and wore a small nose ring and silver bangles on her arms. As a traditional Hindu she would be obliged by custom to touch Sabra's feet as a sign of respect to an elder. But Sabra was a Muslim, and there is no foot-touching in the Muslim religion, so the Hindu students or youngsters would, like Luggi's wife, repeat the words, "I touch your feet," and Luggi's wife had added the Muslim salaam too. She addressed Sabra as "Teacher." On seeing Ayesha she greeted her in the same way and added her congratulations.

Sabra thanked her and said it was very sweet of her to come from so far away and all by herself. "Come to the veranda, Bibi, and have a drink." Sabra asked Mwangi to help fasten the string of flowers and leaves on the front door, which he did with Huma and Farida's help. It certainly cheered the doorway and looked festive and colourful. Ayesha flashed a smile at the woman and thanked her profusely. Later, both Sabra and Ayesha gave her some money, as is customary. Sabra added a coloured dupatta, and some old clothes of Huma's and Honey's for her children. She often did that whenever there were clothes or shoes to give away. Sabra also gave her the bus fare to go back and a packet of mithai and other homemade goodies. The sweeper woman seemed more than pleased and showered thanks, blessings, and good wishes on them all. Sitting on the step she drank a bottle of soda which Shaira gave her. She was not invited for the feast or invited inside and she would not expect that. She was a Harijan, the new name given by Mahatma Gandhi to the untouchables in India. Though her children and the children of the few others like her in the Colony went to the same schools as other Indians, in practice the families still kept to themselves and expected and received a kind of charity from both Muslims and Hindus, especially on festive occasions. It would be ages before they would be integrated into society, if at all.

No sooner had the sweeper woman gone than Mohammed Rafik arrived, lugging the bundle of meat.

"It's all cut up and ready, Masi Jee," he said to Sabra. "I told my brother to make separate packets for the pilau and korma."

"Thank you so much, Beta, that is really thoughtful of you," said Sabra. "It'll save so much time."

Mohammed Rafik was about to leave when Sabra asked him if he'd like a soft drink or tea.

"No thanks, Masi Jee. I have to go back. But I'll see you tonight."

"Oh yes, and don't forget to remind your mother and sisters to come early," Sabra told him as he left. Her insistence that his family come early did not mean that she expected them to arrive early literally, but was a way of showing how welcome the guests were and how grateful she was for Mohammed Rafik's help.

Sabra called Mwangi and asked him to put the meat in the outside cooler. All the rations and cleaned-up rice and spices were kept in the space between the kitchen and the workers' quarters, where Maaja Nai could reach them easily.

At midday Zohra's son, pushing a rickety, noisy wheelbarrow full of cardboard boxes piled high, came into Sabra's backyard. The boxes contained the crockery and dastar khwans, borrowed from one of the mosques, for use at the feast.

Sabra came forward and thanked the young boy, who also helped to off-load the boxes and place them in the kitchen. Sabra called Shaira and Hibba to count the items in the boxes and put them aside. "Please count the different items, Beti. In case of breakages we shall have to replace them."

Maaja Nai arrived promptly as he had promised with his helpers, his sharp knives, and a few utensils. He greeted Sabra and Mwangi and without wasting any time went behind the kitchen where, with his helpers, he made temporary jikos with the blocks of stones—three stones to a jiko. He asked Honey and Majid to bring a few small bricks from the backyard for him to place on the blocks, so that when the big deg was placed on them there would be room for the flames. One of his helpers, named Njuguna, arranged the logs with paper and tinders and lit the fire. The children all came and stood around watching and chatting with Maaja Nai. When the fire was properly alight, Maaja Nai tied on a long green apron and then placed on the fire the big cauldron, in which he had already put the meat from the bigger packet and lots of water to boil for the yakhni for the pilau. He threw several peeled onions, a cupful of peeled garlic, and crushed green ginger into the cauldron. His second helper had been busily peeling the garlic and crushing the green ginger in a stone mortar with a wooden pestle as he squatted on the grass. Maaja Nai lifted the tray containing the masala and, placing it on a box nearby, sprinkled handfuls of the cleaned spices—cinnamon sticks, cumin, dry coriander seeds, cloves, peppercorns, cardamom, and salt—into the cauldron and gave the contents a good stir with a long flat iron spoon. He covered the cauldron with a lid and then he himself washed and soaked the long-grain Basmati rice in two basins, the bigger one for the pilau and the smaller for zarda.

That done, he asked for a wooden board from the kitchen and, sitting down on the grass with the board in front of him, he started to chop the onions which Njuguna had laboriously been peeling into a basin of water. Maaja Nai was very fast and chopped the onions paper thin with even strokes. He kept his face away and did not even look at the onions. Njuguna, however, kept sniffing and rubbing his eyes. "Look the other way, you limb of an owl. I've told you many times not to look at the onions while peeling." Njuguna grinned widely, then said, "We can't be all good at onions like you, Mzee, you must have gone to an onion-chopping school," and the children who were all standing around laughed.

Dr Bashir and Mussavir, who had gone to town together after breakfast, came back at four o'clock in the afternoon. They said they had gone to see someone at the Railway Administration to find out if there were any openings for Ta'Ha when he came. They sounded hopeful of finding something.

Latif and Jamila, who were to come with Latif's boss's son and daughter-in-law, were a bit late. Attia had gone to help Jamila with her dress and makeup. Jamila wore a green Benarsi outfit with a matching dupatta and some jewellery. She looked rested and cheerful and less shy. Latif was his calm self. He was wearing a dark suit with a red printed tie. Leaving Jamila with the women, he went and joined his uncle and Mussavir and the two Hindu doctors who were to go to Abyssinia with Mussavir.

"I'm sorry, yesterday I kept calling you Shaira Apa," Jamila said to Shaira. "I'm told you are even younger than Hibba!"

"It's all right, Jamila Bhabi. I'm used to it now. The young treat me as a grown-up but not the grown-ups."

Attia was surprised to learn that Shaira was not yet fourteen. But she said it was not bad to look older than one's age at that stage because normally at thirteen and fourteen one is sort of between a young person and a grown-up. Not a very satisfactory situation.

"But even though I look older, I'm now in that difficult state," Shaira said, laughing.

"I'm so happy to learn that we are going to be very close relatives," Jamila whispered, bending towards Shaira.

"Oh, I don't know for sure. I'm still at school and propose to study further."

"But Mussavir Bhai is impatient and wants the Nikah before he leaves."

"Are you then engaged to Dr Mussavir, Shaira?" asked Attia, arranging her blue voile dupatta over her shoulders. She was wearing a tilla-embroidered satin suit in blue. She was a tall and big woman with a round face and grey eyes, a pathan girl from the Frontier Province in Northern India.

"No, not really." Shaira shook her head. Her face seemed red and her voice a bit shaky. "I mean . . . it is not definite."

"Oh, don't be so modest and challak. Of course you are engaged in a way. I heard in India you have been named." Jamila was quite vocal for a new bride and Shaira was surprised Latif had not wasted any time and had told her everything on the first night.

Maaja Nai was now busy cooking in earnest. The aroma of food and spice pervaded the grounds of the house, and guests coming from outside said they could smell the delicious aroma from afar. Maaja Nai had earlier fried half the chopped onions and poured them together with the soaked and drained rice into the big cauldron and lowered the heat after the liquid in the rice had dried. He covered the lid and, borrowing a spade from the gardener, scooped some live coals from the fire below the cauldron to spread on the metal lid of the deg. He said that by the time dinner was served the rice would be hot and dried.

Next, he measured the ghee and sugar for the zarda, for which he had already boiled the rice in a big saucepan with some dried saffron leaves and orange food colouring. Placing the smaller deg on the charcoal jiko, he fried some cardamom seeds in the ghee. When the frying cardamom seeds threw forth a sweet aroma, he added the drained coloured rice and the measured sugar, blanched almonds, pistachio nuts, and raisins into the

In the Shadow of Kirinyaga

mixture, turning it all gently to allow air into it. He replaced the lid and lowered the heat, then put some live coals over it like he did for the pilau.

On the second stone jiko simmered the meat for korma he had fried earlier in ghee with chopped onions and tomatoes, chili, turmeric, and coriander powders. He had added enough water for the meat to tenderize and leave some liquid for gravy. His main work finished, Maaja Nai sat on a chair and enjoyed his hookah, which he had dismantled and brought in a bag.

Shahid and his friends, with Mohammed Rafik in an immaculate suit and tie, had begun to arrange the chairs and tables in the garden for the men's dinner. The plates, glasses, piyalas, saucers, and ladles for serving the food were stacked on a table not far from the kitchen. Shaira had earlier given Shahid some bedsheets to be used as tablecloths. Mohammed Rafik even picked a few flowers and greenery from the garden and placed them in the centre.

Inside the ladies and girls sat on the mats and rugs, some of which had been spread with bedsheets. Jamila the bride sat with Attia, Farida, and Huma on a mattress against one wall. The place looked colourful and cheery when the lights were on. Some of the young girls sang wedding songs and beat the dolki. Newcomers greeted and congratulated the bride. Some gave her money in silver for good luck.

Amidst all the activity, suddenly there came screams came from the back of the house in the vicinity of Mwangi's quarter. Huma, followed by other children, ran towards it. Shaira, Hibba, and Munni made for the veranda windows. The singing stopped. Shaira saw her brother Shahid rushing towards the back too, so she hurried down the steps and followed him. Sabra, who was talking to Maaja Nai, called the young ones back, saying this was no tamasha. She asked Honey to call Zaffer.

Huma came back. "Ami, Ami," she cried, "Mwangi is beating Mama Wanjiro with a big stick. He says he wants to kill her and the baby. Ami, please come quickly, before he hurts the baby." Not getting a response from her mother, she rushed to Shahid and said in an excited voice, "Oh, Manjala Bhai, come quickly or Mwangi will really kill Mama Wanjiro. He is very angry."

153

They reached Mwangi's room.

"Mwangi!" called Shahid, "What's the matter? Why are you behaving like that? Stop beating Mama and the baby," he said in Swahili.

"Kihora! You keep out of this. Nenda! Go, leo nita tandika ye kabisa. Hata kama ukiita askari. Potelea mbali," he screamed. "Today I'm going to beat her flat even if you call the police. I don't care."

He hit and kicked her again. Mama Wanjiro, still holding the baby, tried to fend off his beating with her free arm. The other children held on to her skirt and whimpered and whined. Zaffer rushed in and caught Mwangi's hand and pulled away the stick. Mama Wanjiro, on seeing Zaffer, howled and wailed loudly. Sabra, who had also arrived, took the baby from her and told her to be quiet. She told her there were many guests outside for the feast. What would they think? Zaffer pulled Mwangi out and walked him away towards the rear hedge and tried to calm him down and hear his complaints.

Huma sneaked into the room and tried to console Mama Wanjiro, who was still sobbing, saying her husband was beating her for nothing like a wazimu, a madman. If they were in Kikuyuland, he'd have to kill two mbuzi to pacify her parents and clan for beating her.

Mwangi was now explaining to Zaffer, "Fitina yote na toka kwa dada yake." All the trouble was caused by her sister, whom she had visited in the afternoon despite his telling her not to. She had disobeyed him and then she was cheeky and accused him of things he had not done. It was all her sister's doing. Zaffer and Sabra were able to pacify Mwangi and he promised he would go back to the kitchen. But he also said he was not finished with his wife and would deal with her later.

Zaffer was of the opinion that poor Mwangi was perhaps overtired, having worked like a horse these last few days, and Mama Wanjiro had provoked him at the wrong time. However, after a few minutes all was quiet and Mama Wanjiro with her children came to the yard to see the lights and watch the guests arrive.

When all the invited guests had arrived and the dinner was cooked and ready, Maaja Nai asked that one of the elders in the family open the lid of

In the Shadow of Kirinyaga

the cauldron and serve the first helping. Sabra told him Dr Bashir would do it when all the guests were seated. She also told Shahid to collect his helpers, so they could start serving the food straightaway. She told Zaffer to ask the guests to be seated. Zaffer was talking to his boss who had just come and was apologizing for being late. He was a middle-aged Irishman of medium height and wore a bushy moustache. Dressed in a black suit, he carried a small wrapped packet which he gave Latif as a wedding present. Zaffer introduced him to Dr Bashir and Mussavir's colleagues. Mussavir, who had met him earlier, greeted and welcomed him, then introduced him to other guests and found him a seat near his colleagues.

Dr Bashir said a prayer, opened the lid of the deg, and, with a long flat serving spoon, served the steaming fluffy pilau with meat onto the first plate. The aroma of spices was intense. Maaja Nai took over from Dr Bashir. Shahid dished out the zarda into small saucers, the chopped almonds, pistachio nuts, and raisins shining like beads. Another helper dished out the korma mutton, and still another spooned out the spiced yogurt into small china bowls. The bowls of korma and yogurt and the small saucer of zarda were all placed in the enamel plates holding the pilau, which a string of helpers passed from one to the other until they reached the tables in the garden and the sitting room inside the house, where the female helpers took over and passed the food to the women guests sitting on the floor.

The women sat in rows opposite each other and a dastar khwan was spread between the rows on which the enamel plates of food were placed. Young girls passed around glasses of water. Munni and her mother helped with the vegetarian food in thalis and served it to the few Hindu and Sikh guests. She was helped by Shaira and Hibba. Zarda and yogurt were eaten by all the guests but the vegetarian food only by the ladies who were vegetarians. The Brahmin guests came, greeted, and congratulated the bride and groom and the family, but left before the food was served.

The children were surprised to see Zaffer's European boss eating pilau and other food with his fingers like everybody else. But Zaffer got Honey to get him a knife and fork. Honey gave a running commentary about the way he ate the meat with his hands and how he found the korma hot. He said the man must like it for he kept eating despite the fact he was perspiring all the time. Huma and the others laughed and said, "Poor man, he'll surely have problems when he goes to the choo the next morning."

The guests all said the food was delicious and praised Maaja Nai's cooking. By about half past eight all except the helpers had finished their dinner. People mingled and chatted happily. Many of them, after saying their thanks and good wishes, left for their homes.

Later Latif thanked his aunt and uncle, and Sabra and Zaffer, for their generosity and help. He and Jamila took a ride back with his boss. After Maaja Nai and his helpers had eaten, Sabra lent Maaja Nai her tiffin carrier to take food for his family. He had already received the money for himself and his helpers. He was preparing to leave when Mohammed Rafik said he'd take him and his helpers, along with his bicycle, in his van.

18

The Announcements

AFTER THE DINNER was over and all the guests had gone, the families sat in the living room discussing the festivities over coffee. That's when Mussavir announced he was leaving the next day by the evening train for Mombasa, from where he and his colleagues would board ship. And Zaffer told Dr Bashir and Ayesha that he and his mother had decided to comply with their wishes and give them the ceremonial milk to solemnize the engagement between Mussavir and Shaira, before Mussavir left.

Zaffer's announcement brought smiles to the faces of Dr Bashir, Ayesha, and their daughters, who had all gone quiet upon hearing that Mussavir was actually leaving the next day. Mussavir could not believe his ears and looked at Shaira, who also seemed taken aback. She, however, got up to leave the room, but both Dr Bashir and Ayesha stopped her and hugged and kissed her. They thanked Sabra and Zaffer. Sabra too put her arms around Mussavir, and Zaffer gave him a big bear hug. There were congratulations all around. In that commotion no one spoke about Mussavir's departure the next day except Huma, who brought everyone back to it.

"Mussavir Bhaijan, you said you are leaving tomorrow and it's Dusera day tomorrow. An effigy of Ravan is going to be burned in the school grounds in the town."

"Yes, you are right. But unfortunately I have to go. Are you going to see it?"

Huma nodded.

"Go to Latif's flat and watch it from his balcony at the rear. You will get a full view of Ravan from there."

"But I'm going to see it from the grounds with Munni and her family, Bhaijan. There I'll be able to see Sita and Ram shooting arrows to burn the dirty old Ravan."

"It's dangerous to go to the grounds; there will be so many people and you could be squashed," said Shahid. "Why do you want to go at all? Lots of people get hurt every year, this was especially so last year. I heard they were going to stop burning the effigy of Ravan. They should, it's not safe."

"Oh, I'm glad they are keeping it on, Manjala Bhai," said Huma, looking at her cousins. "It's nice to watch it burn and to see the lights and the people rejoicing afterwards. Divali is coming soon too. There'll be lots of mithai to eat and the Hindu houses and buildings will all be lit up with tiny candles and we'll be able to buy firecrackers and phool jaris, the sparklers."

The Mombasa cousins were all ears. Dusera and Divali Hindu festivals were not celebrated so grandly at the coast.

"Do you know why they burn Ravan, Huma? And why Devali is celebrated?" Mussavir asked.

"Oh yes, Mussavir Bhaijan, I know all about it. I have also read in a book about it. When Ram, Sita, and Laxman were still in the jungle by the order of the stepmother Queen Kikei, who wanted her son Bharat to be king, Ravan stole Sita from the jungle. He took her away to Lanka and imprisoned her. Hanuman found her and told her Ram was coming to rescue her. Ram did come and by throwing a burning arrow he shot Ravan and burnt and killed him."

"But Hanuman was only a monkey with such a long tail and he was so ugly," said Majid, the fat cousin.

"He was a Monkey God and a very brave one too," Huma replied defiantly. She made a face at her cousin.

"It is not true, these are all legends," said Shahid.

"But, Manjala Bhaijan, it all happened so long ago. I'm sure it did. When Api tells us about snakes coming out of Medusa's head, I can't believe that, but I think Ram and Sita and Lord Krishna and Ravan were all real people."

"Ravan is supposed to have ten heads! Do you believe that too?" Shahid said angrily.

"He must have had ten heads! Ami told us a calf in India was born with two heads. So I'm sure people can, too," Huma insisted.

"You are right, Huma. Ram, Sita, Krishna were all real. Your brother is only bullying you," Mussavir said and laughed. "And I am glad you like Divali celebrations and fireworks. If one day you go to India you will see much more there. It can be very colourful."

While the children were discussing the Dusera and Devali festivals, the grown-ups were deciding where the ceremonial milk ceremony should take place before Mussavir was sent away. They finally came to the decision that the ceremony be held at Latif's home, and then Mussavir could be seen off from there.

Mussavir was naturally very pleased his mother was able to persuade Zaffer and Sabra. Shaira too was happy and surprised but wondered what had made her mother and brothers change their minds.

Zaffer asked Mussavir if he had any idea how he was going to Abyssinia.

"I'm not sure how, Zaffer. We have all been asked to report at Mombasa, and it is clear it will be a sea voyage and a long train journey."

"That means you will most probably go via Djibouti and not via British Somaliland. Djibouti is a French port where the steamships stop to refuel. My boss told me tourists are often taken to see the big heaps of coal!"

"My colleagues suspect we might go via Kismayao, but it seems the boats are not very regular on that run, and one would have to pass Italian territory," said Mussavir.

Sabra and Zaffer said they would all miss Mussavir but wished him a safe journey and a safe stay wherever he went, and a safe journey home after his mission was completed. Mussavir thanked them all but showed no particular emotion or sign of grief or sadness. In fact, he joked and remained cheerful. He was, of course, elated about the announcement of his engagement. He had met Shaira earlier at their special place near the tank, but they had not known about this development then. They had made sad goodbyes and Shaira had promised to keep in touch through

Latif. That would not now be necessary; they could write to each other directly.

By eleven the next morning, Sabra's house had returned to normal after the previous night's festivities. Sabra got up early and soaked some almonds and pistachio nuts in a bowl of warm water. She asked Mwangi to peel and chop them finely. She boiled about two and a half pints of milk with cardamom and sugar, and when it was cool, she poured it into milk bottles and packed them in a basket to be taken to Latif's home for the engagement ceremony. She put the chopped nuts in a small container and packed it in the same basket.

Huma was persuaded not to go off with Munni but to accompany the family to Latif's flat. Shahid promised he'd take her and their young cousins to see Ravan burning at the grounds after the milk ceremony.

Later at Latif's home, Ayesha seated Shaira and Mussavir on the settee. She then draped a red chiffon dupatta over Shaira's head and shoulders and placed a piece of barfi in her mouth. Shaira sat with her head bent, looking down all the time. Hibba then gave Mussavir the small box containing the ring Ayesha had bought at the goldsmith's. He opened it, took out the ring, and put it on Shaira's third finger on the left hand. It was all solemn and quiet. Even the children and Huma did not utter a word. Sabra placed a piece of barfi in Mussavir's mouth and kissed him on the forehead and gave him fifty-one silver shillings (the odd number for continuation) as salami, which is the first token gift by an in-law-to-be.

Dr Bashir asked all to raise their hands for prayers in the Muslim way and to pray for the couple's health, happiness, and long life, and for the union to be of great benefit for both families. Mussavir and Shaira joined in the prayers. Then the girls, including Jamila, started singing, and Ayesha took out a five-shilling note, passed it over the heads of the couple five times to ward off evil spirits, and recited a couplet from the Holy Book to fend off the devil, shaitan. The five-shilling note she gave to Latif to send to the mosque.

All congratulated Shaira and Mussavir. Sabra then brought out the ceremonial milk in small glasses with a sprinkling of pistachio and almond shavings floating on top. The first glass Sabra served to Dr Bashir and

In the Shadow of Kirinyaga

Ayesha, then she served the couple and all the others. The two were now officially engaged to be married.

At the rear of Latif's flat there was a long veranda with a wooden fence. It faced the back courtyard below as well as the big grounds opposite the Alexandra Cinema and the school where the effigy of Ravan was to be burnt at dusk. The effigy was actually ready and standing—a huge Ravan with a large head on which nine small heads with whiskers and hair were painted in black. The Ravan was made out of bamboo sticks and poles covered with crepe paper in black, yellow, red, and green. Thin kite paper had been used for some parts. It had been made lying flat on the ground and then raised up and held with rope supports pegged into the ground on four sides. It was colourful, but at twenty-two feet high, huge and grotesque and frightening to look at.

Huma, Salim, and Majid were eagerly awaiting Mussavir's departure, so they could then go to the grounds. Huma asked Zaffer for some money to buy aloo choleh from Santoo, a short man very well known for his spiced potato and boiled grams on festive occasions. He always wore a dark pink turban with a long shamla, white kamiz, and shalwar. He carried the tray of aloo choleh and chutney on his head on top of his turban and a bamboo stand in his hand. At the entrance of the grounds, together with vendors of pakoras, chakauries, samosas, and other goodies, he placed his tray on the stand and served his customers. He was quick and served the delicacy on a piece of paper, then spooned chutney over it. He had a round tin for people to put their money in. He was the most popular vendor at the schools.

Salim and Majid were excited, as Ravan was burnt only in Nairobi. The Hindu population was small at the coast. There the Muslim Idds were celebrated more vigorously, with pomp and fun fairs, by the Swahilis and Mshiris and Arabs who resided there. Therefore it was always said that if one wanted to celebrate Idd one should go to Mombasa, and for Divali to Nairobi.

From Latif's veranda there were also wooden steps leading down to the courtyard. Shaira came out and stood near the veranda railing. Mussavir joined her and pointed at the Ravan far away.

"Are you going to see it burn, poetess?" This was their first conversation since their engagement was announced.

"I used to go and see it when I was not in burqa."

"Pity I'm going before they start burning it or I would have taken you. Anyway, see that no Ravan carries you off while I'm away," he warned.

"Are you still worried?" She smiled and then added, "There should be no worry now."

"I would have been less worried if our nikah had been performed. But it was quite a fight even getting the engagement formalized."

He put his hand out and touched hers, which was on the bannister.

"Do you like the ring?" he asked.

"It's all right." Looking at it she said, "It fits me too."

"There was not much choice and this was the only one with a stone. I'll get you one from Somaliland if I go that way."

"Thanks. We must . . . go in now."

"I saw you coming out and waited for the girls to get back. I too have to get ready now. So good-bye, my poetess. Take care and don't study too hard. Remember me."

"I will," she said with a lump in her throat.

"I wish they had announced our engagement earlier, had given us at least one evening together."

She nodded.

"Were you surprised or did you know it would take place?"

"I was very surprised. How would I know? No one even asked me."

"They are terrible, aren't they?" He laughed and added, "I'll write to you as often as I can. The mail will take time but you must reply regularly."

"I'll try, but what will I write about? And it won't be long till you come back."

"Tell me everything. Even about your school activities. Yes, I hope to be back soon, but it will certainly not be before a year or so."

They heard voices, so Shaira moved her hand from under Mussavir's. He touched her cheek gently and said, "Bye, poetess. Remember, you are mine now. And," he emphasized, "I am a very possessive man!"

She smiled and went in. Mussavir remained there, looking down into the courtyard and towards the effigy of Ravan far away.

19

The Dream

AS THE TRAIN to Mombasa rolled away from the Nairobi railway station, Mussavir and the other travellers waved good-bye vigorously to their relatives and friends who had come to see them off. The train gathered speed, and Mussavir went into the cabin he was to share with his two doctor colleagues, Dr Gopalan and Dr Tara Chand, and another passenger. They rang for the steward and ordered drinks. Mussavir placed his briefcase and canvas bedding kit on top and they all sat on the lower berths of a four-berth second-class compartment.

Asians travelling by train could order drinks and coffee, tea and sandwiches in their cabins. But they could not go to the dining car, which was reserved only for European passengers. The non-Europeans also had to carry their own bedding. The four men all settled down and chatted over their drinks until suppertime.

Mussavir was in a peculiar state, halfway between happiness and sadness. He was sad he was going away from Nairobi so soon after his engagement to Shaira, but he was happy that his mother had at last persuaded Sabra to formalize the engagement. He was carrying with him vivid memories of both Nyeri and Nairobi and the short few minutes he had spent with Shaira. He tried to suppress his sadness by talking to his companions, and the beer helped. He was free now to indulge in drinking without fear of his father's discovery. This sense of freedom to smoke and drink was a tonic.

After supper, which they had all brought in boxes, and tea from the train, they settled down on their respective bunks. Mussavir kept smoking and lay awake for a long time. So much had happened in the last five weeks. When he came from India he was carefree, with practically no worries. He had passed his exams and become a doctor, which had pleased his parents a lot. He had come out to work in Kenya and East Africa as desired by them and himself. He had agreed to volunteer to go to Abyssinia after joining the government service, according to his father's wishes. Everything had gone as planned. Then his mother had brought up the subject of his marriage and Shaira appeared in Nyeri. A warm personal relationship had developed between them in a short time. He was still a bit surprised at himself and could not fully understand why he, a stable and sensible person, mature and grown-up, felt and acted like an adolescent boy. He had been overwhelmed by this love for Shaira, which a month earlier he would not have thought he was capable of.

In his college days and holidays in India he had had short and even long affairs with Christian and Anglo-Indian girls; the Muslim and Hindu girls were always aloof and distant in order to safeguard their virginity. It was easier to be friendly and even have affairs with married Muslim and, once in a while, Hindu women. In fact, affairs among married sisters-in-law and brothers-in-law were not uncommon. There were many songs about these affairs in the folklore. But it had to be on the quiet, as family honour had to be preserved. And in these relationships it was often the women who were the initiators, who knew when and where it was possible to meet. But there were accidents and occasions when secrecy was difficult, and when these relationships were discovered there were scandals and divorces and even beatings and thrashings, and in the villages some men even cut off the noses of their wives, daughters, or sisters if they were found to be having affairs with other men.

But much as he enjoyed and felt attached in these relationships for as long as they lasted, there was never any difficulty in dissolving them. He was lucky he had never had any unpleasant or embarrassing moments during his stay in India. As a student doctor he had become somewhat conservative and worried about diseases, so he kept away from prostitutes and suspicious characters. He knew lots of boys who suffered from venereal diseases and went to hakims for treatments, which were never pleasant.

There was quite a bit of homosexuality in the hostels among boys. But because of a bad childhood experience he kept away from boys. Once on holiday outside Hushiarpur his cousins had taken him to a grain store to show him something interesting. The door of the grain store was closed but there was a hole in the wooden door, and looking through it one could see what was going on inside.

His cousins all said one had to be very quiet as there were some older boys performing some tamasha; it was a secret and they made him promise not to tell anyone. His cousins and their friends formed a queue, and one by one each put his eye on the hole and peeped. They covered their mouths with their hands to stop their laughter, but then moved on to allow the next person to peep. Mussavir was the last in the queue, and when he put his eye to the hole he at first did not see anything but some gunny sacks stacked against the wall. Then, as his eye got used to the light, he saw two older boys, completely naked. Their naked bodies shone like the gunny sacks. One lay on his stomach and the other lay on top of him moving his buttocks in a sort of circular motion. Mussavir got scared and moved away quickly. He found the sight revolting and felt like throwing up. His cousins called him a sissy and said he was not a man. The sight still haunted him later in school.

Much later when he was an adolescent he told the wife of one of his cousins and she was very helpful. She gave him a lot of confidence and it was with her that he had his first really fulfilling sexual experience. Lying on the berth of the moving train he thought of India and then came back to Shaira.

Despite her shyness Shaira had reciprocated his feelings and had met him whenever possible at great risk of being found out. During their last meeting on the night of Latif's walima feast, even the last barrier between them could have been broken. He had never intended to go that far, but it nearly happened.

He then began to think of what lay ahead. There would be a lot of work in war conditions in the new country which, he understood, though independent, was still very primitive and even feudalistic. He would have to work far in the interior near the Italian border, where the fighting was taking place. It was not going to be a bed of roses, but he hoped it would not be too bad. With these thoughts he tried to sleep.

He began having a nasty dream. He and Shaira were chained to a rock and stones were being hurled at them by Shahid and his own brother, Ta'Ha. Shaira was screaming for help but he could not break his chains. His parents stood nearby but did not help. A huge black bull then appeared and tried to gore him. Mussavir kept struggling to break the chains but managed to free only one hand. He tried to catch the bull's horn but was unsuccessful. He could now hear people laughing and jeering loudly. He used all his strength to break away from the chains and felt a great jerk. He suddenly awoke from his sleep. The train was shunting and taking on new cabins at Voi. It hissed and groaned and threw out steam, then the engine gave a whistle and with another jerk it started moving faster and gathered speed.

Mussavir was perspiring all over when he awoke. He felt dry and thirsty. He put on his pyjama top and lowered himself down the ladder to get some water from the flask belonging to one of the other doctors. He drank a glass and then, opening the cabin door, went out into the passageway and stood looking out through the window. It was cooler here and he began to feel better.

He smoked a cigarette standing at the window and watched the shrubs and bushes fly past. There were signs of dawn so he went back to his bunk but could not sleep. He kept thinking of the dream. He was not superstitious; in fact, he always made fun of his mother when she worried about dreams. Now he wished she were there to tell him the meaning of his dream. He hoped Shaira was all right. He did not like Shahid much and he had a hunch Shahid resented him, but he had not even thought of Ta'Ha, so he was unable to fathom why he saw both of them in the dream. Then he thought he was being silly. It was just a dream. A lot was on his mind.

When he had been in his berth for about half an hour there was some movement down below. The others started getting up.

In the Shadow of Kirinyaga

"Would you like some tea, Dr Mussavir?" Gopalan asked.

"No, thank you, sir, I do not want any yet." He closed his eyes and dropped off and only got up when the train had reached Maryakani station. His companions were now fully dressed, had tied their bedding bags, and were looking out of the window. Maryakani was a bit more crowded as milk cans were normally loaded for Mombasa from the cattle ranches in the area. Bare-breasted women wearing grey pleated skirts carried small items like fruit and food to sell to the passengers. Mussavir got up and dressed, then wrapped his canvas bedding and, pushing his feet into his shoes, went to the small washroom at the end of the long passageway. Mombasa was only a couple of stations ahead.

"Anybody meeting you, Mussavir?" asked Tara Chand.

"I am staying with a friend of my father who works at the post office. He wrote to my father saying he'll meet me if free, otherwise I could take a taxi and go to his house."

"I am putting up at the Sikh gurdwara, which is in the town and not far from the shipping agents," said Tara Chand. He said Gopalan was staying with some South Indian friends.

"I think before going to the gurdwara we should make an appearance at the agents' and find out about embarkation times and other formalities," said Tara Chand. "Then we can relax and cool ourselves. Mombasa is not a place where you can move about much during the day and on foot."

"You are right," said Mussavir. "I think I had better join you both when you go to the shipping agents. We can take a taxi from the station."

Mussavir's father's friend was waiting at the station when the train finally rolled in and stopped. Mussavir introduced his friends, and Nazar Mohammed, a short man in a khaki uniform and red fez, welcomed them all. He offered to take them to the shipping office and after that drop the others wherever they wanted to go. The office was not far from Fort Jesus. After reporting and getting instructions for the next day, Mussavir and his friends parted and arranged to meet in town in one of the tea rooms by teatime.

20

Mombasa Island

AFTER A COLD SHOWER, breakfast, and rest at his father's friend's home, Mussavir dressed in a light pair of trousers and a white open-collared shirt. Then, in his tennis shoes, he strolled lazily through the narrow but colourful streets and lanes of the old Mombasa bazaar. In this section of the city most of the shops belonged to shrewd, bearded Arabs and their cunning underlings the Mshiris. They sold jewellery and attar, and leather goods, incense and Persian rugs, brassware and pottery, all brought by dhows from the Middle East and India. Men strolled about in long white khanzus and white caps, holding their sandlewood tasbihs in their hands. The Arab and Mashiri women, with their kohl-lined eyes and wearing musk and exotic Middle Eastern perfumes, were wrapped in black buibuis, a whiff of the scent passing with them.

The kahawa sellers wandered about with big brass pots fitted over charcoal braziers to keep the coffee hot and steaming. They held the brass pot in one hand and with the other they rattled the small cups, stopping to serve coffee to whomsoever wanted to buy. A number of small mosques of all denominations were scattered in that area too. Old Arab men and Swahili shehes with their tasbihs sat on cement terraces outside the whitewashed residential buildings and the mosques.

Mussavir leisurely strolled out of the old Mombasa bazaar near the vegetable market on Salim Road, where he stopped to have a glass of fresh cold orange juice at one of the Indian juice stalls. The Salim Road area was much warmer than the old city lanes. The sun shone brightly and the buildings were not high enough to keep the sun away.

From the market down to Kilindini Road most of the shops belonged to Indians, mainly Ismailis, Hindus, and Sindhis. There was also the odd Arab or Sikh shop. Fancy goods as well as sports goods were sold in these shops. A tea house and a couple of hotels strictly for Europeans were situated on Kilindini Road. There was the well-known Manor Hotel, very exclusive and always full of up-country farmers, businessmen, and other Europeans. The other two hotels nearby were usually patronized by sailors from all over Europe, the United States, and South Africa. Many ships called at Mombasa harbour, cargo ships as well as luxury liners, BI and Union Castle ships among others.

The oldest and most exclusive institution of all was the Mombasa Club, situated at the lower end of Fort Jesus Road with the huge old fort, built by the Portuguese in the twelfth century, towering over the cliff. The Mombasa Club faced the sea and had a private beach. It was at this club where most of the British aristocrats and lords who lived up country, as well as the visiting ones from England, often stayed.

Colourful kiosks run by half-caste Arabs and Mshiris were always full of fresh tropical fruit: mangoes, oranges, tangerines, pineapples, bananas, papaya, and of course coconuts, both the pulpy green ones called madafu and the full-grown brown ones. Sailors and tourists walked about freely, buying fruit and drinking coconut juice in the open verandas and terraces.

Despite the heat, Mussavir thoroughly enjoyed the walk. The coast had a special atmosphere, and he felt light and happy. He and his colleagues had agreed to meet at one of the Indian tea shops, the kind the Indians could go to on Salim Road. Tara Chand and Gopalan were already there when Mussavir made his appearance. Like Mussavir, they were dressed in very light trousers and open-collar shirts. Tara Chand, plump and light skinned, had a round face. Like Mussavir, he wore tennis shoes, but Gopalan, dressed in a light blue safari suit, wore sandals and a cloth cap. He was fairly dark, his eyes deep set, and he had an aquiline nose. They compared notes about their impressions of the town, both old and new.

They went into one of the cubicles in the tea house where there was a fan on the ceiling and ordered fruit juice and later tea. There was a table for five in the cubicle but there were not many people even in the main hall so the doctors had it to themselves.

Gopalan, a South Indian who had been in South Africa before, remarked, "Why is it the East African Indians are not enterprising?"

"What do you mean by that, Doctor Sahib?" both Tara Chand and Mussavir asked almost in unison. Mussavir smiled and Tara Chand continued, "They work jolly hard and do not lead easy lives. At times they are exposed to serious dangers in the rural areas and the interior."

Tara Chand, like Mussavir, was from Northern India and the Punjab. And, like most Punjabis, a bit impulsive.

"I don't mean workwise," said Gopalan. "You are right in what you say, but what I am wondering about is that although they have been here for a number of years they have not thought of making decent hotels for themselves, or even clubs for that matter. In contrast, the Indians in the South have done much more for themselves. Here the Indians, and all Asians for that matter, grumble about the colour bar and being refused admission to European hotels but don't do anything themselves. I am told even their sick have to be hospitalized in the wing of the African hospital."

Tara Chand responded defensively again: "Well, the number of Indians in East Africa is not as big as in the South. We do not have the rich merchants like they have. The majority of the Asians here are artisans or craftsmen or involved in petty businesses. The few professionals, the teachers, doctors, and lawyers, all work for the government, which recruited them. They are all family minded. They are not the types who want to sit in clubs and go to hotels."

"You mean they are not sophisticated enough to want to take their wives out?" Mussavir asked Tara Chand and smiled.

"Well, in a way, yes. Most Muslim women are in purdah and even the Hindus, though not in purdah, don't go out to clubs and hotels. They are family minded, as I have said. And for the men there are sports clubs for Indians and Goans. In fact, the railways that employ many Indians and Goans have separate clubs for them."

"No. It's not that. Neither of you have understood what I am trying to say," said Gopalan. "Look at us three, we have come from Nairobi and are putting up with friends and relatives or gurdwaras because the hotels one has access to are so third class and shabby. If there was some decent hotel we could have stayed there and been more independent."

"You are right," said Mussavir, "but as my friend Tara Chand has just said, our numbers are not that large to require separate hotels. If we had access to the already existing hotels it would be all right."

"But even back in India we do not have access to many hotels," said Gopalan, "and I do not see it happening here. The British will never make the Europeans open their hotels to us, therefore we should do something ourselves."

"Would that not in a way be accepting separate racial development?" asked Mussavir.

"Well, we are already a caste-conscious society, so what difference will race separation make?" said Gopalan.

"I don't agree. The existing hotels should be opened to all in a democratic society." Mussavir was emphatic.

"It would be too risky, will be the argument," added Tara Chand.

"What's the risk?" Mussavir questioned.

"If they allow Asians they will also have to allow Africans," said Tara Chand.

"And why not? This is an African country," Mussavir said.

"Oh, yaar, I can't see that happening for years, if at all. Not, I am afraid, in our lifetime." Tara Chand wagged his head from side to side.

"But you know in a way it is also our fault," said Mussavir. "We never agitate or ask for things. We not only accept the situation as it is but also lend ourselves very easily to this racial segregation. It is probably a legacy of our caste system." He went on to say that the South African Indians, despite their early agitation and the fight that Mahatma Gandhi put up with his civil disobedience, and Satyagrahis filling up jails in order to change the laws against the registration of Asians, had cooled down and started having their own separate hotels, clubs, and even hospitals. "I have never been there so don't know much. But if what Gopalan says is true, then they seem to have accepted separate development for each race."

"Oh, my friend, you are not exactly right," said Tara Chand. "We have had agitators all right. I agree we did not have a Gandhi, but we did not have a General Smuts either, or the Black Act or laws which overnight made our mothers concubines instead of wives. The British here accepted the Indian religious marriages, even polygamy. But we have people like Khawaja Shamusdeen, Isher Das, Barrister Mangat, Giddumal, Saleh Mohamed Ladda, Dr De Souza, Pinto, and many others who often make noises both in the Legco as well as in the press. And not only now, but also in the past and after the Great War, when there was prosperity in the country, a lot of public amenities and parks with the statue of Victoria were provided by the various Indian communities, by men like Alladina Visram, Suleman Virjee, and the Jivanjees."

"In fact, that made the Europeans very jittery and fearful. They were scared that the Indians would overpower them politically," Mussavir added, now agreeing with what Tara Chand was telling Gopalan. "There was quite a radical element in the Indian leadership; it pressed for representation according to their numbers and the proportion they paid of the town's rates."

It was now Tara Chand who nodded and agreed with Mussavir, who continued: "My father always talks of those times. In fact, the Indians even boycotted the municipal council for a number of years and withheld payment of rates on the grounds that services were not allocated fairly, and Indians were always offered subordinate status."

Gopalan, sipping his tea, put the cup down and said he had heard something about that in South Africa when still at school. "The Europeans even plotted to kidnap the then governor!"

Both Mussavir and Tara Chand nodded and guffawed, then Tara Chand said that, yes, there was that threat. "It seems the town clerk—Ainsworth—invited more Indians than Europeans to serve on the municipal council." He paused for a moment to cough.

"Yes, yes," Mussavir butted in, saying the Europeans were so incensed they rallied support from missionaries, cajoled, threatened, and even plotted to kidnap the governor. They lobbied in London for restriction of Indian immigration and asked for segregation in residential areas because their attempts at commercial segregation had failed!

Tara Chand, who had recovered from his coughing after a sip of tea, said, "Oh, the Europeans even tried to boycott the Indian traders. They did not want common roll franchise. In this they were supported by the Kenyan government. In fact, Barrister Mangat even wrote some plays about the situation. So no one can say that the people did not try."

But he said he agreed that the majority of the Indians were so involved in their businesses that they were apathetic. They lived in conclaves among their own kind and sects in watertight compartments, did their day's work, and spent their leisure time at home. They attended their own places of worship—the mosques, mandirs, gurdwaras, and churches. Some of these had mussafir khanas, or guest houses, attached to them, where one could live at a small cost. He thought the Indians felt more secure that way. Their only recreation was the cinema, and there were quite a few movie houses in Kenya owned by Indians.

Both Tara Chand and Mussavir told Gopalan that many Indians in Kenya were leftovers from the railway builders who came at the turn of the century. Some went back and some died of malaria and blackwater fever. Many were eaten by lions. The descendants of those that remained asked the government to be allotted land to become small farmers but were refused. It was then they moved far into the interior to remote places and opened up small businesses to buy produce from small African farmers for export or use within the country. They also started petty trading. The Kenyan government encouraged them in that, because the Europeans were not prepared to indulge in trade, and those that did were dismal failures.

The Indians thus helped to open up the country, and the British found it easy and helpful to have them around. The Europeans were either farmers or had white-collar jobs in towns. Professional Indians came much later, among them lawyers and doctors from India.

"The British," said Mussavir, "were clever and made good use of the Indians and in return gave them freedom to build mosques, temples, churches, and even allowed them to buy property in certain areas, but they did not allow them to go into agriculture or mix with them socially. They kept apart and aloof and are ruling here just as they are ruling in India. Oh yes, they have given grants towards schools, but in that too there are racial divisions. Indians go to Indian schools and Africans to African schools. And the education for both the Indians and Africans is inferior."

The trio kept discussing the situation in Kenya and in the process had several cups of tea and filled all the ashtrays with cigarette butts.

"I have always thought of Kenya as my country and home even though I have studied and lived more in India than here. I want to live here and work here too. That is, if I come back alive!" Mussavir said and laughed.

"Were you born here?" Gopalan asked.

"Oh yes, I was born in Nairobi, but we lived in many small towns. I always found the countryside beautiful and peaceful and when growing up one tended to take things for granted."

"Like what?" asked Tara Chand, who was not born in Kenya but came when he was twelve years old.

"Well, one accepted the Europeans as the natural rulers. One was very fond of house servants and ayahs and the ordinary people one came into contact with, but one remained somewhat indifferent towards the Africans as a whole. In fact, one felt superior in a way. Yaar, it was only when I went to college and started taking an interest in Indian politics and thinking for myself that I found the situation in this country and even our attitude towards it ridiculous."

"I know what you mean," said Tara Chand, "but we have not succeeded in India, so this place has no hope whatsoever. The present structure will remain for a long time. Maybe in fifty or so years the African will rise up himself and demand his rights, like the Indians are doing now in India."

"Why fifty years? It will come much quicker," said Gopalan. "I hear there was a lot of trouble in the early twenties when Harry Thukku formed the African Association in 1919 and travelled round the country addressing large gatherings."

"Yes, I remember my father talking about the Kipande riots, and about Harry Thukku's arrest in 1922 when he was taken to the police lines near Norfolk Hotel," Mussavir added.

"It is already legendary," said Tara Chand. "The Africans, it seems, gathered in their thousands and went on a two-day strike. They sat and sang hymns and chanted prayers. When asked to disperse they refused and the police opened fire and many Africans were killed. Harry Thukku was exiled to Kismayo and the other man, the general secretary, Kenyatta, left the country. In fact, he is still abroad in Europe or England. The movement was of course quickly quelled."

"Yes," added Mussavir. "The two even shared a platform with the congress leaders from India when they came. The Europeans were very angry then too and feared the Indians were going to take over Kenya and East Africa!"

The doctors did not realize they had been in the tea room for over an hour. The place would soon be closing. They got up, paid at the counter, and left the hotel.

"It's much cooler now, yaar," said Mussavir. "Let's go to the lighthouse side and have a glimpse of the Indian Ocean."

"How far is it?" asked Gopalan.

"Not very far," said Tara Chand. "But we can catch a bus from right here. It's breezy. The tide must be coming in."

They walked a few yards to the bus stop and waited. There were more people now on the pavement as it was cooler and people had come out for walks. Some of the shops were closed while others were still open and carrying on with their business.

The bus was quite full as most people went to the seaside in the evening to witness the sunset and enjoy the cool sea air. The doctors managed to get seats at the back and, passing the Star of the Sea Mission School on their right, the bus went down the road towards the seafront. The tide was coming in and many boats, big and small, were in the harbour. The bus dropped them at the terminal near a few baobab trees with sea herons perched on their bare brown branches.

The trio walked along the promenade. They feasted their eyes on the lashing waves and deep blue sea and the vast number of people of all colours and shades who had descended there for the sea air. It seemed as if the whole of the Asian community was there: women in colourful saris and buibuis and girls in frilly dresses, men in light clothes and printed shirts all marching up and down the sea front. Some had filled the benches and cement terraces and still others lazed on the grass and gazed at the sights.

The next morning when Mussavir reached the shipping agents with his colleagues they were met by a European doctor, an old retired colonial from India. He was to be their leader. He told them embarkation would take place at three in the afternoon and the French boat on which they were travelling would leave during the night and take them to the port of Djibouti, from where they would travel by train to Addis Ababa.

"Yaar, the train is going to take five days to reach Addis," Tara Chand, looking not very happy, said to his companions.

"Yes, that is long," said Mussavir.

"But the French boat we are travelling in is a big liner headed for France," said Gopalan.

"That should be interesting then. Lots to drink. French wines and who knows what other interesting things too!"

"Maybe." Tara Chand shrugged his shoulders. "But the train from Djibouti is going to be not only crowded but also slow and tedious, not like our frontier mail in India."

"How do you know?" asked Mussavir

"It's common knowledge in Nairobi and I heard this at the Red Cross headquarters. They said since the crisis developed, every train from Djibouti goes loaded with its quota of adventurers, journalists, and mercenaries, as well as genuine volunteers of all kinds. Like moths around a lamp, they are pouring into the country despite embargoes and difficulties. All kinds of European, Slav, and even Turkish mercenaries have surfaced. Some of them are being sent to Harar to replace the Belgians. I hope there is room for us or we'll have to roast in Djibouti, which they say can be like a furnace with no air at all."

"How absolutely marvellous!" exclaimed Mussavir.

21

Mussavir Writes

TWO DAYS AFTER Mussavir and his companions left Nairobi, Dr Bashir rushed back to Sabra's home where his wife and their daughters were packing and getting ready for the home journey the next day.

"Very good news, my dear," he said to Ayesha, "I'm so relieved. Allah Almighty has answered my prayers so quickly, and to my great satisfaction." He looked up towards the ceiling and, moving towards the door, he turned and added, "I had better offer two prostrations in thanks immediately." He went to his prayer mat without even telling her what he was thankful to God for.

Hibba and Farida were surprised and Ayesha made a questioning gesture, but Dr Bashir was already on his prayer mat. When he finished, she asked, "Pray, what wish of yours has Allah granted? May we know too?"

"Oh, I'm sorry. There is a job vacancy for Ta'Ha, and guess where?" He smiled.

Ayesha looked thoughtful, then her eyes glowed: "In Nyeri?"

"Almost. Next door, in Karatina."

"Are you sure?"

"Yes, I saw the department head, and after learning that Ta'Ha had done his intermediate studies, he confirmed it straightaway."

"That's really good," Ayesha said, expressing her relief. She told her daughters their father had been under a lot of stress, with Mussavir leaving and the uncertainty about Ta'Ha. He did not talk about it, but he must be truly relieved. She hoped Ta'Ha would work hard and not let his father down. Railways were good to work for and looked after their workers well.

Together with Jamila the Bashir family headed for Nyeri the next day. Latif was to follow in a week's time for one week's holiday.

After its turmoil, Sabra's home began to get back to normal. The Mombasa cousins, Majid and Salim, went home as their holidays had come to an end. Huma and Honey, too, started school. Shaira still had a week to go before her school started.

After Jamila and Latif returned from Nyeri they often visited Sabra. Jamila liked Shaira and respected Sabra like a mother. Latif told Sabra he had found a small house in the Pangani area where his boss and son lived and which was not too far from Sabra. He said Jamila did not like it very much in the town. She wanted to be nearer people she knew. She was already friendly with Attia, his boss's daughter-in-law.

Now that the familiar routine was established, Sabra felt she had to inform her husband's father and brothers about Shaira's engagement to Mussavir. The matter had been weighing on her mind for many days and could be postponed no longer. She did not want a third party to write to them before she did. She discussed the matter with her sons and asked how best to write. She had got a photograph about Mussavir from Ayesha before she left in order to send it with the letter. She collected her writing pad and pen and sat at the dining table one evening to compose a letter. Zaffer was reading the paper nearby. Sabra asked him what she should say.

"What is there to say, Ami? Just tell them that all of us, including Shaira, like Mussavir. He is presentable and wholesome, a doctor with good prospects and all that, you know . . ."

"I can't say Shaira likes him, and . . ." Sabra glowered at Zaffer and curled her nose.

"Ami, Shaira's liking him is most important. She has to live with him when all is said and done."

"Yes, but they will all start insinuating we have hurried with the engagement, maybe it was a love match. I don't want anyone pointing fingers at my daughter."

"Then tell them exactly what happened and omit Shaira's liking him. Tell them he was going to the war and his parents wanted some shagoon to formalize the engagement before he left. You might add, Ami, that we are lucky, as good matches are not easily available. He could easily have got another girl. We did not want to lose him." That said, Zaffer went back to his paper.

"No, it is not dignified to put it like that, as if to say we had put our Shaira on the marriage market." Sabra's sharp retort made Zaffer look at her again.

"Then put it in your own way, Ami. You are normally quite good at it."

Shahid, who had been sitting with a cup of tea, broke his silence and said he did not want to contradict them but he felt a bit uneasy. He had heard that Mussavir, for all his marvellous qualities, had one great fault. He was fond of alcohol and could drink excessively. He was not sure of his morals either. Zaffer defended Mussavir, saying he was all right and did not drink more than most young men who indulged. "We must not lose perspective, Shahid. You have a habit of being judgmental, which is not very good. The good in the man far outweighs the one little bad habit, if you can even call drinking a glass of beer once in a while a habit."

"That little habit, Bhaijan, is haraam, strictly forbidden in Islam," Shahid said. He knew that Zaffer himself indulged, about which his mother had no knowledge.

Sabra was busy writing and did not even look up or hear what Shahid had said. She had found the right words to convey the news to her old father-in-law.

When Shaira started school, Sabra received a letter from their landlord saying he had sold the Nairobi house, as he had decided to remain in India where he had gone to visit. The new owner would require vacant possession of the premises. He was therefore giving her a month's notice to vacate. The family, though surprised at this sudden development, did not weep or groan. They admitted it was a nice house, in a less crowded area with grounds and a garden, but it was too far from the town and schools. They immediately began looking for another house. Many houses had been built in Nairobi before the Depression and were still available. After seeing several in the Pangani and Fairview areas, they found a semidetached one on Forest Road and moved there. Huma was sorry; she would miss her friend Munni and would also miss visiting Masi Jantey and her orchard of ancient fruit trees. But she was happy that City Park, one of the largest and most well-tended parks, with beautiful lawns and flowerbeds and swings and a bandstand, was very near the new place.

The new house was part of a two-gabled building with a common garden in front and a common courtyard at the rear. The two houses had three bedrooms each and two bathrooms, and bucket-type toilets in the courtyard. A Shia Ithanashari couple and their eight-year-old daughter, Batul, lived in one room of the other house. The other two rooms were occupied by an Ismaili Khoja family with three children. This was not unusual, as some people could not afford to rent a whole house. But the unusual thing with these families was that although both families were Shia Muslims, they were from different sects. Normally these two sects did not mix with one another. In fact, the Ismailis, who were the followers of the Aga Khan, would not even drink a glass of water from an Ithanashari home. So it was surprising that these two families were civil and polite to one another, and that both welcomed Sabra and her family. Batul was Huma's age and they soon became pals. The children of the Ismaili family were three boys, ages five, three, and nine months.

No sooner had they settled then Mwangi got news of his father's death and was required to go back to Kiambu and look after his father's shamba and other matters. He was the eldest son. Sabra and her children were sorry to lose Mwangi. He had been with them for many years and was familiar with their routine and was an honest person. But they had to let him go. After unsuccessfully trying a Kamba and a Maragoli, someone at Zaffer's office recommended a Jaluo named Odera. Mwangi, like most Kikuyus, had warned Sabra not to engage a Luo from Lake Victoria. "They are snooty, Mama, and don't like to work for Indians. They are also not trustworthy." A Luo worker on the other hand would say the same about a Kikuyu. In fact, a Luo would go one step further and say the Luo were a cut above the others. People avoided engaging Kikuyu and Luo workers together in the same house. In actual fact they were both good and hard workers but had age-old rivalries, and so the wars of words went on.

Sabra and Zaffer decided to give Odera a trial. He was neat and clean, a tall man with thick features. He was also much darker than Mwangi and had good references on his kipande, which all Africans working as domestic workers had to carry for record of their work and comments by employers. He seemed a pleasant person, was good with young people, and was single.

After trying him for a week, Zaffer and Sabra engaged him and he moved over to the workers' quarter, which Mwangi and his family had vacated. Odera was a quick worker. He washed and ironed all the clothes well and had no taboos about women's clothes either. His cooking was not as good as Mwangi's, but he was willing to learn. He was very talkative and spoke Swahili in a funny way which made the children laugh. But Odera himself laughed even louder at his own pronunciations. He loved singing and was always humming and whistling tunes. He had a small mouth organ on which he always played English and Swahili and even Indian tunes after work. Sabra recited the Holy Quran every morning, loudly, and at times Huma and Honey joined her. Odera in no time picked up the tunes and would mimic and recite the Arabic ayats and suras while working. He was also quick in picking up Punjabi, Hindustani, Gujerati, and even Kutchi tunes which Huma or the neighbors' children sometimes sang. Some evenings after work he would sit outside his door on a three-legged wooden stool in the courtyard and smoke a foot-long pipe, keeping his arm stretched to hold the head of the pipe in his palm. He would tell Huma, Honey, and the neighbours' children about his home in Kisumu and of boats and fishing in Lake Victoria. The children picked up a lot of Luo words from him. The Kikuyu words and phrases learnt from Mwangi and Mama Wanjiro, like "Ati rey rey, nekwega mno," were replaced by "O mera! Idi kanye. Kel bando, odek!" and so on. Zaffer told the children that in Kisumu all Jaluos, not only men but even women, smoked such pipes.

Ta'Ha, Dr Bashir's youngest son, arrived and stayed with Latif and Jamila.

He visited Sabra's new home before going to Nyeri. He talked with Zaffer and Shahid and gave Shaira a small present. She had met him before and felt warm towards him as he resembled Mussavir in looks, though she thought Mussavir was more handsome and far more pleasant than Ta'Ha, who was a bit serious.

Shaira received her first letter from Mussavir; he had posted it at Djibouti before leaving for Addis Ababa. It was written in Urdu and he requested that she reply in Urdu as it would help her in her study of the language. Mussavir had fine handwriting and he had penned a long letter. She was surprised and amused that he addressed her as "My Poetess" and started by telling her about the train journey to Mombasa and then the sea voyage to Djibouti in French Somaliland.

The ship's journey was a disappointment of the highest order despite being a French boat generally reputed to be good. It was a small poky cargo boat and the deck where we were supposed to spend most of our day hours was more a hold than a real deck. There was a top deck but only for the ship's officers. The only passenger allowed there was the Colonel, who was as unfriendly and lousy as the ship.

Tara Chand and I were seasick the first evening and part of the next day, too. We slept on the deck as the cabin was hot. Gopalan was cool and collected. He slept in the cabin! I have travelled many times from Bombay to Mombasa in a British ship with my parents and alone and not once did I fall seasick, so was surprised when I was the first to get sick on this boat.

We were so happy when we disembarked in Djibouti towards the evening when it was cooler. The ship docked at a bare dock with hardly any big buildings as is usual in harbours. Apart from open lorries there were some long-bodied saloon cars without hoods and red and blue and even yellow in colour. The drive to the town, in an open-hooded taxi, was pleasant. There was a breeze from the sea. And we saw the sunset on the horizon, the sun suddenly dropping away as if sinking into a yellow sea.

But Djibouti was like a tandoor at full heat! The heat was so excruciating that, by God, the three days spent in Djibouti were not only tiresome, hot, and dreary but also depressing. We were forced to remain in the hotel rooms with rickety fans which squeaked like the unoiled wheels of an oxcart in India. We only dared to go out in the late late afternoon and early evening when it was bearable. But on the whole the place was so different from anything I have experienced. It is desertlike. Yet it is full of people of all kinds who have arrived by boat or road, soldiers, and foreign journalists coming from or going to Addis Ababa, by the only train, which takes five days to reach there. They say ever since the Italian invasion the Emperor is getting help from wherever he can. So we shall be travelling in a crowded train.

The few Frenchmen we met were odd. And apathetic. And certainly less suave than the British colonials. They never work after midday. The whole place was in siesta until four in the afternoon! Some villas in the Rue de Beauchamps looked as if newly painted but it is doubtful if the paint will withstand the intense heat. We were told the diplomats live out in the suburbs in big villas. The roads are sandy. One of the Indians told Gopalan that "Djibouti" means "my handiya," a casserole, in the language of the Afars. A common joke here is that not only the mosquitoes and flies but also other insects seem tired and sleepy! The hotel staff keep sprinkling water on the floors to keep them cool.

So much for the French. My poor poetess, I hope I am not sounding a bore myself by moaning so much.

The Afars and Issas too are very different from our Somalis in Kenya. Our guide told us they are mostly from the nomadic people. No urgency about anything. One habit they have in common with the Kenyan Somalis is the constant chewing of khat, which in Kenya we call marungi. The people of Meru in the Frontier Province chew it day and night. The men in Djibouti are all addicted to it like Indians in India are to paans.

In the evenings when the heat was less intense we all moved about in the main square, which was much better than other places, with lots of pavement cafes as well as shops. Journalists from all over the world sat in these cafes and chatted and drank gallons of liquids of all kinds. The French food is surprisingly tastier than the English cuisine. But meat, vegetables, fruit, eggs, and milk are imported. Even the drinking water comes from France! Nothing grows here. I was surprised they have no mango or date trees, and palm trees are scarce too.

We saw a few Indian shops and even women wearing saris and men in dhotis and black caps. Trust the Indian banyas to venture into French territory! The local women are tall and big chested and wear colourful prints like the Somali women in Kenya.

I am sure you are working at your lessons without interruption and with satisfaction, but I hope you will find time to write back and give me all the news as I shall be very lonely otherwise. The mail might not be too regular, but the letters will eventually reach me wherever I am. I'll write again from Addis Ababa. Well, my poetess, I think of you a lot and send you all my love.

Yours, Mussavir

Shaira was delighted. She had not expected such a long and interesting letter. She enjoyed reading about Djibouti and hoped he would write about Abyssinia in the same manner. She read and reread the letter. That night and in school the next day, she kept thinking of him and hoped to get another letter soon. She told Miss Almeida, her Goan teacher of Geography and History, about the letter she had received from Mussavir and asked her if she had a map of that part of Africa. The teacher said she should look up the Horn of Africa and lent her an old atlas. She even opened it and showed Shaira the part of Abyssinia and the various parts of Somaliland which the Great Powers had dished out to themselves after the Suez Canal was built. The heartland of Abyssinia was a vast mountainous plateau, split with gorges, escarpments, and peaks. The Somali deserts were to the east and the jungles of the Upper Nile were in the west. The dry and hot wastelands of Kenya lay in the south.

"Seems a very big country, Miss," said Shaira.

"Oh yes, and its history goes back to biblical times. Tigre or Axam," she pointed a finger at the place on the page, "was the original capital and the religious and cultural centre of the Empire, in fact, the legendary birthplace of the first Emperor Menelick I, son of King Solomon and the Queen of Sheba. Tigre borders the Italian colony of Eritrea in the Northern Province. But the most important place is the Sultanate of Harar, which was governed by Menelick's cousin, Ras Makonen, who added vast portions of Somali grazing lands known as the Ogaden. Ras Makonen's son Ras Tafari, now known as Haile Selassie, the present Emperor, was born in Harar five years after its conquest."

Later, when Shaira tried to compose a letter to Mussavir in Urdu, it was not so easy. She did not even know how to address him! In Urdu the title had to be formal and to the point. It was not as in English, where you just started "Dear so and so." Everybody was not a dear. In fact, the word "dear" was hardly used. She decided she would consult Jamila and ask her how to address him.

22

New Home and Neighbourhood

"JAMILA BHABI, HOW does one address one's fiancé in Urdu?" Shaira asked Jamila when the two were together at Sabra's new home.

"Well, in Urdu male and female are both called 'mangayter'," replied Jamila, looking up from her knitting.

"Does one really use that mouthful of a word?"

"Oh no, silly," Jamila grinned widely. "One does not say exactly that, but supposing I had to write to Latif, I would say, 'Sar taj man, salamat'."

"What! 'Sar taj man'? 'Crown of my head'? And 'salamat', may you live forever? Both in Persian?"

"Literally translated they do mean that and sound funny, but that is how one addresses one's husband or beloved."

"But I'm not married yet. I'm not sure if I want to use that wet title even afterwards." Shaira raised her brows.

"But you will marry him one day. So it does not matter," Jamila said, shrugging her shoulders.

"Sounds rather stupid to me. You know he wants me to write in Urdu, and I want to, but I find Urdu titles flowery and also mushy."

"Why don't you just say 'Mere mehboob', or 'Jannam'?" Jamila said smiling.

"No . . . My beloved, my life, all again in Persian and Arabic. I'm not even good at Urdu, so I don't want to jump to Persian and Arabic."

"Let it be Urdu then, say, 'Mere ham safar' or 'Mere sathi', 'Mere devta', or 'Mere malik'!" rattled off Jamila. "There are so many nice titles, no end to them."

Shaira burst out laughing then said, "My goodness, Bhabi, you want me to raise him to the high heavens, make him a demigod? My fellow-traveller, my lord, my master, my companion!" Shaira began to laugh.

"Well, he is going to be your mujazi khuda, isn't he?" Jamila said. "It means God on earth, you madcap."

"Oh, do shut up, Bhabi," Shaira said, trying to stop her giggles. "You seem to have swallowed a dictionary. That's enough, or I'll break my sides laughing." Then composing herself, she added, "I'm sorry, but I don't like these flowery titles. My God on earth, my owner! As if I am going to be his slave."

"But Urdu and Persian are flowery languages and not cold like English," Jamila retorted.

"At least English keeps you down to earth," Shaira said, and they both laughed again.

When Shaira did eventually write, she skipped the title, hoping that by the time she finished she might have decided on one of the simpler ones. She, did, however, tell Mussavir about the suggested titles by Jamila and asked him if he could help her choose one. She thanked him for the long and most interesting letter. She was sorry he did not enjoy the voyage on the ship and hoped the train journey would be less tiresome and the climate in Addis Ababa cooler. She had heard the altitude was high. She wanted him to write all about Addis Ababa and other places if he visited them. She also wrote that she was finding it frightfully difficult to write in Urdu. He should not laugh at her many mistakes.

Then she told him of the move to the new house, where there were no places like the water tank of the old house. It was also not in the shadow of any mountain. They lived on flat land opposite the Forest Road Christian graveyard. There were lots of eucalyptus and pepper trees, which were shady. She also told him about Odera and how amusing he was. She finished by saying she missed him more than she had thought she would, and at times found it difficult to concentrate on her studies, especially when she got news that there was heavy fighting going on all around him. She was praying for his safety and hoped he would come back soon. She signed: "A poetess in name only."

Huma and Honey settled well in the new abode and soon made friends in the neighbourhood. Huma and Batul, in fact, were always together at one another's home or out at play. Batul went to the Muslim Girls School in Gyan Singh's shamba off Race Course Road, by the school bus. Huma and Shaira went to the Government Indian Girls School, which was on the main Government Road and opposite Jivanjee Gardens. They both walked the three miles there and back. Honey's school was quite far too. He went with Shahid on the bicycle and got a ride back from a neighbour whose son attended the same school. During the long rains the girls took a bus from Pangani, which was not far from the house.

Sabra and her family had been in the new place for about a month before the celebration of Idd ul Azha, the big Idd commemorating the sacrifice of Abraham. Normally Sabra got two sheep or rams for slaughtering, one each for herself and Zaffer, the two adults, as was obligatory in the Muslim religion. That year she told Zaffer, "We have to get three animals, my son."

Zaffer, who was never keen on slaughtering animals at home, asked, "Why three?"

"Shahid is now of age and working."

"Yes, but it will be such a mess slaughtering so many, and moreover, the sheep and goats are more expensive now. Almost double the price." Zaffer thought the price might change her mind.

"It's a religious obligation, Son, and has to be performed. I have kept some money aside and can let you have the extra. I am told they cost fifteen shillings each this year."

"Let's send one to be slaughtered at some mosque, so that the meat can be distributed among the poor. The other two for friends and neighbours and family use can be slaughtered at home as we always do."

"Yes, that seems a good idea," said Sabra.

On the morning of the Idd day, the family got up early and bathed and dressed for the special occasion. Huma had a new set of clothes, in blue, and Shaira wore the suit and jewellery she had worn for the Ghai girl's wedding at Nyeri. Sabra dressed in her simple but neat white shalwar kamiz. Zaffer wore a suit instead of the tweed jacket he often wore, and Shahid, too, had a dark suit on. Honey wore a blazer over his long grey trousers. The children had some breakfast, but the grown-ups were fasting and would break their fast after the sacrifice.

There was less activity and excitement on this Idd than Idd ul Fitr, the festival after the month of Ramadan, when people and particularly the young anxiously looked for the new moon's appearance on the previous night. That Idd can only be celebrated after someone has actually sighted the moon. At times, when no moon is sighted on the first night, there is no holiday on that day and Idd is observed on the following day. So everybody, old and young, black, white, and brown, has to know if the moon had been sighted to find out if it is a holiday. There were a few sects of Muslims who followed the calendar and observed the day according to the date, even if the moon was not sighted. However, the majority of Muslims, particularly in the tropics, followed the tradition of sighting the moon.

The Idd commemorating the sacrifice fell exactly two lunar months and ten days after the Ramadan Idd. Odera was the only person excited. He went in and out of the house fetching hot water and making breakfast for Huma and Honey and chatting away, asking about the festival and what it was for, why the animals were slaughtered. When Zaffer explained to him it was to commemorate the sacrifice of Abraham and his son, he said, "Ala, kumbe? Is that so?" with wide eyes. "I didn't know Muslims believed in Abraham and his son Issack."

"It's not Issack but Ishmael, the son of his second wife, Hajrah," Ayesha told him.

"Did he sacrifice two sons then?"

"The Christians believe it was Issack and the Muslims say it was the second son, Ishmail," Zaffer told him.

"But it's good the Waislamus sacrifice goats and distribute them to the poor. The Christians should slaughter pigs," he said, and before he could ask more there was a call from the next-door neighbour's worker saying the butcher's lorry had come to deliver the goats. He was required to receive the goats and tether them in the courtyard.

The family then trooped to the mosque for Idd prayers and to hear a special sermon heard in mosques all over the world. When they came back within an hour, Zaffer and Shahid went to the backyard to slaughter the animals. Odera and one of the other workers helped to hold the animals down, one at a time, at the edge of the open drain near the water tap outside. Sabra said a prayer and touched the sharp knife, then handed it to Zaffer, who had removed his jacket and rolled up his sleeves. He bent down and, reciting the appropriate invocation, slaughtered the ram, slitting its neck with quick strokes. Blood gushed out into the running water and down the drain. The tap had been opened to run the water for that purpose. Shahid slaughtered the other in exactly the same manner. The animals kicked and made a few strangled bleats. Then they lay still. Odera, making jokes and laughing, pulled the carcasses onto the cement floor under the tap where they would later be skinned.

Huma, watching from a little distance, made a face and exclaimed, "Poor goats, why do we have to kill them? Ami, I am not going to eat any meat from them. It's so cruel. I feel sorry, and look at all the blood."

"You are not supposed to feel sorry, Huma, or the kurbani, the sacrifice, becomes makruh, or forbidden," said Shahid and added, "on kiamat, the day of judgment, these rams will carry us to heaven."

"But they are dead, Manjala Bhai. How will they carry us to heaven?"

"The mullahs say they will wake up that day and come to life again. But I agree with you, Huma, it is cruel to kill so many animals. And I am not as sure as your Manjala Bhai that they will come to life and fly us to heaven. But think of it this way. The meat from these animals will provide food for many people who can't buy meat at all. They would be happy to eat a good meal, wouldn't they?"

"But I'm not going to be happy eating it. I feel like not eating meat at all." Huma made a funny face again.

"You need not eat it, dear daughter, but I'm sure you won't mind distributing the meat?" Sabra said.

Huma did not say anything and left for Batul's place. They too were busy slaughtering a goat and skinning it. The Ismaili neighbours did not slaughter any animals. They had all gone to town.

When the meat in both the two houses was cut up and cleaned, both Batul's mother and Sabra started dividing it in lots and marking them with name tags of people who were to have the meat. Sabra gave a big leg to the Ismaili neighbours. Batul's mother did not bother to give them any because they would not have accepted it from her. She did, however, give a good amount of meat to the Ismaili neighbours' houseboy instead. He was pleased to get meat from her and Sabra.

Sabra asked Odera to choose whatever piece he wanted. He said he would like the head, trotters, and some ribs. The sweeper, Gardi, took the other head, both skins, and the tripes. At home Sabra curried the livers, hearts, and kidneys with dry fenugreek leaves and spices, and they were eaten with parathas as a snack for breaking the fast, followed by tea and katlama. For lunch Odera, helped by Sabra and Shaira, cooked pilau with meat from the neck and briskets. Odera minced some boneless meat from one of the legs for kebabs and roasted the other leg in the oven for the evening meal, first marinating it with crushed garlic, green ginger, spices, and yogurt. A shoulder and chops she kept in the cooler for use during the week. Shahid and Honey went to deliver the meat to friends in the town and in Eastleigh. The rest was distributed among neighbours.

Sabra had invited Jamila and Latif to lunch as it was Jamila's first Idd in Nairobi. In the late afternoon they all walked to City Park through the Forest Road entrance and through the woods behind the Forest Road cemetery. Entering City Park here was like entering a narrow valley with towering trees on either sides. One forgot that it was right in the middle of a residential area. The heavy foliage made it difficult for the sun's rays to pass through. The family strolled down the main road for about a hundred yards, then, stepping over a furrow on the right, they walked along a path which wound its way among tall shady trees. Birds twittered and chirped and there were lots of nests in the trees. Squirrels and mongoose and fimbis and moles dashed past, and from time to time, monkeys jumped from branch to branch. The black soil was always damp and soft and light to walk on and gave off a mossy smell.

In the Shadow of Kirinyaga

The main road led to the Nairobi River bridge in the valley and up the hill to the other entrance on Limuru Road. The car park there was surrounded by a green hedge covered with golden shower vine and its orange-coloured blossoms like a quilt. On Sundays and holidays the park was always full and a policeman had to direct the cars.

Huma led the way, followed by the rest of her family and guests. They walked on the path in single file for about ten minutes and entered the park. It was like the end of a tunnel. Bright sunshine, deep blue sky, and well-trimmed lawns with fresh and colourful flowers of all kinds met the eye. The children ran to the swings. The bandstand was empty as it wasn't a Sunday. But children were perched upon the iron railings and steps leading to the stand. Older people sat on the lawn. Groups of men played cards.

Shaira and Jamila strolled about and then went to see the maze made of kaiapple hedge. Zaffer and Latif joined them, and after getting lost many times they at last found the right path to the centre. They sat there awhile enjoying the bright blue sky and greenery.

When they walked back it was nearing dusk. The Ismaili neighbours were home and had a houseful of guests. They insisted that Sabra with her family and guests have high tea with them. They had brought samosas and kebabs, bhajias, farsan with chutney, and cakes and mithai from town. They all chatted and enjoyed themselves for another hour at the neighbours'. Batul and her parents, who had gone to visit relatives, came back, and Huma and Batul counted all the money they had received for Idd from family members and friends. They had about fifteen shillings each. Batul said she would put all hers in her post office account.

"I shall put some in but not all," said Huma. "I want to buy something nice from Woolworths."

Honey, who had received about a pound, said he would buy a cricket bat.

23

Letter from Addis Ababa

"THERE IS NO postmark except 'Nairobi'," said Zaffer, turning the thick envelope in his hand. "It must have come in a Red Cross bag from Abyssinia to Nairobi," he added as he handed the letter to Shaira.

"Oh, thank you, Bhaijan," she said. Her eyes glowed as she inspected it. "You are right, Bhaijan, it has only Kenyan stamps." Her heart was beating fast.

"Latif got one too. He told me his uncle and aunt got one last week at Nyeri."

Zaffer went to his room and Shaira hurriedly tore open the letter. Mussavir had not received any letter, hers or from anyone else, including his parents, but he hoped some letters would eventually come. He described the journey and Addis Ababa exactly as he had described Djibouti.

At last I am now in the Empire's great city. After reading about its history dating back to biblical days, with Rasses, Dejazes, Princes, and Dukes and nobles wearing grand formal coats and embroidered capes, whom the Emperor meets and entertains in the great banqueting halls with tej, the honey wine, and raw meat, I am disappointed to find it a shabby city even though it sits at the foot of mountains and is surrounded by forests, spread out over a vast area. But I suppose it's wartime and everything is in disorder.

The train journey to Addis was long and tedious, but definitely better than the ship voyage. The first day the overloaded train, pulled by a big but not very strong engine, dragged itself laboriously through miles and miles of desertlike hot and dreadful country, all lava and rock. Occasionally one saw a group of nomad wanderers with pundas and camels overloaded with bundles of goods on their backs and slogging away in the baking sun. Tall men holding long staffs and wearing muddy brown shukas walked behind the animals. The smoking rooms were always full of all kinds of men, soldiers, journalists, doctors, and even engineers. When we could not find a place to sit we would go to our cabin and read and sleep when tired.

The next day, to our pleasant surprise, the scenery took a sudden change—green and wooded with lakes that looked still and absolutely like sheets of glass. As the train rolled further south, we passed wooded hills and soon even green fields began to appear. To our great delight the nights were cooler and the food palatable. The French love food and drink. We played cards in one of the train's dusty old smoking rooms. The other passengers told us that in the 1920s the train did not travel at night but stopped at some stations because there was great danger of being attacked by bandits and shiftas.

As we approached the upward climb to Addis Ababa, ascending slowly, range after range of craggy mountains came into sharp relief. They say coffee is grown on the higher reaches. It was very cool there.

Addis Ababa is much bigger and certainly much cooler than Djibouti, that handyia! but it is very different from our East African towns. The city seems to have been laid out around the Menelick and the great ghebbes (clusters of noblemens' residences). It is populated by a large and mixed community of foreigners. Diplomatic residences are spacious and spread out over wide parklands on the fringes of the capital.

There are trees all over but mainly eucalyptus. In fact, one can smell burning eucalyptus in the air at night. Must be jolly good for people with colds! Legend has it that Emperor Menelick ordered everyone to plant this distinctive tree when Addis Ababa was built. It is supposed to drain the swamps and destroy mosquitos and also to provide wood for fuel. He must have been a very feared man because even now when the people want to call for attention or to clear a way in a crowd they say, "Ba Menelick!"

Abyssinia also has its own brand of Christianity and apparently no foreign missionaries, Christian or Muslim, ever preached here. How lucky!

The people are lighter in colour and have delicate features. A Frenchman on the train told us that Ethiopia, which is another name for Abyssinia, is derived from the Greek words "to burn" and "face"—the land of the people with burnt faces! The same man told us that in the Amharic language Addis Ababa means "new flower." The Emperor's palace stands on the hilltop. There are a few modern buildings occupied by the Princes and Princesses who own a lot of land and the few old cars and vehicles. We were told they work the people like slaves and are feudalistic all right. There is more poverty and four times more people here than in East Africa. The men all wear long white robes called shammas.

The mud huts, and there are hundreds of them everywhere, are inferior, more filthy and squalid, than the ones in our Pangani and Pumwani areas in Nairobi. The rough roads in Pangani and Pumwani at least have street lighting and order and the city council keeps the drains clean. But what one sees mostly on the rough streets of Addis are cavalcades of pundas, camels, and mules plodding along loaded with sacks of grain and wheat. I have never seen so many pundas, even in India! They must breed these donkeys like one does cows and buffalos in the East. That reminds me, you'll be amused there are lots of sepoys walking about in the city. Our desis from India! Mostly Sikhs looking very smart in their stiff army uniforms and neat red turbans. Tara Chand told me the British ambassador, Sir Charles somebody, has always been wary of the natives, so he strengthened his embassy guard by two companies of 5/14th Punjabis from Aden! And Lady C, his wife, has organized the Abyssinian ladies as bandage makers for the medical units, and we, the Red Cross units, are quartered in the Menelick school about half a mile from the embassy. Dr Markwalder, a Swiss, is in charge of the overall unit.

There are lots of Indian shopkeepers running their various businesses like in Nairobi. In fact, I am told that most of the lorry drivers are Hindu Punjabis. The more I see of these territories the more I realize how much better off people are in East Africa, which is like heaven compared to here. The British, with all their arrogance and snobbery and show of superiority, are far better rulers than the French and Italians. At least in this part of Eastern Africa. One can't help giving the devil his due. My poor poetess, sorry I seem to have become a schoolteacher of civics.

I do miss my family, particularly Mama, and of course you who have come into my life. I can at least look forward to the future with hope of happiness and peace if not at present. Now I have to go for the drill practice. I have to don a military uniform and do the duty it demands of me to the best of my ability, but I am not sure if I can become a wholehearted and pukka warrior. Do say a prayer for me.

I shall be going to the interior shortly and might not be able to write again soon. The

hospitals and medical facilities are reasonable in Addis, but I am not sure what they are like in the interior.
Yours, Mussavir

Mussavir ended the letter with endearments, saying he missed her and hoped she had got his first letter and would write soon.

Shaira read and reread the letter. She had always wanted a pen pal but could not get the confidence to write to someone and share thoughts and secrets. She felt elated at the God-given opportunity of being not only engaged to a nice man who cared for her so, but one with whom she could look forward to an interesting and happy life. She also felt Mussavir had the instinct for teaching, like his father. She had seen Dr Bashir teach his daughters, and thought he was very good at explaining.

Occasionally the papers and radio put out small items of news about the Italians massing and moving their armies and tanks to the border of Italian Somaliland. There was also news of heavy fighting and heavy casualties of the Abyssinians. There seemed to have been an uproar in Europe and America about the bombing of a European hospital in Abyssinia.

24

Muharram

THREE WEEKS AFTER the Idd ul Azha, also known as Bakra Idd, the Muslim New Year, Muharram started. The Muslim New Year starts with a sad note and there are no celebrations. It is the month of the Martyrs. The Shia neighbours had been getting ready for their ten days of mourning for the Martyrs. Batul's mother aired the family's black garments, hanging them on the clothesline. Shirts, coats, kurtas, and shalwar kamizes for herself, Batul, and her husband. She had stitched some new clothes for herself and Batul, all black, in cotton, silk, and satin. On the afternoon of the first day of Muharram, Huma rushed in, all excited, and said, "Ami, Batul and her mum want me to go the Imam Barra for majlis with them. They say I can, if you allow me. May I go please, Ami?"

"It is at night, Huma, they will come back very late. They will eat there and carry on with the prayers till midnight. You have to do your homework and also go to school tomorrow," Sabra told her.

"I don't have much homework, Ami. I can do it now. Batul says it's very nice. They'll recite and sing lots of marcias and perform the physical mattam in the end. Ami, I have never ever been to a majlis or seen mattam. May I please go, please, Ami," she pleaded.

"Huma, my dear bitya, it is a religious majlis and not a tamasha. It's a serious prayer meeting. You'll be tired and bored after a while. And you have never witnessed a mattam, the self-flogging. You'll be scared."

"What will Huma be scared of, Ami?" Shaira asked.

"She wants to go with Batul and her parents to the Imam Barra and see mattam," Sabra told Shaira.

"Actually, Ami, I too would like to go. I've heard it's touching and moving. But I'd like to go on mattam day. They do not have it every night."

"Not you, too?" Sabra said with a scowl. "What's come over you both? Anyway, ask Zaffer when he comes," Sabra said, passing the difficult decision to him as she sometimes did.

Before Zaffer had even set foot in the house, like a shot Huma and Shaira made their request to him.

"There's no harm in attending a majlis, but it is quite morbid, and why do you want to go at all?" Zaffer asked.

But the girls insisted and Huma pleaded that the neighbours had invited them. He told Sabra the neighbours might think they were prejudiced and so it was better to let them go once.

Shaira said she'd ask Batul's mother which day was best for mattam, other than the ashura, or tenth day. But Huma was also allowed to accompany the neighbours that day.

Huma wanted to wear black clothes like Batul and her mother, but she had none. Sabra said it was not necessary for non-Shias to wear black. But as a courtesy to the neighbours, Huma could wear a navy blue or green suit and dupatta. She could not go in a dress like she did to school. Her feet and head had to be covered.

So, hurriedly finishing her homework, Huma donned her navy blue suit and trotted off excitedly with the neighbours in the evening. She came back at about eleven. She was even more excited than when she left. Not about the majlis and mattam, but because she had seen the Embu men, many of them, near the railway quarters, emptying the buckets! Huma would have woken up everybody if Sabra, reading in bed, had not quietened her.

In the morning Huma got up earlier than usual and while still in bed asked Sabra, "Ami, why don't we observe Muharram?"

"Who says we don't observe Muharram? We do in our own way." Opening the Holy Book she started to turn a few pages.

"Don't we believe in the Imams?" asked Huma.

"Of course we believe in the Imams and their martyrdom, Beti," Sabra said. She put the open book in front of her, ready to start.

"Then why don't we have any ceremony on ashura day and during Muharram in our mosques?"

"I've told you, my dear daughter, we all observe Muharram in our own way. It is a very sad time. We remember the Martyrs through prayers, giving of alms and sherbet, and even fasting. But we don't gather together and mourn by weeping and flogging and whipping ourselves." Sabra closed the Holy Book. "In the month of Muharram we don't perform marriages or any kind of happy celebrations."

"But we believe in Hazrat Ali and Imams Hassan and Hussein and all that happened in Karbala Sheriff, don't we?"

"Of course, Huma, you know we do. And you also know who Hazrat Ali was and his wife and sons."

"Oh, I know all that," said Huma. "Hazrat Ali was our Holy Prophet's son-in-law, married to his daughter Bibi Fatima, and father of Imams Hassan and Hussein. But I want to know why we do not do any mattam at all," Huma insisted.

"I've told you it is not necessary. The imams were destined to die as martyrs. It was God's will that they became shaheed and in a way it is a lesson to all of us. We are supposed to be proud of them that they passed the high test of a cruel ordeal. It is not necessary to relive the incidents physically and make them into rituals."

"But the marcias are so moving, Ami, and so sad. When everybody stands in a circle and beats their chest, one feels like crying. I cried too," she said, and waited for Sabra's reaction.

"Crying, even weeping and sobbing quietly, is all right, but I hope you did not beat your chest, Huma. I told you not to," Sabra said firmly. "I won't let you go again if you did that."

"Batul told me to keep my right hand on my chest, but I did not beat hard like they all did. One woman beat herself so much and so hard, her chest was bruised and even blood oozed out."

Honey, who had come in and perched himself at the end of Sabra's bed and was still in his pyjamas, said, "Some Shia boys at school told me that some men beat themselves with ropes which have tiny knives tied to them."

"They do that in India and in Shia countries, not here. It's not allowed." Sabra added, "Anyway, you both better get up and get ready for school. Odera and Shaira are preparing breakfast. Hurry up." She started reciting from the Holy Book.

Huma and Honey got up and went to the bathroom to wash and brush their teeth. While waiting for Honey to finish with the tap, Huma started to hum the tune of one of the marcias she had heard at the majlis the previous night. Odera passed by the bathroom to go to the veranda with the tea and milk.

"Odera! Jambo," said Huma in greeting.

"Ah, jambo, Ooma, jambo sana. Where did you go last night?"

"Last night, oh, usiku mimi kwenda mosque ya Batul," chirped Huma.

"Kweli? Now really? You went to Batul's miskiti. Did you pray well?" Odera asked.

"Ndiyo, yes, lakini baado wakati sisi rudi sisi ona watu ya Embu! Mingi sana." She told him she saw a lot of Embu people on her way back.

"Watu ya Embu? Nani hawa? Who are they?" Odera did not comprehend.

"You don't know? Wewe hapana jua? They come at night to take . . ." and she dissolved in giggles. "Na chukua . . ." She started to laugh again.

"What do they take?" And Odera, who needed no coaxing to have a good laugh, started to laugh too. "Wey sema tu! Go on, tell me, why do you laugh so much?"

Huma pointed towards the toilet in the courtyard and giggled again and Odera, finally understanding what she was saying, laughed again and said, "Oh I see. Kumbe! Uliona hawa machura? You saw the churas?" Odera saw Zaffer coming for breakfast and went towards the dining table. Zaffer asked Odera what he was amused about so early in the morning. Odera chuckled and said Huma had seen the Embu men collecting the night soil from the toilets.

"Did she?" Looking at Huma, who was about to enter the bathroom, Zaffer asked, "Where did you see them?" He sat at the table for his breakfast, which Odera rushed to the kitchen to get for him. Shaira came back with him. She went in to get ready for school.

"Oh, Barre Bhaijan, we saw so many of them coming along the road holding hurricane lamps and wearing long cloaks of gunny sack cloth. They held big reed broom in one hand and a huge bucket on their head," Huma said in one breath.

"They didn't throw the bucket at you? They would if you laughed so much," said Zaffer, taking the plate of fried eggs from Odera.

"No, Bhaijan, we didn't laugh. We kept very quiet. I covered my mouth with my dupatta. They were emptying the buckets from the toilets of the railway quarters."

"What a fine subject to be talking about at breakfast!" Shahid said, coming in and hearing the tail end of Huma's talk. "It would have been really nice if they had thrown some of the contents at you." Huma laughed and Shahid went on, "What are you laughing at? They are jolly useful people; if they didn't come and empty the buckets we would be riddled with diseases."

"For a man who didn't like the subject being discussed your details are not exactly appetizing either, my brother," Zaffer said.

Huma ignored what Zaffer had said and asked, "Why are they called Embu people, Bhaijan?

"Because they come from Embu near the Muranga and Fort Hall area. They're the only ones who do this kind of work. Even Gaardi, our day sweeper, is from Embu."

Odera, who had brought some toast on a toast rack, understood what Zaffer was saying, for he told Huma that the Embu people were cousins of the Kikuyus but the Kikuyus considered them inferior and look down on them. In fact, lots of people thought they were a dirty people. Odera chuckled again.

"Have you not got any such people in your Luo land?" Zaffer asked.

"Oh no, hapana, the Luo don't indulge in this kind of work." He smiled broadly and added, "In the villages and rural areas they go in the bush. Having a toilet inside a home is not considered good in Luo culture. A father-in-law cannot use the same toilet as his daughter-in-law. And a mother-in-law cannot use the same toilet as a son-in-law." He said the town people had pit latrines and the Wazungu in Kisumu and the surrounding areas had water tanks in the latrines with a chain attached.

Shahid again objected to this kind of talk at the breakfast table and he sent Odera to get more toast and tea.

Huma visited the Imam Barra again with Batul and her parents and once even Shaira went with them. During the first week Huma kept humming and reciting the marcias which she had heard, especially the couplet:

Saad haif zalimoone sataya Hussein ko
Bulwa ke pani tak na pillaya Hussein ko

A hundred woes at the cruelty shown by those cruel people.
Inviting Hussein they did not even give him a drink of water.

The other marcia she sang frequently was about the young man who went to his martyrdom after being married to his bride for one night. His bride the next morning went out wailing to the other women:

Aey bibio mara gaya ikk raat ka dullah mera

Oh women, my bridegroom of one night has been murdered.

Huma repeated the marcias whilst working at her homework and playing with her dolls. In no time Odera picked up the two tunes and he was humming them too. He kept repeating them whilst washing and ironing clothes and cleaning and sweeping the rooms. At first he only hummed the tunes but then he started using the words, and he made his own versions of them. The marcias were sad but Odera hadn't a clue what they meant. At first everyone smiled, but then Sabra explained to him that what he was singing was a religious song—he should only hum the tune, not sing the words. So he asked Huma to teach him the right words since Sabra was worried the Shia neighbours would object.

Luckily, they were tolerant, but Shahid was irritated and one evening told his mother she would have a daughter converting to Shia religion.

"What difference will it make," said Zaffer. "We are all branches of the same root and tree. In fact, all of us are like the five blind men of Hindustan."

"Yes, but the Shia branch is not straight and natural," Shahid retorted.

"Don't be such a bigot, Shahid," said Zaffer. "There are over fifty sects in Islam, do you mean to say they are all not straight?"

"They are all straight with minor differences, except the Shias," argued Shahid. "They don't accept the first three Khalifas after the Holy Prophet Mohammed—they won't even name their children after the first three Khalifas—and they raise Hazrat Ali almost to the rank of God. Worst of all, they have muta, or pleasure marriages!" Shahid's eyes showed fire.

"Not accepting the first three Khalifas is more a political than a religious difference. And as for raising Hazrat Ali to the rank of God, the Ismailis say Aga Khan is God and the Christians say Jesus was the son of God, or God himself. They have been saying that for centuries and will go on saying so. It is their point of view. Had you been born a Shia, my dear and righteous brother, I am positive you would have beaten yourself to death, because I am sure you would have been a real fanatic. Grow up!"

"Ah yes, some of their sects do allow muta," Zaffer added as an afterthought. "It was to stop prostitution, when there were more women than men after the wars."

Sabra told them to stop arguing.

"Shahid, your brother is right. You are becoming dogmatic. Beta, you have to be tolerant of other people's religions. Prophets Musa, Issa, and our own Prophet Mohammed, peace be on all of them, brought their own religions, and Prophet Mohammed has said there is no compulsion in religion, so it's no use arguing over them."

"One has a right to discuss them and have a view of one's own, even if no one agrees. Bhaijan has his views and I have mine."

"This has all come about because of Huma singing the marcias. Well, Huma, as you well know, goes for novel things, and marcias are novel to her and she learns songs quickly. She has a good ear for them. Before long she will learn others."

"Manjala Bhaijan, I'm not going to become a Shia," said Huma. "I only like the marcias and feel sorry for the Martyrs."

"There you are, Shahid," said Zaffer. "I told you that Huma, like all of us, is not going to change her religion. She has faith just like the blind men of Hindustan."

"Who were the blind men of Hindustan?" Huma quickly asked before Shahid could say anything.

"Now there she goes again! I knew she would ask that," Sabra said, and she looked at Zaffer. "Why do you have to start kufr talk now? You can't leave well enough alone."

"It's not kufr talk, Ami, it is good for Huma to know the story of the wise men of Hindustan." He smiled widely and asked Huma if she knew the story of the blind men who wanted to know what an elephant looked like.

Huma shook her head. Shahid, who had finished his breakfast, got up to go, saying he had heard the story many times.

"Huma, once upon a time there were five wise men, all blind, who wanted to know what an elephant looked like. They took a long journey and reached the elephant."

"But, Barre Bhaijan, you said they were all blind, how could they see?" Huma interrupted.

"Well, they thought if they could feel the elephant with their hands they would know what it was like."

"But did the elephant not kick them?"

"The elephant must have been a tame one, it must have been an Asian elephant"

"And then what happened?"

"The first man put his hands out and touched the body of the great beast. It felt like a big wall. He came and told his friends the elephant was exactly like a wall. The second man must have touched the foot. He argued the elephant was not like a wall but it was absolutely like a tree. The third man, who touched the ears, said the elephant was neither like a wall nor a tree, it was in fact like a big fan. The fourth happened to catch the tail and said the elephant was like a rope. The fifth man passed his hand over the trunk and said all the others were talking nonsense, the elephant was definitely like a snake. You see, Huma, all these wise blind men felt different parts of the elephant, therefore each was sure the elephant was like the part he had touched and felt. But they were actually all wrong too. Weren't they? I think religions are like that."

"Yes, Bhaijan, the wise men were wrong because they were all blind." Huma was so absorbed in the story that she forgot why it had been told in the first place. Zaffer, to his mother's great relief, left it at that.

Shortly thereafter both Huma and Odera started singing ginans, which the Ismaili neighbour's wife sang on and off. They were about Raja Jasrath and his seven brothers from Hindu mythology. The marcias were forgotten.

25

Casualty

ONE MORNING IN February 1936, Zaffer was scanning the English papers in his office. The caption read that the Italians were advancing with tanks and guns towards Addis Ababa, causing heavy casualties to the already weak Abyssinians. Addis Ababa, at the foot of the mountains and surrounded by forests, was almost impossible to defend, at least against an attacking army possessing artillery. The Abyssinians possessed no artillery and the weather was bad. Later, Zaffer learned that the Italians might soon take over. Appeals and desperate requests by the Emperor for help went unanswered by the international community.

Zaffer, before going home, went to see Latif at his office. Latif told him Dr Bashir had bad news too. Mussavir was injured and hospitalized. Latif and Jamila were planning to visit Zaffer's home to inform his mother.

Zaffer rushed home and gave the grave news to his mother. Sabra was shocked and upset. "I shall straightaway send some sadqa money to the mosque and offer special prayers," she told Zaffer, "but we should not tell Shaira yet. Who knows, it might only be a rumour."

"I don't think it is a rumour, Ami. Tayajan Bashir has been notified by the Red Cross authorities."

Mother and son were discussing the matter when Latif and Jamila arrived and confirmed what Zaffer had told his mother. Latif said his uncle did not want the news to leak out. The authorities had informed him in confidence. They were not sure how Mussavir had sustained his injuries, but they suspected a bomb had fallen on the hospital or camp.

Jamila went inside to look for Shaira when the others were talking, and found her reading a book on her bed.

"Oh, hello, Jamila Bhabi, salaam alaikum," Shaira said, offering the obligatory Muslim greeting. She sat up and invited Jamila to sit.

Jamila did not realize that Shaira did not know, so in her normal way she said, "I'm so sorry, Shaira, we came as soon as we got the bad news. I wish to Allah that it is not true, or if it is, then let it not be too bad."

"What bad news, Bhabi?" Shaira asked.

"You don't know?" Jamila asked and looked towards the door as she removed her burqa.

"Don't know what, Bhabi? You look worried. What has happened? Is it bad news from India?"

"No. It is not from India. The news is from—"

"From Abyssinia then?" Shaira blanched.

"Mussavir Bhai is injured and hospitalized."

"No. How do you know?" Shaira realized Jamila was serious.

"Tayajan rang up and told Latif."

Shaira sat down on her bed, her mouth dry, unable to speak.

Sabra came in and, realizing Jamila had divulged the news, told her daughter not to worry but to pray quietly for Mussavir's recovery. "He is in hospital, thank heavens, and not on the field. It is very unfortunate and worrying, but these risks are always there on a war front." Sabra impressed upon both of them that the news should not be allowed to leak out. Sabra did not want tongues wagging and people casting taunts that Shaira had been unlucky and the cause of Mussavir's bad luck. "I shall write to Ayesha and Bhai Bashir this evening, and I shall send some charity money to the mosque," Sabra said to Jamila.

Shaira knew she could not expect more from her mother; she was a hardened person. Many a time she related incidents of the Great War when she and Shaira's father lived at Makindu. There was always danger of being attacked by the Germans from the border, and many a time

Shaira's father had to go on the train, leaving her on her own. At times she was not even sure he'd return the next day. She would describe the incidents without emotion.

After Jamila and Latif left, Shaira went to her room and lay in bed and tried to pray.

Soon there were rumours that the Abyssinians had lost the war and Emperor Haile Selasse was about to abscond. This was soon confirmed. Apparently the Emperor had left on the third of May by train for the French port of Djibouti. Addis Ababa fell to the Italians two days later. The war was over. It had lasted seven months.

Sabra wrote to Dr Bashir expressing her concern and asked him to keep her informed. She got a reply that Mussavir had been moved to a hospital in British Somaliland; he had not suffered any physical injuries, but some kind of shell shock. This was more worrying, Dr Bashir said. He had therefore delayed his leave and was planning to go to Somaliland himself to see how his son was.

Zaffer told his mother since the war had ended the other doctors who went with Mussavir would be returning to Nairobi, so some definite news would soon be forthcoming.

Dr Bashir left by road and took over a week to reach Hergeisa in British Somaliland. Ayesha and the girls came to Nairobi and stayed with Latif and Jamila. Ta'Ha was transferred to Magadi, so he came to Nairobi with his mother and sisters and then proceeded to Magadi. And later Ayesha and her daughters went to Magadi to be with Ta'Ha and wait for Dr Bashir's arrival.

Shaira was shocked to see how much weight Ayesha had lost. She had gone quiet and hardly smiled. It was obvious she was suffering greatly. Ayesha and the girls came to Sabra's home for a meal, and when Ayesha hugged Shaira, she lost control and wept.

Zaffer put his arms around her.

"Taijan, you must be brave and not lose hope. Mussavir will, God willing, be better and himself again."

"I hope you are right, Beta Zaffer. It is through sheer willpower that I have kept going so far," she said, wiping her eyes with her dupatta. "I knew my son had gone to a war, not a picnic, and there were risks. And I could understand physical injuries from which one does recover from eventually. But this mental injury really baffles me. Will he recover from it and be normal again? He is in a hospital all alone far away from home and heaven knows in what condition. He may not recover." She sighed and said she was not even sure if in those hospitals they could cure such things.

"I know, Taijan. Yes, it is very worrying, but I was talking to my boss only the other day and he says that during the Great War a lot of men suffered from shell shock. He said it takes time but people do recover from it. We have to be patient, and thankful that he is alive. I'm sure Allah will listen to our prayers, Inshallah."

Shaira was upset but had to keep calm and carry on with her studies. At night in her bed she wept and prayed. Work in school was becoming difficult and exams drew nearer.

Dr Bashir came back from Somaliland and, after staying with Latif, he visited Sabra. He looked strained and did not talk much about Mussavir except to say he was in no danger of dying. In fact, he was recovering normally under the circumstances and the medical people were satisfied with his condition. It was only a matter of time now. He was confident Mussavir was in good hands and under good medical care. In fact, he would soon be transferred to a hospital in Northern Kenya, not far from the border with Somaliland. Dr Bashir also told Sabra and Zaffer he was going on leave with his wife and daughters and was confident that by the time he returned Mussavir would be out of hospital. He left for Magadi the next day to fetch Ayesha and his daughters.

Sabra asked him if she could arrange a prayer meeting in her home for Mussavir's recovery before he and his wife left for India. He agreed, so Sabra organized a recital of the Holy Quran and the chanting of the Ayat Karima 125,000 times. Sabra sent out invitations to female neighbours and friends for the afternoon. She got the whole of the living room emptied and spread white sheets on the floor. Small earthenware bowls with a little hot charcoal and incense were placed in the four corners of the room.

In the middle of the room the thirty siparas of the Holy Quran, bound separately, were placed on a small table where she kept three empty glass bowls. Later, before the prayer started, one glass bowl was filled with dried peas.

The females all sat around the room and first they read the chapters of the Holy Quran which Hibba and Shaira distributed to the women. Some women read two chapters each, others recited at least one, until the whole book was recited. They got out their tasbihs, which they had brought in their pouches and bags, and started to recite the ayats and verse Karima. When a woman completed one tasbih, which had one hundred beads, she would rise from her place and take one pea from a bowl of dried peas and place it in a second bowl. After a while the peas in the second bowl were counted, and for every ten peas, one pea was put in a third bowl (marking the ten-thousandth reading of the verse Karima). This went on until the ayat Karima had been recited by the women and girls 125,000 times.

Then all stood up and started to chant the Muslim creed and the droods—the showering of blessing and peace upon the Holy Prophet Mohammed—followed by common prayers for Mussavir's health and recovery. The whole ceremony took two and a half hours. Tea was served in the end and money was sent for charity.

Shaira took part in the prayer meeting but was unable to concentrate. Her mind would wander and she would think of poor Mussavir on his own in a hospital among strangers in a new country, with no friends and family. She wished he had been in Nairobi. Though she would not have been allowed to visit him in hospital, she would at least have known how he was faring. Shaira also noticed Hibba was at times sarcastic with her. She realized Hibba was upset about her brother and had cried a lot during the prayers. Shaira heard her saying that someone's evil eye had cast a spell on her brother, as he was the only one among the doctors who was injured. She even said to Shaira that some of the women said Mussavir should not have been engaged before he left. Jamila had told her that in India Shaira would be considered unlucky for Mussavir. Shaira was hurt that her friend and sister-in-law-to-be should feel that way. She did not, however, say anything to her. She was fond of Hibba and she knew Hibba adored her brother and the anguish had clouded her judgment.

Later Huma got wind of this bad-luck business and when in bed one evening told her mother, "Ami, people are saying Api is unlucky for Mussavir Bhaijan. Can that be true?"

"What nonsense, who says that? Luck and bad luck are all in Allah's hands."

"I heard Jamila Bhabi talking about it to Attia Bhabi."

"It is not true. You must not listen to them, and don't worry," Sabra advised Huma.

"I didn't believe them, Ami, but I was very angry with them. Ami, will Mussavir Bhaijan be all right?"

"Of course he will, Inshallah. Just keep praying for him."

"I shall, Ami. I shall pray my hardest."

The prayer gathering was supposed to give consolation to both the families, and they all appeared calm and collected.

Dr Bashir told Sabra and Zaffer that Mussavir had blackouts and lapses of memory and at times he was withdrawn and did not talk much. He also had nightmares and was sometimes uncontrollable. They had to treat him with electric shocks. But he said he had faith in Allah and prayers, and he was sure the Almighty was going to help and cure him.

Before leaving, Ayesha told Sabra that during their leave in India, if a suitable match was found for Hibba, she would be married. Ayesha was also planning to bring a bride for Ta'Ha.

When Mussavir's two doctor colleagues returned from Abyssinia, Zaffer went to see them to find out how Mussavir had been injured. They were both very sad at their friend's fate. According to them, although Mussavir was not at all happy that his father had pushed him to the war front, he nevertheless did not shirk the work. Casualties were more than the surgeons could cope with, and conditions at the hospitals were bad and supplies insufficient.

"He worked harder than any of us," Tara Chand said sadly. "He spent a lot of time in the hospital operating and helping. If only he did not have this weakness after work . . . you probably know about it . . . he drank more than we did, and after he came back from the field his drinking became heavier than before. He also went funny. Very quiet and thoughtful at times. He did not joke as much as he used to. At times we thought he was in some kind of shock."

"And there was no shortage of liquor. It was available in great supply," offered Gopalan.

Zaffer said he had been reading the English papers which his boss received from time to time, as he fished for news from wherever he could all these months. He had the impression the war was a messy one. He asked what it had really been like there.

"Yaar, kutch na pooch. It was more than messy, and terrible is not the word, my friend," said Tara Chand. "Such a vast undeveloped country, with donkey and mule trails rather than roads, and such a mountainous country with hills and valleys and hundreds of hairpin bends where it was almost impossible for the vehicles to travel. And the Abyssinians were used to fighting hand-to-hand with swords, rifles, and daggers, guerrilla-type tactics that were no match for a modern war fought from the air. Yet they did fight and faced tanks and even killed some Italian officers. The morale at first was high. But when the Italians used mustard gas, so many were burnt and scalded . . ."

"Did they really use mustard gas?" asked a surprised Zaffer?

"Oh yes," said Gopalan. "At the British legation they said the Italians used it first in the Takaze Valley to avenge an Air Force pilot whom the Abyssinians beheaded publically in Dagghabur, the place he had bombed and strafed. And from then on all hell broke loose and atrocity followed atrocity. Even the Swedish hospital was bombed twice, and mostly women and young girls were killed."

Tara Chand added that the Abyssinian army had only primary medical services of its own. The various units of the Red Cross from Europe helped. The volunteers were a mixed group of all races and colours, so Sweden, Britain, Holland, and Finland organized their own Red Cross units while the Swiss doctor took charge of the others.

"That's when we three were separated," said Gopalan. "Mussavir went with Dr Markwalder and his team to Quoram on the plateau where the

British field hospital was established. Mules and foot were the only way of travel in the Tigre Highlands. Dr Markwalder managed to get his eighteen lorries up the escarpment, where he was met by the English Major and his Red Cross unit. All around them, Bitowed Makonen's well-armed men were encamped. They marched further north when the assault began. By morning they had lost half their force; hundreds of wounded were exposed on the ridge. Bitowed was mortally wounded and some say he died soon after, but his death was kept a secret; others say he was taken to the medical base where he died and his demoralized men forced the Major and an assistant doctor to perform a most macabre operation on him. His body was cut in two while still warm and packed in a drum to be buried in his home base."

"We both suspect Mussavir was the assistant doctor. And that is why he was so quiet, shocked, and disoriented when he came back," Tara Chand added.

Dr Markwalder was a brave man. He told the two Indian doctors that Mussavir was in an air-raid shelter when a bomb fell into it and killed one of his assistants. Mussavir rushed out screaming and dragging the body of the man, whose guts were hanging out of his split belly. Another shell burst near him. It was surprising he himself was not torn to pieces. He was unharmed, but he lost his head and became so hysterical they had to calm him with strong sedatives.

"Luckily Dr Markwalder was at hand," said Tara Chand. "With the help of the British legation, he sent Mussavir to a proper hospital in British Somaliland. We never saw him again."

"But poor Dr Markwalder himself was later shot when picking up the wounded," added Gopalan.

"It is a shame and great pity about Mussavir," said Tara Chand. "I understand he is engaged to your sister. He seemed very happy and had told us about his engagement just before leaving for Abyssinia."

"Yes, that's true, my mother and I are so worried, as are his parents and family," said Zaffer. "There is no hurry about the marriage. My sister is young and still studying. The marriage can wait till he is fully recovered."

"I don't know, it's perhaps not fair to say . . . but I think some damage may be permanent, or may cure very slowly," Gopalan said thoughtfully. "I would think twice if it was my sister who was to be married to him, especially if she was young and inexperienced. You could have another mental patient in your hands."

"Oh no, my friend, you are pessimistic," Tara Chand said. "He won't become a loony. In a couple of years or even less he should be all right again. In fact, a loving wife could be very helpful. I don't think any of his damage is permanent."

"You both were in Addis Ababa when Italy took over. Was it peaceful?" Zaffer asked, to change the subject.

The doctors told him they were there when the Emperor left for Djibouti. They said the British consul at Harar came to meet him. The troops started to go back to their homes. Some ran into the forests and joined the bands of hostile Abyssinians.

In the capital there was much looting and plundering, especially of the foreign embassies. The Turkish legation was attacked first, then the American. Indian shopkeepers barricaded themselves in their stores. There was great destruction at the French embassy, but at least the French had underground bunkers in their cellars.

When Zaffer came home he told his mother and sister all that the two doctors had told him, but omitted Gopalan's doubts about the marriage. His mother wept and said she was praying very hard all the time. Shaira did not say anything but went to her room and offered special prayers and wept whilst praying. She did not leave her room for a long time.

Latif and Jamila visited Sabra again, and Latif told her he had received a letter from his uncle in India. Dr Bashir, his wife, and the girls had all been quite sick on arrival, due to the very hot weather. In fact, Hibba contracted dysentery, but was recovering. Jamila had heard from her mother who told her a cousin of Jamila, a lawyer by profession, had expressed a desire to marry Hibba, but Dr Bashir had not made up his mind.

Later Shaira got a letter from Hibba herself and she had a different story to tell. She sounded disturbed and unhappy. She said she did not like India and she did not want to stay or settle there. It was so hot and life was so different from East Africa.

One of Jamila Bhabi's cousins has asked for my hand in marriage. He is a lawyer and is soon to become a magistrate. He is not only much older than me but also a widower. His wife died in childbirth and the child died too. He did not marry for a long time but wants to now. Mama does not seem to be interested in anything. She still weeps and prays for hours and wants to go to the Dargah of the Peer to offer prayers at the shrine. I told her I don't want to be married and would like to go back with them. But Abu is adamant that I be married off and soon. How I wish Mussavir Bhaijan were here to help me. I know he would. Just because I am not educated in a school here they think I am uneducated and I should consider myself lucky. What good is it to me if he is a magistrate when I don't like him and find him old . . .

Shaira was sad to read Hibba's letter and very sorry for her. She spoke to Jamila, who became defensive and said her cousin was a really nice man, a vakil and a magistrate. "I don't know what she is raving about, she who is not even educated. She must consider herself darn lucky my cousin is prepared to marry her."

"But he's much older than her, Bhabi," said Shaira in defence of her friend. "Not many girls want to marry someone much older than themselves, but I suppose he is your cousin. I'm sorry, I shouldn't have told you."

Sabra came in and they discontinued the conversation, but Shaira felt very bad about Hibba and desperately wanted to help her. She wished Mussavir had been around; he would not have agreed to such a match for his sister. She thought of writing to Dr Bashir herself. After all, she was to be related to Hibba and could act on Mussavir's behalf.

Shaira had not even replied to Hibba when Latif told Sabra he had another letter from his uncle, who told him Hibba's nikah had been performed and the date for Hibba's marriage had been fixed. Dr Bashir and his wife would be coming back soon after the marriage and spend the rest of their leave in Kenya. They had also found a bride for Ta'Ha. She would be coming out with them.

26

Hibba's Misfortune and Zaffer's Visit to Mussavir

SABRA HEARD VOICES and banging on the back door one night. When she looked out of the window, she found the backyard all lit up. Odera was standing with two askaris. She presumed the police constables were doing their rounds checking if there were any extra people in the workers' quarters; they did that now and again. She was about to go back to bed when she heard a knock on the veranda door and Odera called, "Mama, mama . . . Bwana Jaffa . . . Mama!"

Sabra rushed back to the window and asked Odera what was the matter. Odera told her the police wanted to see Zaffer. Sabra asked why they wanted to see her son.

"The askaris want to take me away, Mama."

She immediately woke Zaffer. Shahid woke up too and both brothers rushed out in their pyjamas. Sabra could not hear what the policemen said but she saw them go inside Odera's room, and they came out holding Odera's pipe and a small tin. Zaffer was talking to the askari in charge. Odera was holding his sweater, which Sabra had given him on Idd day. He had put on his rubber shoes, but one of the askaris made Odera remove the shoes and put them back in the room.

Sabra put on her shawl and came out and asked what was going on.

"Ami, please go back and rest. I'll come in and tell you all about it," said Zaffer.

The askaris walked with Odera out the back door and Shahid locked it. Both brothers came into the house. They told their mother Odera was arrested because he had been smoking bhang.

"Smoking bhang," Sabra exclaimed in surprise. "Where did he get it from? Did he steal it? Why have they taken him?"

"Ami, having bhang in your possession and smoking it is a criminal offence," said Zaffer. "There was bhang in his pipe and also in the tin. He is very stupid. Now he will be in for at least six months."

"No wonder he was always singing and cheerful," said Shahid.

"Six months!" exclaimed Sabra. "He has not harmed anyone and is not a criminal. Did you not tell the askari he is a good worker and has never stolen from us ever in the short time he has been with us?"

"Ami," said Zaffer, "what difference would that make? They have caught him red-handed and he did not deny anything. I am only sorry that they are going to stamp his kipande, which so far has been clean." Zaffer shook his head in frustration.

Shahid went back to sleep. Shaira, who also had got up with the commotion, asked what was wrong. Sabra told her about Odera's arrest.

"Zaffer Beta, you had better go to the police station and pay a fine on his behalf," Sabra told Zaffer as she sat on her bed.

"Ami, it is very unlikely that they will fine him. It will be a prison sentence after a trial. Bhang is punishable by imprisonment," Zaffer emphasized. "I shall of course go to the police station and see the Indian superintendent."

They all went to bed and Sabra did not sleep for a long time. She was worried about getting a replacement for Odera. She knew many workers would come to seek work the moment they got wind of Odera's arrest. But a really good worker was hard to find.

In the morning Sabra and Shaira got up early to get breakfast ready. Huma and Honey were upset to hear about Odera's arrest.

"Why is it a crime to smoke bhang, Ami?" Huma asked. She said she was so sorry, as Odera was such a nice man. She was worried he would be beaten in prison and not get enough food, and it would be bad food, she

216

was sure, as Mwangi once told her. "What will happen to his things now? Was he allowed to take his mouth organ and pipe?"

"It was that blasted pipe that got him into trouble," Zaffer said. "He was not even allowed to wear shoes and it was so cold. He asked that his belongings, including his mouth organ, be kept here."

Shahid shouted from inside saying that even if they had allowed him to take his things they would definitely have been stolen in the prison, and they would not let him use his shoes. Prisoners went about barefoot. Sabra said she would collect all his belongings and store them away.

Zaffer was right; Odera was not fined but imprisoned for three and a half months. Zaffer's visit to the police station did not help. The Indian superintendent said the Luos were great smokers of bhang. They had to be sent to prison to be punished as a deterrent to others. Sabra had no alternative but to look for another man.

The neighbours' workers all came to sympathize, and even the vegetable vendors and chicken sellers were sad that Odera had been arrested. Tongues wagged and they all said someone must have reported him, otherwise the police would not have known. The Ismaili neighbour's worker suspected the ayah of the Goanese neighbours who lived three houses away. She was a Kikuyu and did not like him. Poor Odera was the talk of the neighbourhood for a few days. But in Sabra's home he was much missed. They engaged a Maragoli, not a fast worker or even clean and neat like Odera. But he was willing, so they hired him on a temporary basis.

Sabra and her family had barely settled after Odera's arrest and imprisonment when to their great surprise Latif told them his uncle and aunt were coming back to Kenya soon. They had gone to India for five months but were returning after three. Tragedy dogged their steps. Hibba was married and given away despite the fact that she was running a high temperature on her wedding day. A week later when, according to tradition, she came back for her first visit to her parents, the fever had still not broken. She was shown to a specialist. The tests showed she was suffering from typhoid, and she was immediately admitted into the local hospital. Her condition deteriorated and she died in a fortnight, a bride of less than a month.

Dr Bashir and Ayesha, shattered and disoriented, wanted to leave India soon after the funeral. But family and relatives persuaded them to stay for a while to recover from the shock. Accompanied by Ta'Ha's bride and Farida, they left for Bombay to await transshipment to Mombasa.

Latif's parents wrote to him about this tragedy. And Ta'Ha, too, heard from his brother Zahir, who described in detail what had happened. Sabra's family were naturally upset and went to Latif and Jamila's home to offer condolences and to partake in the fatia ceremony. Everyone was shocked at the turn of events and how such bad luck had struck the family twice. Ta'Ha had arrived in Nairobi in a distressed state and immediately left for the Frontier Province to be with Mussavir. He told Sabra he was not sure if Mussavir had received news of their sister's death. He wanted to break the news to him personally.

Dr Bashir, Ayesha, Farida, and Ta'Ha's bride eventually arrived in Nairobi and put up with Latif and Jamila for a couple of weeks. Hordes of well-wishers and friends visited them to offer their sympathies. On completion of their leave, they went back to Nyeri and on to Isiolo, their new posting beyond Nyeri and Nanyuki. Before the family left, however, Ta'Ha and his bride, Sharifa, went to Magadi. There was neither a giving-away ceremony nor a walima. The couple just took a bus to Magadi.

Before leaving Nairobi, however, Dr Bashir summoned Sabra and expressed a desire that Shaira and Mussavir should be married. He reported that Mussavir was back at work and had almost completely recovered. Dr Bashir insisted that Mussavir needed a wife.

"Had he and Shaira not been engaged, Ayesha and I would have brought a bride for him from India as we did for Ta'Ha," he said.

"I fully appreciate your wish, Bhai Bashir," said Sabra, "but both my sons and I are of the opinion that under the circumstances Mussavir should be given more time and the marriage should not be hurried. You are also aware she is still a minor according to Kenyan law."

"It is not necessary to register the marriage. We can perform only the nikah, in which case her being fourteen is all right."

Shaira was waiting for her Preliminary Cambridge results and was in her fifteenth year. Despite the stress and strain about Mussavir, she did not do badly in her studies. Her family and teachers were pleased with her success. She had applied for admission to go on to the Junior Cambridge the following year. She was, however, very surprised that Mussavir had not written her since his letters from Abyssinia. At first she had presumed he was too sick to write, but now he was apparently back in Kenya and already working. So what could the reason be? Sabra and Zaffer were both apprehensive, even though they were sad about Mussavir's predicament. Zaffer had liked him very much as a person and as a suitable match for Shaira. He had no intention of calling off the marriage, though a number of their friends, and even one of the doctors who had gone with Mussavir to Abyssinia, suggested caution.

However, both Sabra and Zaffer were surprised that Mussavir had not come to Nairobi to see them. They felt Dr Bashir was keeping something back, not telling them all. Latif and Jamila too seemed to be in the dark. Shaira had deduced her mother's and brother's feelings. She was in a dilemma. She loved Mussavir more than ever and wanted desperately to help him get well. She had ignored the taunts of some who said she was unlucky for Mussavir. Her intuition told her Mussavir liked her and had wanted to get married to her even before he left. She did not believe he had become indifferent in a matter of a year or so. She yearned to meet him, even though she knew her mother would not allow her to see him if he came to Nairobi. But she was sure if he was still normal he would find a way of seeing her.

After the two long and detailed letters in the beginning, he had not written to her again. Could it be that the shell shock had wiped her from his memory? She could not think of any other reason for his indifference. She prayed and thought of him daily and she missed him desperately. She felt helpless, like a caged animal.

Farida, Dr Bashir's younger daughter, sometimes wrote to Shaira and gave her news of the family. She said her parents missed Hibba and she herself found her sister's absence painful. She felt lonesome. Her eldest brother neither visited nor wrote but her father received reports that he was well and working. Their cheerful and happy home had become like a morgue. How she wished her brother Ta'Ha and his wife Sharifa would come for a visit. She had become fond of her new sister-in-law during the sea voyage and stay in Bombay. Her father gave her a lot of lessons and assignments to do so she was kept busy. She also helped her mother, who had become quiet and was not her usual cheerful self.

Jamila once hinted to Sabra that Dr Bashir and his wife would not themselves talk of breaking their son's engagement to Shaira, but if Sabra wanted to withdraw from the agreement, she was sure they would understand and not blame her. Mussavir had broken a fundamental and important religious covenant and become an alcoholic. Muslim parents can refuse to give their daughter in marriage to such a man. Jamila felt there was also some mystery regarding Mussavir's stay in Somaliland. She was unable to guess, and Dr Bashir had not told her husband anything. Latif had wanted to visit Mussavir but Dr Bashir discouraged him. Mussavir had never come to Nyeri or to Isiolo. She maintained that if he was well enough to work, surely he was well enough to visit his parents, and he had some responsibility to Shaira and her family. She had also heard Dr Bashir say that Mussavir would need a very strong wife, one who could handle him in his drunken state. He thought a strong village girl who was used to a tough father and brothers would be ideal. That had made her suspect that Mussavir may have suffered some injury that had rendered him impotent. A marriage to a tough village girl could help; that was a belief held by older people in India.

Sabra mentioned this to her sons. Shahid was in favour of breaking the engagement straightaway; he had never liked Mussavir. "He is welcome to his tough village hussy. Over my dead body will my sister be a co-wife or marry a drunk." He had found out there was more to this shell-shock business—Mussavir was involved with a nurse, perhaps already married to her, and was perpetually drunk after work and during the evenings. That was enough reason to break the engagement on religious grounds. Zaffer did not argue with Shahid. He told his mother he was planning to go to the Frontier Province and to Isiolo. He would see for himself and then decide. It was not fair to do anything in a hurry and based on hearsay.

The following month Zaffer went to Garrisa in the Northern Frontier. He went straight to Mussavir's hospital and then to his home and spent one night there. He saw Mussavir at work and at home after work. He was satisfied that whether Mussavir had recovered fully or not, his marriage to Shaira was out of the question. At first he was angry that Mussavir had kept everybody in suspense instead of being honest and explaining the real reason for his silence. But after hearing Mussavir out he believed him and understood his problem. It had all been so unfortunate.

Shahid was partly right. Mussavir had become involved with the nurse who had looked after him when he was shell-shocked. Later, at Mussavir's home, Zaffer met Halima, the half-Somali, half-Italian nurse who had accompanied him to Kenya. She was educated, well groomed, and attractive. And she was pregnant, and about to deliver at any moment. Mussavir was indeed addicted to drink, but that made him discuss the whole matter freely with Zaffer. They talked well into the night. And at the end Mussavir asked Zaffer to take a letter to Shaira. He felt he owed her some explanation as to why his engagement to her had to be dissolved. Zaffer agreed to take the letter, but thought he would give it to Shaira only as a last resort. He hoped to convince her without the letter.

On his return journey Zaffer stopped at Isiolo and stayed one night with Dr Bashir and his wife in order to resolve the unfortunate matter completely.

"Beta Zaffer, I owe you an apology," said Dr Bashir. "When I spoke to you and your mother in Nairobi about Mussavir and Shaira getting married straightaway, I was not aware of what we now know."

"It's all right, Tayajan. It's not your fault, just sheer bad luck. I had always thought Mussavir was a strong person, but it would seem that something in his system must have cracked badly. I have fully accepted his explanation. But what is unforgivable is that he did not tell us; in fact he kept us all in suspense, especially Shaira."

"I agree with you and I am very sorry, believe me. But he must have suffered extreme pangs of guilt that made him drink more, and there is definitely a flaw, a weakness, in his makeup. He must have been very scared of me. He knows I shall never forgive him even if Allah does. My whole life's work is undone. I have all my life been a devout and God-fearing Muslim, and to have produced a son who has become an alcoholic! I don't ever want to see him again."

"Tayajan, you must not be that harsh. He is your eldest son and a good human being. Maybe once he is relieved of his engagement he will settle down and then drink less and eventually give it up. He feels so guilty at the moment."

"That is possible, but then he could get worse too," Dr Bashir said. "When he was shell-shocked, they overdid it with electric shocks. When I saw him in Somaliland I was not aware of this other matter, as I have said, but even at that time, there was one saving grace. While at work, Mussavir was normal and completely committed. I was told he operates with precision and skill and his hand does not shake and his reflexes are normal. He was not at all nervous."

"Yes, Tayajan, I was told that too, by his doctor colleagues. In fact, the Somalis I met in Garissa like him very much."

"I hope your mother will accept the situation just as you have. It's not going to be easy for her or for poor Shaira—we all love her so much, but fate has played us a trick." Dr Bashir sighed.

"Shaira is still young. She'll be upset, no doubt, but will hopefully get over it. We plan to let her go for further studies. That will be best for her. It's better she suffers now than later on."

Ayesha, who had been sitting quietly, began to sob. Zaffer got up and sat with her. "Don't worry, Taijan, Allah's ways are slow but sure. He will, Inshallah, help Mussavir get normal again. You don't have to worry about Shaira. As I have just said, she will be upset for a while, naturally, but I am confident she'll eventually be all right."

Zaffer told both Dr Bashir and Ayesha that after he had discussed the matter with his mother he would write to tell them that the engagement had ended.

"Thank you, Zaffer. That seems to be the best course now," said Dr Bashir, looking relieved.

The following morning Zaffer left for Nairobi.

Shahid was not only relieved but delighted when Zaffer told his mother and him that he had broken off Mussavir's engagement to Shaira. Sabra looked sad. She had liked Mussavir very much. A fear also gnawed inside her about tongues that would wag, and she was sure some embarrassment would have to be faced. Not everybody was going to judge them kindly. There would be considerable gossip, and to crown it all, she herself would have to do a lot of explaining to her relations in India for the broken engagement. That was not going to be pleasant at all. However, the problem had to be faced.

Zaffer told Sabra and Shahid that he would himself like to break the news to Shaira. But he told his mother if she felt she should do it then she should use tact and be gentle. But tact was not a very strong point with Sabra when it concerned her elder daughter. The next day when Zaffer and Shahid had gone to work, she called Shaira. "Shaira Beti, you had better take off your ring from your finger now and put it in a box. It will have to be sent back."

"Why, Ami? What did Bhaijan say? How is . . ." and her throat tightened.

She looked at the ring on her finger and, covering it with her right hand, said, "Has Bhaijan broken our engagement then? Broken it completely?"

"After staying with Mussavir for one night and then another night in Isiolo, Zaffer found it necessary to do that straightaway."

"But Ami, why in such a hurry? I thought we were going to wait for a while and . . ." Her voice broke again.

"It's no use to continue with the engagement when we know you cannot marry him," said Sabra, "You have to forget him now and accept the fact that he was not destined for you."

"But Ami, that's not fair. I don't want my engagement to be broken. In fact, Tayajan is right. We should be married now." Shaira was surprised she could say that straight to her mother. "I am confident he will be all right soon. You have not told me what Bhaijan said. What did he see that was so wrong? I have a right to know."

"You don't have to know anything. You have to trust us. We know what is best for you. Shahid was right. Mussavir drinks heavily and has become an alcoholic and—"

"But Ami, drinking can be stopped. I've read that people drink excessively because they are upset or unhappy. The war must have upset him very much. We must give him a chance to get better," she pleaded.

"Enough, Shaira, don't get out of control," said Sabra. "If people hear you defending a man who indulges in drink, a heinous crime in Muslim eyes, no one will want to marry you. Get the ring off your finger and place it in the box and let me have it. I shall put it away."

"I'll take it off after I have talked to Bhaijan Zaffer."

"What difference will that make now? The engagement is already broken. Knowing Bhai Bashir, he must have already made other arrangements to get a wife for him, from India."

Unable to bear it any longer, Shaira burst into tears and rushed to her room. She felt hollow and heavy inside. It wasn't fair; she thought, her mother was impatient and refused to see things from her point of view.

Later in the evening she went to see her brother Zaffer in his room. He guessed from her looks that she knew. He put out his arm and patted her. She started to cry. "Bhaijan, it's not fair. Not fair at all. You should have asked me before doing what you did."

"Take it easy, Shaira, my sister. I know it is very painful but I had no alternative. It was the only thing to do now."

"Bhaijan, for nearly a year and a half I've been thinking of him as my future . . . husband, and you have gone and broken it so suddenly. I had so much faith in you. I thought you would at least tell me and let me decide."

"I know I should have, Shaira, but though you are not like other girls, you are still young and also very emotional. You have no idea how serious the whole thing is. I meant to talk to you and to explain to you in due course."

"It'll be too late then, Bhaijan. I want to know now. I am not really that young, am I? I've been engaged to be married for over a year now. Have I become suddenly younger?"

Zaffer patted her shoulder again. He explained to her that it was possible Mussavir was a bit unstable even before he went to war, because he used to drink even under minor stress. "I used to think he enjoyed drinking because Islam forbade drink and, as the saying goes, 'forbidden fruit is always sweeter'! I have heard from reliable sources that he was drinking excessively on the journey to Addis Ababa as well as in the camps. After work he was always drunk. I have no doubt the conditions in the hospitals were bad and many people were killed. He himself escaped death a few times. Then he had shell shock, which can be very traumatic and can disorient a person and much more."

Shaira listened to Zaffer quietly and did not interrupt, occasionally wiping her tears and blowing her nose. Zaffer went on in a subdued voice to tell her he would not have broken the engagement if it had not been for something that happened to the poor man on his return journey when he was staying with some Somalis. "Now, as a result of that, he is unable to marry you. It is my opinion too that you will not be able to cope with it all and control him when he is drunk. He now needs a different kind of woman. Tayajan is in a hurry and wants his son to have a wife soon, someone tough and strong." Zaffer related it this way, thinking he could soften the blow.

"But does he agree with all that himself?" she interrupted. "Has he said he wants to marry a tough girl or a village girl, as Ami says? I know for certain he would never marry a girl whom he had not met, seen, or known. He used to say he was not like Latif."

"My sister, he may not feel like that now. Providence has made a decision for him."

"In what way? I don't understand. What happened on his way back? What did the Somalis do to him? What could it be that was so awful? I want to know. It is my right to know."

Zaffer was thoughtful, uncertain whether he should tell her or not.

"Bhaijan, I wish I could see him," she said, interrupting his thoughts. "I can't believe he has changed so much. Please, Bhaijan, let me go and see him. Please, Bhaijan." She begged and pleaded and cried. She said she would take off her ring only in Mussavir's presence. He had put the ring on her finger so he should be the one to remove it.

Zaffer had to go out to meet some clients. He asked her to calm herself and pray and try to understand what he had told her. He would talk to her again later in the evening.

27

The Letters

ZAFFER RETURNED LATE, so Shaira did not see him that night. The next morning she got up with a headache and did not want to go to school. Her mother did not press her and let her stay in her room. Sabra did not ask her again to remove the ring either. But at about midday Sabra called her to help in the kitchen and pantry. She told her it was good to work when one was unhappy. Sabra was gentle and her irritation too had abated. She told Shaira, "You are too young to feel so strongly and deeply. Life is long. One has to suffer unpleasantness and unhappiness at one time or another. One has to learn to face disappointments." Sabra went on in a calm tone, "I know it's not easy, but one must leave some things to fate too. And trust in God. It is possible there are better things in store for you in the future, my daughter."

Shaira kept quiet and did not reply. Her mother continued, "Beti, whatever Allah does is for the best. Maybe Mussavir is not right for you. I'm so sorry we agreed to solemnize the engagement. Perhaps we got carried away with events at that time. The Bashirs were in such a hurry to perform the nikah, it is they who are now too impatient to break. They want to marry him to a more suitable girl."

"But Ami, why have I suddenly become unsuitable? Supposing I had been married to him or my nikah performed, would they then have divorced me? Or would you have asked for a divorce on my behalf?"

"You would never have been married to him at the age of thirteen, Shaira, so the question of divorce would never have arisen. Bhai Bashir is, I am sorry to say, a hard man. With all his piety and regularity in prayers and whatnot, he lacks sensitivity. Look how he first sent Mussavir to this Abyssinian war so soon after his studies. Then in India he forced Hibba to marry a man much older than herself and sent her away when she was sickening with typhoid. And in that scorching hot weather. They had five months' leave. They could have postponed the marriage and given her away later. The poor girl died within a fortnight. Not only tragic but horrific." Sabra paused and sighed. "And then see how they treated the new daughter-in-law. They just sent her off to Magadi by bus. The more I think of it the more I feel that it is perhaps better that the engagement ended."

Sabra had never talked that much and so intimately with Shaira before. She was forever scolding and criticizing her. Shaira was surprised that her mother could be gentle and considerate. It lessened her anger and she plucked up courage. "Ami, I have asked Bhaijan to let me go there and ask him myself why he does not want to marry me."

"Have you gone out of your mind? Where is your self-respect, and the respect of your family, your khandan? Do you want to grovel before him? I'm already worried about what I'm going to say to your grandfather and uncles." Sabra stared hard at Shaira and said with emphasis, "You know you come from the Rajputs, and we don't bend in front of anyone. You read these English books," Sabra pointed at some books on the shelves, "so have begun to think like that. A self-respecting woman never begs a man to marry her. It is unheard of."

"But Ami, we are Muslims. Was Bivi Khadija not a self-respecting woman? Didn't she ask our Holy Prophet to marry her? I don't only read English books. I'm aware of what other women, even religious ones, have done in their time."

"Shaira, stop talking kufr talk and never ever compare yourself to Bivi Khadija. Those were different circumstances."

A neighbour came to the door and Sabra took her to the courtyard and started chatting. Shaira remained where she was, dusting the shelves in the pantry cupboard. If she could not go to see or meet Mussavir she could ask Zaffer to let her write to him. She could write even without permission, she thought, and post it from school. She could look up the address in the post office directory.

Back in her room she brooded as to what she would write. She would remind Mussavir of all that he had said to her in the shadow of Mount Kenya; of what he told her when they secretly met. She would ask him to think back on what he told her on the bank of the river in Nyeri, under the Nandi flame trees. Then she could remind him what he had told her in Nairobi near the water tank and in the garden of the Eastleigh house; of his parting words in front of the Ravan when he was about to leave. Some word or sentence out of all that might startle the memory of his feelings for her. She was absolutely sure he had not forgotten her completely.

When Zaffer came home from work, Sabra told him Shaira had gone to see Jamila and come back looking very tired, and she had not eaten, or come out of her room since. Zaffer went to her room straightaway and found her more in control of herself, but she did look very pale. She got up and greeted him but did not say anything.

"I have given a lot of thought to your request, Shaira, but have come to the conclusion that it is of no use. You'd be only more miserable and unhappy, and it is not fair to Mussavir for you to confront him. Most of all, it is against all norms, our tradition and culture."

He told her that though she was already in purdah and was using the veil, she had more latitude in many things than other girls in the community. And she must not ask for things that were not done. She must accept his and their mother's advice and immerse herself in her studies. He was planning to try to get her admitted to the Aga Khan Girls School—they might allow her to go in Punjabi dress. Zaffer thought this would cheer her, but it did not seem to. It seemed as if she were not even listening to him.

"Bhaijan, why didn't you tell me . . . Mu . . . is married already, married to a Somali nurse?" Shaira stared straight at him. Her eyes looked tired. "Is he, Bhaijan? And is it also true she is with him in Garissa?" Zaffer, surprised, took time to reply.

"Yes, Shaira. It's true. I wanted to spare you unnecessary suffering and pain. I'm sorry."

"Did you think I would never know? How long would it remain a secret?"

"Not for long, you are right. I should have told you."

"I would have liked you to tell me the straight truth instead of saying in a roundabout way that something terrible had happened to him on his way back and all that you said . . ." She sat down on the edge of her bed and covered her eyes with her arm. "You and Ami should have told me he had found and married a better and older girl than me."

"She is older but not necessarily better than you. Don't you ever belittle yourself." Zaffer sat beside her and put his arm around her.

"Why did he do that, Bhaijan? He told me he loved me even in his letters," she said sadly.

"He had to marry her, Shaira, was made to marry her otherwise they would have . . . killed him." Zaffer was uneasy. He decided to give her the letter.

"Why would they want to kill him?"

"Shaira, I wasn't going to tell you, but I have a letter for you from Mussavir. I now think you should have the letter. But you must promise me one thing: you will not reply to him. There must be no correspondence between you and him now. Your engagement to him is broken and this letter is going to confirm it." He pulled out an envelope from his inner pocket. Her face lit up and she looked anxiously at her brother.

"Oh, thank you, Bhaijan, thank you very much. The letter can't give me more pain now. At least I shall know why all this had to happen. I hope he has given a good reason."

"He has, my dear. But you have not promised me that you will not write back. I don't want it known that you have been writing to him even after your engagement was broken off. I want no blemish on your name. Ours is a small community here, and word will soon pass around. Remember, you have to be married one day, and you must not do anything to spoil your chances. A broken engagement is already a small blot, but it will pass."

Sophia Mustafa

"If you say I must not write to him, Bhaijan, then I will not write unless you give me permission. But please don't make me promise."

Zaffer handed her the envelope and said, "I have a rough idea of what Mussavir has told you."

"Thank you, Bhaijan. Thank you very much."

She took the letter with trembling hands, and held it tight while Zaffer walked out of the room. She sat on the bed and, tearing open the envelope, she started to read. The letter this time was written in English.

Poetess,

I feel I must write to you now and end the suspense. Fortunately, your brother Zaffer has come and I am grateful to him. We have had an honest man-to-man talk, and he has been a patient listener. He assures me he understands my predicament and says he will try to explain it to you and your mother. However, I feel you are mature enough, despite your tender years, to understand what I am going to reveal to you.

I know I am going to cause you a lot of pain and embarrassment. But, again, I know that young as you may be, you possess a very big heart and have a deep understanding of a lot of things. So I hope one day you will forgive me and not think too unkindly of me.

You have been hearing of my injuries and hospitalization in different places, so I will not bore you by going into it all again. In one of these hospitals I was looked after by a nurse, Halima, who was the daughter of an Italian father and Somali mother. She helped me and was the only person able to control me during my mad and hysterical moments. In fact, it would not be an exaggeration to say that I owe my life and recovery to her efforts and help.

I began to depend on her and we became friendly and even intimate, as a result of which she got pregnant. The Somalis, as you know, can be wild and ferocious where honour is concerned. They are a proud people. When Halima's uncles got wind of it they accused me of rape and threatened not only to kill me but also to castrate me before doing so. Halima's stepfather was a kinder man. He had married her mother when the Italian had run away to avoid being stoned to death. He was fond of his stepdaughter. Unlike other Somali girls, Halima was sent to school and later trained as a nurse.

Halima's stepfather suggested that I marry her immediately, and if he undertook the responsibility of permitting it, there would not be any problem. He was Halima's

In the Shadow of Kirinyaga

legal wali. He said I could then take Halima away to Kenya with me. He said this was the only way I could save myself from a painful death.

You might ask: was I frightened of death after being in a war? Yes, I was frightened, even before I went. Living in Kenya, a heavenly peaceful place, one can hardly imagine the unrest that has been going on over there and how disturbed the people are. In those parts, despite their being ruled by British, Italians, French, and free Abyssinians, justice can be doled out on the roadside, and very summarily. It is not at all difficult to get people to preside over these so-called courts and to procure witnesses. When Halima told me she was pregnant I was shocked, but I accepted my crime and would have married her in due course. But the threat from her relatives and people hurried matters and we got married the same night in Harar. I came under the protection of Halima's stepfather, who later helped me return to Kenya.

I did not go to Isiolo or Nyeri, because my parents were not there. Later, when they returned, they were terribly shattered by Hibba's death. So was I, and I was very angry too with my father's stubborn behaviour in giving away Hibba first to a much older man and then sending her away when she was so sick. It was inhuman. If I had gone to see them I would have had a confrontation with my father. I did not want to pain them more. I knew my Abu has not fully accepted my story—he feels I chickened out and was trapped by Halima's relatives. He says he cannot be sure if the child is mine. He has not seen or been through what I have witnessed, so it is not easy for him to understand.

You too may ask, poetess, why I did not think of you and tell them I was committed to be married to you. I did not do that as it would not have made the slightest difference to them, or even to Halima, to whom I did talk about you. A man can have more than one wife, and it is a common feature of life there. In fact, Halima still tells me I should ask you to come and live with us. She thinks you will eventually.

As a Muslim I am allowed to exercise my privilege to have more than one wife, but I know you will never be allowed to marry me now, even if you are willing. I can't ask you to do that. You are under age and legally still a minor. As a proud Punjabi I am not a man if I break my formal engagement and let someone else marry my fiancée. In India I would have been deemed a big coward and not allowed to wear a moustache! But, thank heavens, I am not that kind of a Punjabi. I am also not in India, and we are not living in the Middle Ages.

Before I close I want to say one thing more, poetess, and that is that whatever happened in Nyeri was real. I am not likely to forget it. I am sorry that our great mountain did not perhaps like our union. It is said the mountain can be angry and cast a curse.

231

But I also want to tell you that what happened in Somaliland was also real, and though I still love you I am also absolutely beholden to Halima. I need her. I cannot do without her. And then there is the child to think of.

I wish you the best of luck and pray that you will not suffer unduly. You are interested in your studies, which is a blessing, and who knows, you may even go for medicine and become a doctor one day. If you do that you will understand me all the more and forgive me.

I propose very soon to ask for a transfer to a more remote place than this, maybe in the Turkana country. That will be better for both Halima and myself. That also will prove less embarrassing for my parents. I shall miss Mama very much but that can't be helped. In time I hope they will understand and forgive me.

Mussavir.

Shaira finished reading the letter. She felt weak in the legs and had a hollow feeling in her stomach. She held the letter tightly in her hand and lay down on her bed, curling her legs up to ease the funny feeling. After a while she reread the letter. She stopped at the place where Mussavir had said she was a minor legally and he could not ask her to . . . what? she thought. Maybe to elope with him? He had once told her in Nyeri that he would suggest they elope if on his return there were any more objections to the marriage. That was before they were formally engaged. She asked herself what her reaction would have been if he had asked her to go to him, against her family's wishes, knowing Halima would be there too. She knew no one was going to believe her if she said that she understood the situation. It was, in fact, a load off her mind that he had written a perfectly sane letter and did not sound sick or hysterical. And though she knew she had lost him, she was happy that it was not due to any fault in her or because he had stopped loving her.

She then remembered what her mother had said. She came from Rajput stock and Rajputanis don't bend before others. Was her mother right? Did Shaira feel like a Rajputani, a woman from a warrior tribe? The answer was a big *no*. She did not care who she was. All she knew was the way she felt. If she were free to decide her own future, she would have gone to Mussavir without hesitation. But she was not free. She was like a caged bird whose wings were clipped. The law would bring her back if she disobeyed her family and went to Mussavir. She wished she were seventeen or eighteen.

All her thoughts were in a jumble. She put out her hand to hold her head. She noticed the ring on her finger and remembered the day it was put there. She remembered when she and Mussavir were saying good-bye in front of the effigy of Ravan. Fate must have been roaring with laughter when Mussavir said he was a possessive man and that she was all his.

Shaira got up from her bed and picked the small box out of the drawer. She removed the ring from her finger and looked at it in her palm. She put it in the slot in the velvet, then lowered the tiny lid until it clicked. She opened the wardrobe and took out the red dupatta that had been draped on her shoulders by Ayesha before Mussavir put the ring on her finger. She took the ring box and the dupatta and put it in her mother's wardrobe. Her mother would soon see the two articles. She walked back to her room. Outside there was a commotion. Huma sounded happy and was greeting someone in Swahili. She shouted with excitement, "Ami, he has come back. Odera has come back from the jail . . . Odera is here."

Shaira went to the window and saw her mother, Honey, and Huma all gathered around a weak and thin-looking Odera. He was smiling widely, chatting and as cheerful as before. Batul, the neighbour's daughter, also came and greeted him.

Shaira was happy to see him out of prison and back but was not in a mood to go out to greet him. She made up her mind to wait until she was of age to make her own decisions. But she felt she must inform Mussavir of that. She would have to disobey her brother, maybe only this once. She sat down at her desk and penned a letter in English.

Dear Dr Mussavir:

I have read your letter many times. I am relieved that you wrote in detail and saved me from learning about you from others. I want you to know that I do appreciate and understand all that you have said. It is a load off my mind that you are safe, alive, and well.

It is true that neither my family nor the law will allow me to do what I would like to. I am not free to make my own decisions. My brother gave me your letter on condition that I not write back to you. But I am disobeying him this once. I have removed the ring from my finger and soon it will reach its rightful owner.

I would be a hypocrite if I said I am not angry, unhappy, or miserable. But I hope my mother is right—she says time is a great healer. She must know because she has been through quite a lot. I was interested in further studies. But I am not so sure now. There is no more to say, is there?

Shaira.

P.S By the way, our houseman, Odera, the cheerful one, has come back from prison and looks frail and ill, but he is lucky to be free. I am envious of him.

Shaira folded the letter, put it in an envelope, and set it aside in her book. She would post it from school.

She had been in her room for a long time so decided to go out and welcome Odera and hear of his ordeal in jail. It might take her mind off her own misery.

Acknowledgments

The idea of writing a novel of containment such as *In the Shadow of Kirinyaga* germinated in my mind in the late 1940s, even though I only started to actually write it in the mid 1980s. I was old enough in the 1930s to be aware of what was called the Abyssinian War and the toll it took within the larger region, including its devastating effects on two Muslim families of second generation Asians living in Kenya during that period; they are the main source material for my fictional characters. I also remember my late uncle Sher Mohamed Butt, who was a transporter. His overland runs from Kenya to Abyssinia and Somalia, carrying produce and merchandise to other Asian traders, were the source of the many stories he returned with. One was about the wells at Wal Wal, and the incident that led to what was subsequently named the "mini" war of 1934-5 in Abyssinia, the Ethiopia of today. My novel is therefore based on true events, though all the people from whom my characters are drawn are now deceased. I have retained the real names of only the historical personages directly involved in the political events of the time and place; all other names I have changed.

I have necessarily supplemented my personal knowledge and recollections with further research into the historical events surrounding my story. The list of political and historical studies from which I have benefitted and drawn includes the following: On Ethiopia (chapters 12, 16, 21, 25 in particular): Anthony Mockler, *The Wars of Haile Selassie* (Oxford, 1984), the collection of essays, *The Ethiopian Crisis: Touchstone of Appeasement?* edited by Ludwig F Shaefer (DC Heath, 1961), and which includes contributions by GM Gathorne-Hardy, Winston Churchill, Arnold J Toynbee, Gaetano Salvemini, Luigi Villari, DW Brogan, Sigmund Neuman, Elizabeth Wiskemann, Alan Bullock, Herbert Feis, and Richard HS Crossman. On Kenya: Errol Trzebinski, *The Kenya Pioneers* (Norton, 1985), and for their immersion in the colonial ambiance of the time, Elspeth Huxley, *Nellie: Letters from Africa* (Weidenfeld and Nicolson, 1973), and *The Flame*

Trees of Thika (Penguin, [1959] 1989), Beryl Markham, *West With the Night* (Virago, [1942] 1986), and Isak Dineson, *Out of Africa* (Penguin, [1937] 1985). Further consultation for events depicted in chapters 21 and 23 includes, Genesta Hamilton's diaries: A *Stone's Throw (Travels from Africa in Six Decades)* (Hutchinson, 1987), and David Lamb, *The Africans* (Vintage, [1982] 1987).

I am indebted to my family in a variety of ways. Here in Canada, my eldest daughter Rehana and her husband Mustafa, as well as their daughter, Kaneez, were each helpful in reproducing the manuscript during its various stages. I am grateful to my son Kemal, daughter-in-law Jacqueline, grandson Dashiel in Namibia, for introducing me and my work to Irene Staunton of Baobab Academic Books, Zimbabwe. Irene Staunton was instrumental in getting the manuscript read by her editor, Eileen Haddock, my grateful thanks to both of them. My other daughter, Fawzia, in New York, read the manuscript in its very early stages. I thank her for assisting me in gathering research materials for my background reading and in helping with the compilation of the final draft.

Among my friends, I thank: Telford Georges, Yash Ghai, Zaffer Ali, Fatma Aloo, Maryam Tejani, Fatima Harji, Saeeda Jamal and Memoona Moola for their encouragement. In particular I am indebted to William (Bill) Robertson, an accomplished poet and fiction writer himself, for editing the final draft and offering invaluable suggestions, changes, and encouragement during his wonderful workshops and seminars. I am also grateful to the anonymous script reader of the Saskatchewan Arts Board, whose detailed critique was most helpful in my subsequent revisions. I owe an especial and enduring debt to Nurjehan Aziz for taking the risk of publishing the work of someone entering her eightieth year.

Finally, I must also thank my husband Abdulla for his patience and unflagging support.

Sophia Mustafa

Of Kashmiri origin, Sophia Mustafa was born in India in 1922 and grew up and went to school in Nairobi, Kenya. She was married in 1940 and moved to Tanganyika in 1948 with her husband. She was one of the first women members of parliament in Tanzania, when she wrote The Tanganyika Way published by Oxford University Press in 1961. She moved to Canada with her husband in 1989 and currently lives in Brampton, Ontario. She has three grownup children.